PRIDE

AND

FALL

PRIDE

— AND —

FALL

CATHEDRAL LAKE
BOOK THREE

STACI
TROILO

RADIANCE

RADIANCE
an imprint of
Roan & Weatherford Publishing Associates, LLC
Bentonville, Arkansas

Library of Congress Cataloging-in-Publication Data
Names: Troilo, Staci author.
Title: Pride and Fall/Staci Troilo | Cathedral Lake #3
Description: Second Edition | Bentonville: Radiance, 2023
Identifiers: LCCN: 2020935335 | ISBN: 978-1-63373-616-0 (hardcover) |
ISBN: 978-1-63373-617-7 (trade paperback) | ISBN: 978-1-63373-229-2 (eBook)
BISAC: FICTION/Thriller/Suspense | FICTION/Thriller/Medical |
FICTION/Romance/Medical
LC record available at: https://lccn.loc.gov/2020935335

Radiance Press trade paperback edition November, 2023

Cover & Interior Design by Casey W. Cowan
Editing by Amy Cowan

For Samantha—My favorite daughter.
With all my love.

ACKNOWLEDGEMENTS

I AM GRATEFUL TO SO many people—those who supported me through the process of writing this novel and those who support me every day through love and friendship.

Casey—designing, and publishing the book you now hold in your hands. Aaron—for your patience and medical expertise. Mom and Dad—for your support and love. All my family and friends—for putting up with a temperamental writer.

And, most importantly of all, Seth and Sammi— you mean more to me than you'll ever know.

PRIDE

AND

FALL

CHAPTER 1

THE CATHEDRAL LAKE HIGH CROWD swept Faith Keller along with the rowdy masses. She linked arms with her best friend, more for safety than camaraderie. "I'm reconsidering."

"What?" Kacee shouted over the scaled-down marching band tucked behind the far court hoop. Drums pounded, echoing through the arena. Horns blared "We Will Rock You" while the cheerleaders danced a synchronized routine.

Faith stopped and scrutinized the girls. When she was in school, cheering wasn't nearly so X-rated. Of course, she went to a private school, not the city school. Her squad wore pleated skirts and shook pompoms. These girls wore—well, to call those skirts would be an exaggeration, and it wasn't only pompoms they shook so vigorously. "I. Want. To. Go."

Kacee sighed and dragged her friend through the raucous crowd toward the bleachers. "It's the championship game. These tickets weren't cheap."

"I don't care about the money."

She squeezed Faith's arm and climbed through the stands. "Look. Your brother saved us seats."

Faith had no choice but to hurry after her. Each step brought her closer to the edge of panic, and she battled to maintain control. The crowd closed in, the noise deafened, the air thinned. The room spun, tilted, grew and shrank at the same time.

Control. She needed control.

As though through a long tunnel, she heard Kacee's voice. "Hey, Jensen, Bella. Thanks for saving us seats. Austin, Miles, it's been a while. Where're Brett and Simone?"

Faith panted for air, but none came. Too many people. Any of them could so easily jam a gun into her back and abduct her. What if it happened again? What if this time her rescuers were too late to save her? What if no one came at all? Or what if instead of abduction, her attacker pulled the trigger?

She leaned forward, ready to bolt to her feet, when someone whispered in her ear.

"Ssh."

Frantic, she whipped her head around.

Jensen shook his head, a small, sad smile on his face. Bella, his fiancée, climbed down to sit beside her and grabbed her hand. He rubbed warm circles on Faith's back and again whispered to her. "Deep, slow breaths, sis. In and out. Nice and slow. Just breathe."

Faith closed her eyes and squeezed Bella's hand while she let her brother's calming voice and soothing touch relax her. God, she was such a mess. After a few minutes, and more than a few silent tears, the panic attack passed. She wiped her face, nudged her brother's knees with her back, and leaned toward Bella. "How do you do it?"

"Do what?"

"We were both abducted, but you were shot. Yet I'm the basket case and you're totally fine."

"I'm not fine, Faith."

"You're better than me. What's the secret?"

The announcer interrupted them to ask them to stand for the National Anthem. They turned and faced the flag and listened to a local legend belt out the lyrics to "The Star Spangled Banner."

Hand over her heart, Faith mouthed the words along with the singer. The song always moved her, made her both proud and sad at the same time.

"And the rocket's red glare, the bombs burst—"

Shots fired into the gym, dropping players, cheerleaders, band members, and fans with pink mist explosions, red blotches blooming on their clothing.

Pandemonium.

Chaos.

People ran in every direction to avoid the attack. Faith remained rooted to her seat, terror paralyzing her. Without knowing where it came from, they could be running right into it.

Kacee yanked on her arm. "We have to get out of here!"

Jensen hauled her up from behind and half-dragged, half-carried her down the bleachers.

Fear tasted metallic on her tongue, and the acid in her stomach roiled. When they reached the gym floor, she stopped, bent over, dry heaved. Shots plowed into the players' bench beside them, splintering the wood. Her brother yanked on her arm. They dashed for the nearest exit, frantic cattle without cowboys to herd them.

The steady and rapid spit of bullets rained down on them. All Faith knew was Jensen had his hand on her head and was pushing her toward the door. She made out Detective Cooper and various other members of Cathedral Lake's police department making their way inside, fighting against the tide of people trying to force their way out.

"Tony!" Jensen stopped.

"Not now." All business. Didn't mince words. "Get them out of here."

"Wait!" Jensen grabbed his arm. "I only count one shooter. Bastard's in the rafters of the ceiling above the press box. Has at least one automatic. Doesn't seem to have a specific target."

"Thanks. Now go!"

Someone fell into Faith, knocking her and a few others down. The crowd surged, trampling over the man who'd fallen into her, pinning her underneath him. Oh, Lord! She'd be crushed under the weight of the exodus. She turned her head to yell at him, ended up with a face full of his jacket. She yelled a muffled, "Get up!" but it got lost in the folds of his coat and the cries of the crowd.

And he didn't move. Had he been shot? Trampled to death?

Would she die there, trapped beneath a stranger?

"Help!" But no one could hear her. She had no lung capacity, no voice. The man's dead weight combined with the weight of the people climbing over him effectively suffocated her.

"Faith! Faith!" her brother called for her, but she couldn't answer.

She only had enough strength to make one last feeble attempt to push the man off her. Shoving with all the force she could muster, her hand touched something hot, sticky—blood. Mortified, she flung him and rolled, somehow getting out from under him even as people continued to step on his body and on her. A foot on her calf, another on her rib. She'd rise to her knees just to be knocked down again. Someone ground her hand into the concrete.

Concrete! Through her tears, she realized they'd made it outside.

Hands reached under her armpits and hauled her to her feet.

"Faith. What the hell?"

"Jensen!" She threw her arms around him.

He squeezed her, then pulled away. "What's the matter with you? You could have been trampled to death. You can't just drop to the ground in relief the second you cross the threshold."

"I didn't. I—"

"Here and now isn't the time and place, J," Bella said.

"No, I suppose not."

"But I—" Faith started again.

Jensen dragged her over toward the ambulances. "You've got blood on you. Are you hurt?"

Her ribs, hand, and calf throbbed. Her head pounded, her stomach roiled, and her heart ached. But physically, she would heal. "No. It's not my blood."

"Come on, then. They're going to need all the help they can get."

"Help?"

"Faith, there are only so many EMTs here. We need to assist."

"So go. You're a doctor. I'm sure they'd appreciate it."

"And you're a vet."

"I treat animals."

"You know how to assess conditions. Triage. Suture a wound if you have to. Besides, you have your CPR certification."

"That hardly qualifies me to remove bullets."

"No one's asking you to perform cardiothoracic surgery. Just help out. They're short-handed."

She knew he was right, but she didn't know if she could muster the calm to help.

God help her. God help them all.

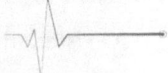

THE AFTERMATH WAS BRUTAL. COULD they even call it an aftermath? Faith wasn't sure. The term implied the situation was over, but from the rolling report of the automatic weapon and the return bursts of the law enforcements' firearms, it was still going on.

Even though the distance muffled the sounds of the gunfire, Faith still cringed at the violent sounds.

She wrapped a child's wound with gauze and tried her best to reassure a set of traumatized parents. "It's only grazed. Doesn't even need stitches. She'll be perfectly fine. She was very lucky."

Lucky. The girl was only seven years old, and she was shot, for Pete's sake. In her hometown. In her parents' care. How is that lucky? How does she move on from that?

The little girl smiled. "Does that mean I can go now? Can I have ice cream?"

"Two giant scoops!" Her mom gave her a big hug and kiss, her eyes shiny with tears she no doubt didn't want her daughter to see.

"With sprinkles!" Her dad picked her up and spun her in a circle. They both thanked Faith and hurried off.

Faith shrugged. Maybe ice cream and sprinkles would help. It had been years since she'd eaten dairy. She could give it a try.

"How you holding up?" Jensen hurried past her on his way to someone else being escorted out of the gym.

"Fine." Yep. She lied.

Each shot reminded her of Bella's shooting, of how helpless she felt seeing the blood blooming on her chest. How frightened she was of losing Bella. Even more terrified that it could have been her.

That any day it could be her.

Wonder what flavor ice cream fixes that.

Officers rushed through the lot, ushering everyone to the next parking venue. They were already in a lot adjacent to the prime parking area beside the gym. Faith didn't realize a third even existed until she was herded to it.

Once the new triage unit was established, she moved on to another patient. A tall, muscular man with close-cropped hair. "Hello. My name is Faith. Can you tell me where you're hurt?"

"Hi. Name's David. David James." He held out his hand to shake hers, but in doing so, took his hand off his arm which gushed blood. "Sorry. Don't know what I was thinking."

"Don't be sorry about that. Shows you were raised with good manners, shaking hands when you meet someone. However," she rooted through the supplies the EMTs gave her, "I don't know if I'm going to be able to help you. That looks pretty bad. I don't think butterfly strips will hold. You're going to need stitches."

"Can't you do that? I don't want to go to the hospital."

Faith slipped on a fresh set of gloves and examined the injury. She'd seen more than her fair share of gunshot wounds that evening, and his didn't look like all the others. It looked more like a clean slice than the path a bullet would gouge out of flesh. "What happened?"

"Bullet just winged me. Lucky I wasn't an inch to the left, I guess. Would have hit muscle or bone, I suppose."

"Hmm." Strange, but who was she to question? "Well, David, I'm a veterinarian, not a doctor. I'm just pitching in. So I really shouldn't."

"A vet? Do you have a practice here in Cathedral Lake?"

"Actually, yes. I graduated last May and opened my practice in June."

"How's it going?"

Faith swabbed his wound with alcohol and wrapped it with gauze. No way was that bandage going to hold for long. "Really well, thanks. I'm actually at the point where I could use some help."

"Well, I'm not a vet, but I used to help out Doctor Jones at the shelter. And I could use the work. Can I fill out an application?"

She looked up at him. "You worked with Zeke?"

"Yeah. Weekends and summers for a few years. I loved the animals. Just wish it was a no-kill shelter."

Faith took a deep breath, remembering when she met Dr. Zeke Jones. He was putting down a severely injured dog shortly after she'd lost her sister. She and her brother staged a protest trying to save its life, but in the end, her father and mother insisted it was the humane thing to do. They compromised— Zeke euthanized the dog, but then they took him home and gave him a proper burial. She never felt like she did enough for that poor creature. Despite not agreeing with the decision, over the years, with volunteering and internships, she'd developed a fondness for the vet.

"I couldn't agree with you more. Every animal deserves a loving home." She cut some tape and secured his bandage. "So, you grew up around here?"

"Born and raised."

"Here to watch your alma mater tonight?"

He nodded.

"Did you play?" He was tall and fit. Looked like an athlete.

"No. Just a fan."

"Huh. You're so tall, I figured you had to have played."

"Nope. But I get that a lot." He cleared his throat. "So, whatdaya say, doc? Can I fill out an application?"

She shook her head. "No."

"No?" His face fell.

"No. I heard all I need to hear. Job's yours."

He grinned. "Great."

"Now go get this arm taken care of." She patted him on the back and turned to leave.

"Hey, doc."

She turned again. "Name's Keller. But you can call me Faith."

"Okay, Faith. Since we're not strangers anymore. Thanks."

"You're welcome. Now go." She shooed him along.

"Wait."

"I've got tons more people to help."

"Well, since I'm technically your employee now, why don't you just stitch me up and save me the trip to the ER?"

"How does our working arrangement change anything?"

"I'm not just some random person you're out here looking over for the EMTs. You're just cleaning up a colleague."

Faith bit her lip. "I don't have anything to numb your arm."

"I'm a tough SOB. I can take it."

"I don't know."

"Come on. I'll be waiting all night at the ER. They've got who-knows-how-many seriously wounded and dead on their hands. I'll be the last on their list."

She took a deep breath and looked around. For the first time since she met David, she realized the night around her had quieted. An occasional siren still sounded when an ambulance arrived or left, but the constant alarms had ended. The gunfire had stopped. People no longer screamed, and sobs were fewer and farther between. The news media had arrived—harsh camera lights illuminated reporters who spoke into microphones, their monotonous broadcasts blending into the din around her.

It was well and truly the aftermath.

She'd survived. Again.

"If the needle hurts, I don't want to hear about it."

He grinned. "Won't even see me wince."

Faith gave props to David. She didn't see him wince. Of course, that was because she didn't look at him. For all she knew, he grimaced in agony the entire time she worked on him. But when she finished, he thanked her, gathered his things, and started to leave.

She stopped him only briefly to exchange phone numbers so they could discuss his work schedule. The fact that she had the presence of mind to do that impressed her. Most of the night she'd been on autopilot.

And that was being kind.

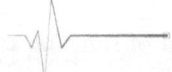

FAITH LEANED AGAINST THE BUMPER of Kacee's car. Her friend sat inside behind the wheel, sound asleep. Had been in there for an hour or more. Faith wasn't sure. She'd lost track of time. She was just glad Kacee was safe. Would have been happier if Kacee had gone home, but she'd flat out refused, saying she wouldn't leave without Faith. She had walked around offering counseling to people for a while—social workers were always among the first people to jump into a tense situation—but toward the end of the night, most of the conscious victims had dispersed, and the unconscious ones obviously didn't need her. "I'm just in the way," she'd said and climbed into her car. Faith and Jensen continued to help where they could—Jensen being much more helpful than Faith felt.

When she was no longer useful and thoroughly exhausted, she trudged over to Kacee's car, leaned against the hood, and watched her brother finish up with the EMTs. Her father would have been so proud of Jensen if he had been there watching him with the victims. Well, if Dad had been there, he wouldn't have been watching. He would have been working right alongside everyone else. But he'd have been proud. He'd always wanted Jensen to be a doctor. Was over the moon when he became one—after about eight years of barely speaking to him when he thought he was studying to be an engineer. She was so glad they'd finally mended their relationship.

And to think it only took her being kidnapped to make it happen.

She shuddered and tried to bury the thought. Again. But tonight's trauma, exhaustion, fear… it was all too much. Her heart, her lungs—they seized, constricted. She couldn't breathe, couldn't move. Every muscle froze. Body paralyzed, rigid. Only her thoughts raced. Synapses fired rapidly—zoom, zoom, zoom! Blinding flashes of horrific memories, terrifying possibilities, crippling history, and incapacitating potential.

Faith closed her eyes. Gasped for air that wouldn't come. Grasped her throat and collapsed to the ground.

She woke to the tangy scent of smelling salts. Jensen and Kacee hovered over her. The back of her head throbbed more than it did from her earlier injuries, and shame flamed her cheeks. "I'm sorry," she whispered.

"Can you sit?" Jensen asked.

"Yes. Yes, of course."

"You say 'of course' like it's obvious." Kacee offered her hand and helped her up. "You collapsed."

"It's been a long night. Do we know yet what happened in there? Is the shooter—Did they get him?"

"They got him," Jensen said.

"And don't change the subject," Kacee said.

She sighed. "I said I was sorry."

"I called Tod."

She shot her brother a hard stare. "That's not necessary."

"He's waiting for you."

Faith glanced at her watch. "It's three in the morning!"

"Then we better not waste any more time." Jensen opened Kacee's passenger side door and gestured for Faith to get in.

She hung her head. No point in arguing. And honestly, she probably needed the visit.

Faith had first gone to see Dr. Tod Jeffers nine years earlier when her twin sister died in a motorcycle accident. Well, it was hard to call it an accident when the motorcycle had been tampered with. By a family "friend" no less. Not that Hope had been the target. She'd been collateral damage. Didn't hurt any less, though. In fact, it hurt more, maybe. Her death and the ramifications of it had almost destroyed their whole family. Faith found Dr. Jeffers—Tod—to be a comfort in those trying times. And she'd needed him sporadically through the years. Frequently since her abduction almost one year ago.

That he'd agree to see her in the middle of the night was a testament to his commitment to both his profession and her health.

"We'll be out here when you're done." Jensen pulled up to the curb in front of Dr. Jeffers' posh brownstone home/office.

"Don't be ridiculous. I'll call a cab when I'm through." Faith got out and closed the door. She heard the whirr of the automated window rolling down.

"You don't be ridiculous," Kacee said. "We'll wait."

A light was on in Dr. Jeffers' downstairs window, so he was clearly ready for her. He opened the door before she knocked. His feet were bare, and he wore plaid pajama pants and a well-worn gray Carnegie Mellon University t-shirt, but he looked alert. "Hi, Faith. Come on in."

"Hi, Tod. Sorry to disturb your sleep." She stepped past him into the foyer and waited for him to close the door. The faint and familiar scent of lemon furniture polish enveloped her, warred with the aroma of coffee wafting out of the mug he held in his hand.

"You didn't wake me. The sirens started just after seven this evening. I've been watching the news ever since. Can I get you some coffee?" He gestured to his office.

She shook her head and walked the familiar path to a comfortable leather couch. The cushions were soft, and she nestled into them. A glass of warm milk, and she just might get some sleep. Instead, she glanced at his bookcase. "You release a new book?"

He smiled. "Yes, but is that really what you want to talk about right now?"

Faith shrugged. "I don't really want to talk at all. Jensen made me come."

"Probably because you had two panic attacks in one night. One of which made you lose consciousness."

"There was a terrorist attack at a basketball game. Gunfire. Right in front of me! You can hardly be surprised I'd take it badly."

"No. It doesn't surprise me at all. Why don't we talk about your first episode."

"What about it?"

"Why did being at the game bother you? What was the problem with sitting with your brother and friends in a public venue?"

"Well, clearly it was a problem. Look how it ended."

"Faith. You know that's highly unusual. Almost unheard of, not the norm. No one could have predicted that."

"And yet it happened. How many people are kidnapped in their lifetimes? Not many. But kidnapped and in a terrorist attack? Bet those odds are even slimmer. Like getting hit by lightning and then bitten by a shark a year later."

"You're right. I'm sure the chances someone experiencing even one of those crimes are small, let alone living through two. So don't you think you've had more than your share of bad luck? Don't you think the odds are now in your favor to be safe?"

"Who are you? The lady from the Hunger Games?"

Tod sat back and laughed. "Don't try to deflect, Faith. Think about it. Why did you really panic at the game? Before the gunfire."

Why did she panic? Too many people. Too many variables. "I lost control of the situation."

"You understand you can't always have control, right?"

Tears welled in her eyes, and she blinked them away. She nodded.

"We've talked about you trying to stay in situations where you maintain total control."

"I'm fine, then."

"And that's great. That's progress."

Faith took a deep breath. She had control at Tod's. She could see the entrance and exit to the room. She had a clear path out. She could see his hands and knew he had no weapons within reach. And she knew he wouldn't try to hurt her. That was the biggest point.

She was safe.

"But what about the tools we discussed for when you can't control your surroundings? Did you try to use those tonight?"

She shook her head. "They flew right out of my mind. All I knew was I couldn't breathe, and I could be a target."

"Okay. We have to work on you remembering your tools."

"I remember them now. The breathing. The hand taps and eye movements. The humming—"

"All good. And all not worth a damn if you don't remember them when you need them. Will you reconsider group therapy?"

"No. I'm not sharing with strangers. It's too weird."

"All right. Medication, then?"

"No. I told you. I'm not putting that crap in my system again. I hate how the pills make me feel detached, numb."

"It's not crap if it helps you cope."

"Big pharma is just a—"

He held up his hand. "I'm not having this argument again. Especially in the middle of the night. I have a suggestion that I want you to consider. One you shouldn't object to."

"What?"

"Get a service animal."

"What? Why? I don't need a service animal."

"Consider it."

"Those are for people with vision or hearing impairments. People who have seizures. People with PTS—" She blinked. Swallowed.

"D. PTSD, Faith."

"I don't have… PTSD."

"A year ago, I would have just said you needed time to get over the shock of your trauma. Now, I think it's time we call a spade a spade."

"I'll think about the group therapy."

"Think about the service animal. You're a vet, you must know the benefits of them."

"Who's going to want to go to a vet who needs a service animal?"

"I don't see how the two are related."

"I wouldn't want to have my horse treated by a lady who is clearly afraid of something."

"There is nothing to be ashamed of. Besides, the two situations are mutually exclusive. Doing your job well and recovering from a trauma have nothing to do with each other."

"I think people would be afraid to trust me."

"I don't think that's how people would look at the situation, but if that's how you see it, tell people you're training the dog, or that the dog is just a pet."

"That's a lie."

"We're talking about your health. Would you rather lie and have a job or not have a practice or a life at all?"

She jumped to her feet. "I'd rather not have been abducted in the first place! I'd rather not have been in a terrorist attack tonight! I'd rather my sister not be dead!"

Tod put his mug down, rested his elbows on his knees, and looked up at her. "I can't take you back in time, Faith. I can only help you move forward."

The pounding in her head grew worse than it had been all night. She rubbed at the sore spot, sat back down, and closed her eyes. When Tod's fingers pressed gently against the painful part of her skull, she winced. She hadn't even noticed him cross the room.

"You didn't mention you'd been injured tonight. I'll get you an ice pack before you go." He headed toward the kitchen.

"Thanks."

He returned with the ice a moment later. "So, do you want me to refer you to service dog providers, or do you have breeders you prefer to work with?"

"I didn't agree to getting a dog."

Tod stared at her through narrowed eyes.

She'd forgotten how tenacious he could be. "I know who to call."

CHAPTER 2

CARTER EMERSON SCRATCHED HIS K-9 partner behind the ears. "One more sweep, Max. In case we missed anybody." The dog nuzzled his handler's hand, enjoying the affection before snapping to attention and making another round of the gym.

The officer let the dog do his thing. Max sniffed and searched for incendiary devices while Carter looked for survivors of the terrorist attack. In all his years in Cathedral Lake, he'd never seen such senseless destruction. He'd joined the police force because he wanted to help people, wanted to make a difference. Wanted his brother to be proud of him. Never expected to have a night like this, though. What the hell was the world coming to? He was just glad they'd put the bastard down before he did worse. Didn't feel like it could get worse, but he knew better.

Max's ears perked. He snuffed, tugged the leash, poked his nose under the bleachers. That wasn't his signal for a bomb, but something had caught his attention. Looked like hardly a foot of room back in the corner under the retractable seats. Carter tugged the leash and Max obediently stepped out of the way. Contorting his large body down around the bleachers' support framing, he bent and twisted until he saw what Max sensed.

A little boy.

"Hey. Hey, kid. Are you awake?"

No movement.

"My name's Carter. I'm a police officer. I know you can't see my badge because it's dark back there and I can't really bend down that far, but if you come out, I can show it to you."

Still nothing.

"It's safe. It's all over now. We got the bad guy, and I want to get you help. Are you hurt?"

Did he wiggle? Carter wasn't sure. He tried climbing through the cross-supports, but he just got tangled. Stupidest design ever. Had to scoot back and reassess. Took his flashlight out and shined it on the kid, who blinked against the beam and cringed away from the brightness.

Okay. Good news. Maybe. The kid was awake. He was just terrified of Carter. Hoped he wasn't scared of dogs.

"What's your name, son?"

Still nothing.

"You like doggies, kid?" Carter was going to scream in a moment. He took a deep breath and gestured to Max. "This is my dog. Name's Max. Want to pet him?"

He beckoned Max and sent him through the supports, letting him approach the boy, then he trained his flashlight on them. The boy's eyes widened, but he didn't recoil. Good sign. Max allowed the boy to pat his head. Then Carter called him back.

"Looks like Max likes you. Why don't you come pet him some more?" If that trick didn't work, Carter didn't know what he'd do. Maybe climb up on the bleachers and start dismantling them from the top.

The boy didn't move. Carter thought about radioing for a toolkit. Then the kid took a step toward him. Just one. Carter didn't move. Didn't want to scare him. Kid took another.

Carter backed up. Wanted to give the kid some space. The beam of his flashlight caught something on the floor. Shiny, but bigger than shells from the shooter. Didn't have time to examine them, though. Trained the light on the kid again. The boy took a few more steps, and Carter climbed out from underneath the bleachers completely, then he whispered to Max to join him. Max, agile creature, gracefully leapt over the cross-supports and jumped out into the gym. The boy crawled out after him. Before the kid could change his mind and crawl back, Carter scooped him up.

The wail he let out nearly pierced Carter's eardrums.

Max rubbed up against his handler's leg.

Carter took a deep breath, grabbed Max's leash, and said, "It's okay. I got you." He wasn't sure if he was talking to Max or the boy. He walked outside and deposited the kid with the first EMT he found. "I'm not sure if he's hurt or not. Found him under the bleachers. Hasn't stopped hollering since I got him out."

Someone else could deal with that problem.

He could still hear the kid screaming as he walked back inside.

"Finish the sweep, Max."

They'd already made it almost to the concession stand by heading right, so Carter figured they should go left and end at the stand. He'd pop under the bleachers to check on whatever that stuff was, then they'd come back through the middle of the gym offering assistance where they could. Heading left, Max didn't find any other victims trapped or hiding behind any of the bleachers, so that was a good sign.

Tony caught up to them when they were nearly finished with their sweep. "All clear?"

"Just found a little boy. Took him out to the EMTs. Looks like the rest of the gym is clear."

"Good. The coroner and CSU are going to be busy for a while."

They rounded the corner of the bleachers and headed past the concession stand. Max pulled on his leash and sat, stared at the counter.

"What's up with him?" Cooper asked. "He hungry or something?"

Max barked, rose on his hind legs, put his paws on the counter. He pushed his nose toward the kitchen and whined.

"Damn it." Carter shook his head and pulled Max down, started running around toward the concession stand door, and called to the detective over his shoulder, "Call the bomb squad."

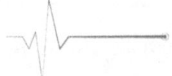

CARTER REWARDED MAX WITH ONE of the treats he kept in the car while he waited for the bomb squad to give the all clear. They'd been moved to the far parking lot, the area deemed the minimum safe distance from the device. While he was far from ground zero, he scanned the parking lot. Might only have been one shooter inside, but that didn't mean he didn't have any accomplices. And if he did, this is where they would be.

It boggled his mind to see so many people rushing around looking for loved ones. So many injured. So many dead. The ambulances couldn't keep up with the tragedy. Nor could the first responders. That was why volunteers from the crowd had stepped up.

This was the stuff of major metropolitan areas, not nice suburban towns like Cathedral Lake.

Was one of the stragglers involved? How sick to perpetrate such violence and then stick around for a first-hand look at the aftermath. He gave the people a closer look. Most looked like they were just doing what needed to be done.

Most.

One of them looked out of sorts.

Shock? Or glee? He squinted to get a better look at her.

"Carter."

He turned when he heard his name called.

Tony gestured for him to approach. "Bomb squad gave us the go-ahead to get back inside. Lucky for all of us, the bomb was mis-wired. If it had gone off, tonight could have been much worse."

"We ID this asshole yet?"

"No, but it won't be long now. CSU is processing the scene. They'll have his prints run as soon as they get him down."

Carter shook his head. Senseless.

"We're done with K-9. You can take off."

"There's one more thing I want to check before I go."

Cooper shrugged. "Don't touch anything. It's CSU's building now."

"Then I'll have them accompany me. I saw something in there."

"I'm coming with you."

"Suit yourself." Of course Tony would stay with him. He watched over Carter like it was his mission in life.

"Come on, Max."

The three of them headed back through the three levels of parking lots until they reached the main gymnasium. The place crawled with more blue jackets and Tyvek booties than Carter had ever seen in one place. More puddles of blood, too. He didn't know if he'd ever get over the carnage.

Rather than bother anyone or get in anyone's way, Carter headed straight for the bleachers where he'd seen the weird cylinders. He started to crawl under when Tony grabbed his arm.

"What are you doing?"

"I told you I saw something under there."

"And I told you not to disturb anything. This is CSU's scene now."

"I just need to see what I saw."

Tony gestured to one of the crime scene investigators, who came right over. "Officer Emerson here saw something under the bleachers that he needs you to document and retrieve."

"Sir, I—" the tech looked around the gym helplessly at all the work he had yet to process.

"I know, but if you don't do it now, I'm not going to be able to keep him from getting it himself, and I don't want to hear you bitch about it. So just get it and move on with your night."

The tech sighed and checked his camera and bag supply. "Where and what, Officer?"

Carter took the CSU tech over to where he'd seen the shiny objects with his flashlight. After the tech documented the objects, photographed them, and bagged them, he showed them to Carter and Tony.

"What's a supply of ketamine doing here?" Carter asked.

"Hell if I know," Tony said.

"Think it has to do with what went down tonight?"

"No idea. But we'll find out."

"This much ketamine could be cooked down to a hell of a lot of powder," Carter said.

"But what's that have to do with a mass shooting?"

"Guess we've got some work to do. Come on, Max."

The tech snatched the bag out of Carter's hands. "Chain of custody."

"I wasn't going to take it."

The tech mumbled something and walked away.

"Whatever. Say, Tony?

Cooper looked at him.

"You think that came from a local source?"

"Don't know. We'll have to run it down. What are you thinking?"

"There was someone acting strange in the other parking lot. Working triage for the EMTs. Is it possible that there's a connection?"

"Sometimes criminals will stick around to witness the effects of their crimes. Problem is, I don't see what the connection is between the drugs and the terrorist."

"Want to come with me and check out the woman in the lot?"

"It's a woman?"

"Yeah. Problem?"

"Pushers around here are all men."

"Pushers you know about. I'm going to see if she's still there. Come, Max."

"Hold on, hot shot. I'm coming." Detective Cooper followed him out of the gym and through the parking lots. When they got to the triage center, it had mostly cleared out. "So, where is she?"

"Looks like she's long gone."

"Maybe she'll turn up on some of the news footage and we can track her down that way."

"Maybe." Carter grabbed one of the volunteers. "Excuse me. Have you seen the female volunteer wearing the purple sweater. About this tall—" he held his hand up to his chin "wavy, light brown hair?"

"Sorry. No." The guy ran off.

Tony shook his head. "V-neck sweater? Good looking? Blue eyes?"

"Couldn't see her eyes. Too far away."

"You're barking up the wrong tree, Emerson."

"Oh? How do you know?"

"I know her. Know the whole family. For years. Almost a decade. She's a veterinarian. Just opened a practice over on Hawthorne."

"A vet? You mean, like someone who would have access to a large supply of ketamine?"

"No. I mean a vet, like someone who has a high regard for animal life and would never do anything to hurt a living creature. You've got it all wrong. Let it go."

"Sure you don't just have a soft spot for this girl and aren't turning a blind eye?"

"Believe me. This family has been to hell and back. No way is she involved. With the shooting or with drugs."

"Then you won't mind telling me her name."

Tony stared him down.

"I'm a cop, too. I can track her down with or without your help. But if you're so certain she's innocent, you've got nothing to hide."

"If you trust me, you won't go harassing her."

"If she's innocent, a few questions won't matter."

Tony sighed. "Her name's Faith Keller. And she's innocent."

Carter loaded Max into his vehicle. "We'll see."

"Let it go, man."

He closed his door and started his vehicle. Waved goodbye as he pulled out. But he made no promises. With or without Tony's approval, he was going to talk to Faith Keller.

CHAPTER 3

FAITH YAWNED, STRETCHED, AND RAN one finger down Salem's spine, their predefined morning greeting. Salem was Faith's best and only version of a security system—he was a big black tomcat who came with the barn she bought and converted into her veterinarian clinic. He had no interest in getting in her car or going home with her, he disdained snuggling or playing with jingling bell toys or yarn, and he didn't care for any of the scratching posts or towers she'd bought him. What he did enjoy—relish, was more like it—was chasing away field mice, terrorizing the smaller dogs that came to the clinic, and devouring the scraps of cured salmon that bothered her on vegan principle to buy but still delighted her as a pet owner to feed him.

"Long night last night, Salem. Wonder if you heard the sirens all the way out here." She opened a can of food for him, which he looked at with scorn. A chuckle burbled out in the middle of another yawn. "You're spoiled." She opened the mini fridge she kept behind the counter, pulled out a sliver of salmon, and dropped it into his bowl with the chicken stew. "Hope the fish doesn't clash with the bird."

Salem didn't seem to mind.

Faith checked her calendar and then her supplies, making sure she was ready for her morning appointments. When the bell on the door jingled, she turned, surprised a client was in so early. "I hope nothing's wrong—"

David James stood there, looking far more awake and alert than she felt.

"David! This is a nice surprise. I was worried a client had an emergency. I'm about fifteen minutes from opening yet."

"I know. I saw the hours posted. I just thought I should come in and get my paperwork filled out."

"Of course. That's a great idea. Paperwork. Um—" Faith looked around. Salem hissed up at him.

David glanced down, smiled kind of nervously at the cat. "That is, of course, unless you changed your mind."

"What? Oh, no. I'm just tired. And a little scatterbrained today."

"Looks like you could use me, then."

"God, yes. And sooner rather than later."

"I can start today, if you'd like."

Faith sighed and plopped down behind the desk. "That would probably be a big help. I'm just dragging from last night."

"How long were you there?"

She bit her lip. Lies really bothered her. Instead of revealing her whole traumatic past and talking about where she'd really been—and the fact that once she got home she didn't manage to sleep, anyway—she just answered a different question. "I got home around four-thirty, I think. I don't know. I was too tired to really keep close count."

"Did you see the news today? They revealed the shooter's identity."

"No. Who was it? Do they think it was ISIS or Al-Qaeda? Here? In Cathedral Lake?" She logged onto the computer and looked up generic forms for hiring a new employee. Man, she really did need an office assistant.

"No, they don't think it was a terror cell at all. Just a lone gunman. Guy by the name of Eli Yavin. Used to coach at Cathedral Lake High. Lost his job a few years ago because of budget cuts. Media is speculating whether he left a manifesto, but the cops or feds or whoever's in charge aren't saying if one was found."

She printed the forms and handed them to David to fill out. "Was the job loss his motive? Why'd he wait so long?"

He shrugged and picked up a pen. "I don't know. The cops haven't released much information yet, and the news has as many opinions as they have reporters. All I know is we've got fifteen dead so far, five more critical. Sixty total spent the night at three different local hospitals. Seventy-three others were treated and released. They say it was the worst attack western Pennsylvania has ever seen."

"No kidding. There hasn't been anything this brutal since the school stabbing at Franklin Regional in 2014."

"I think this one is going to end up worse than that."

"Me, too." She sighed. "I should really check in with my dad. I'm sure he got called to the hospital last night."

"If he did, he's probably sleeping it off."

Faith yawned. "Good point."

David passed his paperwork over to her, and she glanced at. Everything looked in order. Meanwhile, the door opened and Mrs. Heffernan came in with her Chihuahuas—Snickerdoodle and Gingersnap. Leashes tangled and wrapped around Mrs. Heffernan's legs. She only managed to keep from falling by clinging to the door handle. Instead of extracting herself and admonishing the dogs, she laughed about it, her cackles adding to their yaps.

And Faith's growing headache.

Before she summoned the energy to deal with it, David reached over the counter and spun the computer screen to see the calendar. Then he approached the woman and shook her hand. "Missus Heffernan. It's nice to see you this morning. I trust you had no trouble getting here. The police still have some of the roads blocked after last night's incident. And how are Snickerdoodle and Gingersnap today?" He bent down and petted the little monsters on their ever-moving heads.

Mrs. Heffernan just blinked.

Salem darted in, flattened his ears, and swished his tail. He hissed at the dogs, who took no notice and continued to flounce around their owner's legs.

Dumb dogs.

So Salem pounced, adding to the melee, swiping his paws at the already hyper dogs, who promptly amped up their energy and ran further circles around Mrs. Heffernan. Faith hurried over, swooped a spitting Salem into her arms, and ushered him outside while David untangled the leashes.

Mrs. Heffernan batted her overly-mascaraed lashes at Faith's new assistant and fanned herself.

"Well, as I was about to say," he said, slightly breathless, a little more red-faced and sweaty, "I'm David, Doctor Keller's new assistant. Right this way, please." And like nothing had happened, he led her down the hall.

He was going to work out just fine.

Faith didn't even question if he knew where to take them. She didn't care if he led them right out to the horses' paddock. She'd find them when she was good and ready. At the moment, she needed to take something for her migraine-in-the-making and maybe get some caffeine in her system before she crashed.

She walked down the hall to the very back of the barn-turned-clinic. The entire structure had been divided into sections. In the front was the entry, a decent-sized area which she'd furnished with a homey cane porch set covered in apricot and olive striped cushions. Down the hallway from the waiting area were exam rooms, the kennel, her OR, the pharmacy, the break room, and of course, her office in the very back. She entered the lounge and set the coffee pot on to brew. Then she went to her office, opened her desk drawer, and took out four Advil. Knowing that was too many, although sorely tempted, she put one back, then went and stared at the coffee pot until enough had dripped into the carafe to make a respectably-sized mug. Scalding her throat, she downed the ibuprofen and replaced the carafe to let the rest of the coffee finish brewing.

Only then did she feel ready to deal with the not-so-sweet cookie twins. She set off to find the Chihuahuas, but stopped in the middle of the hall.

"Damn it."

There was a problem in the pharmacy. She tried the door. It was still locked, but she peered through the window and assessed the situation. A circle had been cut into the glass of the drug cabinet to unlatch the lock and open the door. From where she stood, she could tell some of her inventory was missing.

She unlocked the door, walked into the room, and strode to the cabinet. She didn't have to unlock it or open the door to see her worst fears realized.

She'd been completely cleaned out.

FAITH HUNG A TOWEL OVER the cabinet door so no one could see that she'd been robbed. Satisfied she'd hidden the problem, she headed for the hall. When she opened the door, she almost ran into David, who stood there, hand poised to knock. She jumped and clutched her chest.

"Sorry," he said. "Didn't mean to scare you. But the cookie monsters are making a bit of a racket."

"Cookie monsters. That's funny. I call them that, too." She made to step around him.

"Everything okay? You seem rattled."

"Fine, fine. Listen, stay out of the pharmacy. I, uh… I have some work to do in there before I teach you my system."

He shrugged. "Whatever you say. I'm going back up front to look through the files, try to familiarize myself with the system and the client list."

"Thanks, David. After you look through things, please file your paperwork."

"You got it."

She waited until he walked down the hall before she headed toward Mrs. Heffernan and her twin nightmares. Cookie monsters. Funny. And accurate.

While Faith walked down the hall, she kept making mental notes to herself to call the police. To try to remember the other dates that she'd been hit. To try to remember what else she'd noticed missing.

This was big. It made four times her clinic had been hit. That she knew of.

Okay, after all the nasty history her family had with drug thefts at work, she should have been much more meticulous. She knew that. Mea culpa and all. But she'd been so busy getting her practice up and running. The last thing on her mind was tight security, fastidious record-keeping, and constant surveillance of her drug cabinet. She ran a tiny veterinarian practice in rural Cathedral Lake. Hell, she was surprised her mailing address was even Cathedral Lake proper. Another mile, it wouldn't even say Hawthorne Road, it would just say Rural Route 1. Bet half the town didn't even know she was there, and she'd been open for almost a year.

Who was doing this? And why would they steal from her? Well, she knew what they wanted, but why her? Surely the shelter or a bigger practice would have a larger stash.

And surely they would have better security and better records.

God, she was so stupid!

But the other thefts were so small. She'd barely noticed them. That's why she didn't report them. She figured she just miscounted or misplaced things.

Now she knew better.

Another mental note—she needed to trust her instincts.

She let herself into the exam room, but her thoughts were in turmoil. A particularly loud yap and a little nip on her finger brought her attention back to what she was doing.

"Are you feeling all right, dear? You usually dote on little Snickeykins and Gingerpoos." Mrs. Heffernan leaned down and let her face get laved with dual Chihuahua kisses.

"I'm fine. Just thinking about the attack."

She sat up, face wet with dog slobber, and didn't wipe it off. "Oh, I know. Isn't it just awful? Did you know anyone there?"

"I was there."

"Oh, you poor dear!"

Faith found herself wrapped in a suffocating hug, hands pinned at her sides. The dogs nipped at her heels.

"Oh, you puppies hush now." Mrs. Heffernan pulled away, her damp cheek sticking to Faith's hair and taking a few strands with it. They clung to her face, the loose tendrils hanging off her chin and wafting in the air conditioning.

Faith had to look away so she didn't laugh. She finished vaccinating the dogs and gave them each a treat, still listening to Mrs. Heffernan prattle on about the terrorist. She repeated everything David had already mentioned.

"You weren't hurt, were you?"

"No." She thought about her head and ribs and calf and absolutely refused to mention the bruises. "We were all fine. I'm just glad it's over." She bent and made notes in the chart, still not willing to look at Mrs. Heffernan despite her mood having darkened. "You're all set to go. I'll ring you up out front and get the boys their tags."

David was at the desk when she went out. A familiar man with a German shepherd sat in the waiting area. He wasn't a customer—of that much she was certain—but she knew him from somewhere. "Hello. I'll be right with you. I just need to finish with this client."

He had dark hair and piercing blue eyes that seemed to stare into her deepest thoughts. Even though she had nothing to hide, it unnerved her, and she looked away.

"Here, David, let me show you how to do this." She showed David how to enter the charges into the computer, how to create the tags for the dogs, and how to handle a credit card payment. When Mrs. Heffernan was gone, amid another tangle of leashes and a cacophony of barks and laughter, Faith turned to the man. "My apologies for the delay. I'm training a new assistant so there is bound to be a learning curve and some slowdowns for a while. How can I help you?"

He unfolded his tall frame from the woven cane chair and walked over to her. His dog stayed obediently at his side. "Doctor Keller. I'm Officer Carter Emerson. I'm here about some ketamine that was found last night at Cathedral Lake High."

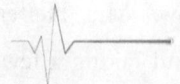

IF THE ROOM WASN'T ALREADY whirling from Faith's lack of sleep, it would certainly have started to spin then. She felt the first stirrings of a panic attack coming on and remembered what Tod had said.

Deep breaths.

Find the exits.

Know it's safe.

She took a deep breath. She was in her barn, her clinic. With the police. She was safe. But what did he want with her? Breathe!

What the hell were those other techniques?

She closed her eyes and took another deep breath. Why couldn't she ever remember the other—oh, yeah.

Hand taps to the rhythm. *Tap. Tap tap. Tap tap tap. Tap tap. Tap.*

Eye movements with the taps. *Tap. Tap tap. Tap tap—*

"Doctor Keller, is something wrong?"

"I forgot to hum."

"I'm sorry?"

She took another deep breath and shook her head. Damned if she didn't feel better. Not great, but at least well enough to deal with whatever this fresh hell was. "No, I'm sorry. Last night was a nightmare, and I didn't get any sleep. This morning started out just as badly. I'm just not myself today. Please excuse me. Why don't we go to my office?" She gestured down the hall and mentally berated herself for babbling.

He started walking, his dog at his heels.

Faith turned around. "David, when the next clients arrive, please just show them to the exam rooms. Tell them I'll be with them as soon as I can."

"Assuming anyone gets past all the roads the police closed down. It's still a mess out there."

Officer Emerson turned and looked at him. So did his dog.

Faith just raised her eyebrows and shrugged. "Well, we all made it. Let's just see who turns up, shall we?"

She led the officer to her office, taking care to block his view of the pharmacy when they passed it. If he noticed their awkward position in the hallway, he didn't mention it.

When they were seated, she said, "Your dog is beautiful. What's his name?"

"Max."

"Hi, Max. Are civilians allowed to pet police dogs?"

"They are, with the handler's consent. But we're here in an official capacity, and I'd like to ask you a few questions."

"Surely that can wait a few minutes, Officer."

He leaned back in his chair and gestured for her to acknowledge Max before they got started.

She got the feeling that the way she treated the dog was somehow still part of the interview, but she didn't care. After treating two high-strung, high-maintenance dogs and dealing with their even higher-strung, higher-maintenance owner, she could deal with one attractive and surly officer.

And his gorgeous dog.

She walked around her desk and squatted down in front of Officer Emerson, close to the dog. Instead of looking at Max, she kept her gaze locked on the cop's. His eyes were the deepest blue, flecks of peacock and jay a bright pop against the dark fringe of his long lashes. He didn't smile, didn't flinch, didn't look away. Faith maintained eye contact while raising her closed hand to the dog and allowing him to sniff her fist, to catch her scent without being intimidated by her looming over him, by her staring him down, by her open hand threatening him.

This was the test. Would he accept her?

Max sniffed. Sniffed again. Neither came toward her nor backed away.

Faith lowered her hand to his shoulder, opened her fist, and stroked his fur gently. He didn't relax, but he did shuffle toward her. Only then did she break eye contact with Officer Emerson and really give Max some love.

"Aren't you a gorgeous boy?" She put both hands on him then and gave him a good scratch on the shoulders and then behind the ears.

Could have sworn he half-closed his eyes and tipped his head back.

He definitely let his tongue loll out.

She dropped to one knee to better support her weight. Probably going to be there for a while doting on him.

Gave her a pretty nice vantage point for gazing at another gorgeous boy, too.

"Doesn't your daddy ever love on you like this, huh, Max? Has Daddy been neglecting you?"

"I don't think he knows me as his father."

She looked up at him. "Well, what does he call you?"

His brows drew down in dark mirrored slashes. "I don't know. I never asked him before."

She laughed. "He's pretty smart. He might surprise you and answer."

"Doctor Keller, if you wouldn't mind, I'd like to talk to you about—"

Faith kept petting Max, who was much calmer and better behaved than the Chihuahuas from earlier. And she had no doubt training was a big part of it, but she was beginning to suspect there was more to his sedate behavior.

"Who is this dog's vet?" she interrupted.

"Pardon?"

"His vet? Has he had an appointment recently?" She might be a nervous wreck in all the other areas of her life, but when it came to animal health, she was an expert. It was the only time she felt in control, and she wouldn't back off on a diagnosis, even if she did anger a cop. "Do you even pet him often or check him regularly?"

Officer Emerson's gaze darkened and he stood.

Max took his cue from his master, and he also got off his haunches, although his gaze didn't harden and his hackles didn't rise.

"What, precisely, are you implying?"

"I'm not implying anything. I'm flat-out stating that your dog could be so docile not because of his training, but because of his condition. He needs treatment and both you and your vet missed it."

CHAPTER 4

CARTER SAW SEVEN SHADES OF red. He came to her clinic to question her, not to be berated about how he cared for his own dog.

He looked down at her, and she looked ready to fling her arms around Max and save him. Like he was in danger.

Hell, Max wasn't just his partner. He was his best friend. Didn't refer to himself as "daddy" like she insinuated was an injustice, but still… All right, now he was defending himself? No fucking way.

"Listen, lady. I didn't come here to—"

"Now I'm 'lady' to you? You were polite when you wanted to question me, but now that I want to help your dog, you call me names? Isn't that kind of backward?"

How the hell did this interview get turned around so fast? Carter ran his hand through his hair and marveled that this girl got under his skin as quick as she did. He'd busted guys with rap sheets longer than the Monongahela River who weren't able to rile him like she did.

"You seem to think you're the one calling the shots, here. I came here to ask you a few questions."

"Well, you're in my house, now, Officer. And you can ask me anything you want. But not while you're mistreating this animal. So you can let me treat him, you can call your vet to come get him and treat him, or you can watch me call Animal Control and report you for neglect. Which is it?"

One, two, three... nope. Ten was not going to be long enough. He breathed out slowly. "What are you talking about, neglect? Max is in prime condition. There's nothing wrong with him. His weight is perfect. His shots are up to date. I feed him holistic, grain-free food. Filtered water. Exercise him regularly. He gets regular screenings, extra ones, even. As well as training classes. He's the perfect dog."

"He's also got a sialocele."

"A what?"

"A sialocele. A salivary gland cyst."

"No way."

"Don't call my competence into question. I know what I'm talking about."

He stooped down in front of Max. "Show me."

She grabbed his hand and placed it in Max, buried it in the warm fur at his neck. "Feel right here. This lump."

He felt around and found a soft lump under the dog's left ear. Checked the other side... Wasn't one. "Are you sure that's what it is? Maybe it's a lymph node infection. Or maybe he got hurt in training."

"If it's a sialocele, training could have caused this. I'd have to aspirate to know for sure that's what it is."

"Aspirate. You mean, stick a needle in him?"

She met his gaze. "Yes."

"There's no other way to diagnose it? You have to poke him?" Carter felt for the lump again. Damned if she wasn't right. There was some kind of mass or swelling there. But did she really know what she was doing? Maybe he should take Max to his regular vet. Of course, if the vet was doing his job, he would have found it a few days ago at his appointment.

"Or surgery."

"You aren't cutting open my dog."

"Look, you're already here. Let me do a quick aspiration and confirm that's what it is. Then you can decide what you want to do."

He didn't want Max to suffer. If he was suffering. His demeanor seemed fine to him, despite what the vet thought. But some of that could just be training. Carter sighed. This was not what he expected to be doing at the moment.

"Better to know, right?" she asked. "You're already at a vet. This will save you from making an appointment elsewhere."

She was right. And what harm could she possibly do to him by sticking him with a needle? He didn't want to think about it. "Fine. What do we do?"

"Not we. I. Go wait in reception, and I'll take care of it."

"Not going to happen, Doc. If you're working on my dog, I'm going to be in the room."

"That's highly unusual."

"Well, that's the deal."

She stared at him for a moment, then she shrugged. "If you pass out, you're on your own. Max is my patient, not you."

If he passed out. What did she take him for? "Don't worry about me. Needles don't scare me."

"Said every man who ever passed out from giving blood. Suit yourself. Let's get him to the operating theater."

"You have an OR?"

A scowl crossed her face. "What do you think I do for a living? Give shots and offer treats? I have to have a designated operating room for, oh, I don't know… operating on animals." She shook her head and took the leash from him. "Come on, Max."

Both dog and master followed her out of the room and into a well-appointed surgical unit. She might be a new vet, but she seemed to have her shit together. "Where do you want me?"

"In the waiting room."

He sighed and swallowed his scathing retort. Instead, he crossed his arms and stared at her.

"Fine." She turned her back and began preparing something at a counter. "Get him up on the table and stand by his belly. I'll need unobstructed access to his neck, and I can't have you in the way."

Carter hated to admit it, given he was so suspicious of her, but she made the very picture of efficiency and competence. He watched her prepare a needle—a very large needle—for Max, and the room lurched.

She approached Max, and the dog looked up at her. He was far more trusting than Carter. Faith petted his head and whispered sweet nothings to him. Such a soothing technique before doing whatever she was about to do with that needle.

"Easy, boy. This will be over in just a minute." She moved the needle—the giant, massive needle—into position.

And Carter's world went black.

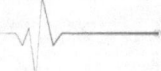

CARTER BLINKED, RUBBED HIS EYES. Where the hell was he? And why did his head hurt like a—

That vet's place. Max!

He bolted upright, and his stomach flopped. A groan escaped him, and he closed his eyes to make the room stop spinning.

"Easy, now," Faith said. "You had a rather nasty fall."

"Max." He didn't open his eyes, but something wet bumped his hand. His dog's nose. Max was there, and hopefully doing okay. The dog snuffled and Carter went to rub behind his ears.

"Careful," Faith said. "His neck might be a little tender for a while."

Carter opened his eyes and looked at his dog. The German shepherd stood there, eyes bright and alert, staring at his human partner. Relief flooded through Carter and he looked at the vet, who had her back to him while she busied herself with equipment at her counter. He looked around the room. She'd somehow managed to get him onto a large table, much like the one Max had been on. He knew he should be grateful, but he had so many questions. "I planned on watching you perform the procedure."

"I told you it wasn't a good idea. You passed out when you saw the needle."

He frowned and drew down his brows. The change in his expression hurt his already pounding head. "I don't know why that happened. I've never been bothered by needles or blood before. And I've seen more than my share of blood on the job." Hell, he'd been shot once and he hadn't passed out. Not that she needed to know that.

"Probably because you never saw someone you care about endure a procedure. It's sometimes different for ourselves or for strangers than it is with loved ones."

Max licked his hand and wagged his tail.

Damn, but that animal was smart. He scratched under Max's ear on the unaffected side of his head and swallowed the guilt at not being there for his K-9 partner when he needed him. "Well, Doc, how'd it go?"

"The fluid I extracted was ropy, thick. It had traces of blood in it. I drained the sialocele for now, but he should have surgery for a more permanent solution, otherwise it will just fill up again."

"Surgery? Isn't that risky?"

"Not for an experienced veterinary surgeon. Max should make a full recovery with no lasting effects. If your vet isn't familiar with the procedure, or isn't trained in surgery, I can do it."

He raised a brow and again was hit with a throbbing pain in his head.

"Or if you aren't comfortable with that, I can recommend someone."

Okay, he'd suspected her of a crime and had gone there to question her, but now he was just being rude. She'd taken care of his dog, recommended follow-up treatment, and apparently helped him when he… fainted, for fuck's sake. He was being an ass.

Not that her compassion and competence made her innocent.

He needed answers.

"I'm sorry, Doc. I've been a little surly. Maybe we can start over?"

She put down whatever it was she'd been so focused on and turned to face him. "Very well."

"I guess I should thank you for taking care of Max. And me."

Faith smiled. She had a pretty smile. It lit up her whole face.

"You're welcome."

"How'd you get me up on this table, anyway?"

"My assistant helped. The hardest part was containing Max. You collapsing upset him."

Carter again scratched behind his dog's ear. "He's very loyal."

"Most dogs are to their owners. He's a sweetheart, though."

"He's an officer. He's not supposed to be sweet."

She frowned. "I fail to see why he can't be both. Just because he's good at his job doesn't mean he can't have a lovable temperament. Especially with you."

Maybe he just didn't get their relationship. The K-9 was his partner, and he'd lay down his life for anyone on the force—even Max. But he'd never looked at the dog as anything more than a dog. Not until this lady forced him to. Okay, so he wasn't Max's "daddy" like she'd called Carter earlier, but they did have a bond. A strong one. An unshakable one.

How the hell had she seen it before he realized it himself?

Man, he hated that she read him better than he read her. Time to turn the tables and get down to business.

"Well, all business about Max aside, I'm here to talk to you about your ketamine supply."

She crossed her arms over her chest and tucked her hands under her arms, but not before Carter saw a slight tremble in them.

"What about it?"

"A large amount of ketamine was found at the gym last night. Enough to crystalize a huge supply of Special K. We thought we'd been doing a good job of controlling the drug market here in town, but finding a stash like that..." He shrugged.

"So what's that have to do with me?"

Carter tired of her looking down at him and rose to his feet. The room only rocked a bit, then he found his footing. He walked to the counter and looked down at her for a change. More like loomed over her. "You were the only vet who stuck around last night. I have to wonder if you were there to look after your investment."

Her face paled, and she cleared her throat.

"Should I take your silence as affirmation?"

She uncrossed her arms and balled her hands into fists at her side. "Absolutely not."

"Then you wouldn't mind if I had a peek at your pharmacy. Just to see—"

"Sure," she said and opened the door. "If you come back with a warrant."

He didn't have probable cause to force his way into her pharmacy, and he'd never get a warrant when Tony insisted she was clean. Not with him as the lead on the case. Not without making an end run around him, which could cripple or kill Carter's career. No. Had to do it another way. "So that's the way you want to play it, huh? Don't want to cooperate? Makes you look guilty."

"You can think whatever you want. Just do it somewhere else."

"Very well, then." He turned to his dog. "Come on, Max."

Max looked up at Faith and wagged his tail.

She petted him, leaned down, and kissed him on his head. "Bye, Max. Be well."

Carter whistled, and Max followed him out the door. While they walked toward the lobby, he looked at his four-legged partner. "Traitor. You're supposed to be on my side, not loving on our suspect."

Max just wagged his tail and kept trotting beside him.

No customers waited in the lobby. Faith's assistant sat behind the counter doing something on the computer. Might as well kill two birds with one stone. "Hey, man."

The assistant looked up. "Hello. Can I help you?"

"Sorry. I didn't catch your name earlier."

"Actually, you did. But after the fall you took, I'm not surprised you forgot."

Carter raised an eyebrow and immediately regretted it.

"David," the assistant said. "Name's David."

"Well, David. I suppose I owe you my thanks for helping me after I fell."

The guy shrugged. "No problem."

"Don't suppose you could answer a question or two for me."

"I think I should be asking you questions. Day of the week, month of the year. Who the president is."

"I'm not concussed."

"Never know. You might want a human doctor to check you out."

"Speaking of the non-human doctor—"

"Were we?"

"I was," Carter said. "What can you tell me about her?"

"Look, I needed a job and she hired me. This is my first day. We barely know each other. So if she's in trouble or something—"

"I won't know that until I get some answers. Don't suppose you'd let me into the pharmacy?"

David looked around, presumably for Faith, and lowered his voice. "I don't want to get mixed up in anything."

"If you just started, then you aren't mixed up in whatever I discover. But if you impede my investigation, well…"

"I don't think Doctor Keller would want me to let you into the pharmacy. She was in there earlier, and when she came out, she seemed particularly upset."

"Upset how?"

"I don't know. Off. Startled that I was there. Told me not to go in."

"Why don't we go take a look?" Carter asked.

"I don't know… Did you ask her?"

Carter just stared at him.

"I better not. Not without her okay. Or a warrant. Besides, I don't have a key and she keeps it locked."

Of course. He slipped his hand into his pocket and produced a business card. "Change your mind or think of anything else, and you give me a call. Okay?"

"Will do," David said.

A black cat jumped up on the counter and hissed at David. He pulled back, then shooed the feline. It jumped down to the floor and hissed at Max.

Carter laughed. Max didn't flinch.

The cat skulked away, and Carter and Max left the vet's office.

He needed to make an appointment with his vet.

Then he needed to figure out a way to get into that pharmacy.

CHAPTER 5

AFTER A LONG, HARD, TROUBLING day, Faith needed a break.
Hell, what she needed was advice. A confidant. She called Kacee to go out for
a drink, but she was hours away on a difficult custody case and didn't know
when she'd make it back. Instead of waiting, she called her mother.

"Hey, Mom. What 'cha doing?"

"You're a doctor, Faith. When in thw world are you going to learn to
annunciate your words?"

She bit back a sigh and wondered why she'd bothered calling her mother in
the first place. Any one of her other friends would have been a better choice,
even if she didn't feel comfortable confiding her police troubles to them. They
were ideal for kicking back and having a good time, putting away her woes and
just enjoying the evening.

"Faith?"

"Sorry. Something caught my attention." Not a total lie.

"So, what's up? Are you through with work for the day? Little early, isn't it?"

It was four o'clock. Not noon, for Pete's sake. "My client load lightened
considerably because some of the roads are still blocked."

"That's one of a number of reasons you should've had your practice in town."

Forget this crap. "Okay, well, I was just checking in—"

"You weren't just checking in. What do you need?"

"Why do you automatically think I need something when I call?"

"Because you don't often call unless you need something."

That time, Faith did sigh. "I just thought it might be nice to grab a drink and unwind. I thought you might be interested."

"Is Kacee or one of your other girlfriends going?"

"Nope. I asked you first." Okay, that one was a total lie, but just a little white one.

"Well, I'm flattered. The roads weren't blocked this close to town. My full staff made it in today but business is light, so I can cut out early."

Had to get another dig in about the location of her practice. "So, do you want me to pick you up, or do you want to meet somewhere?"

"Why don't you come here, then we can decide if we want two cars or one."

"Fine."

"There's a new little bistro on Maple that I've been dying to try. Want to grab dinner, too?"

A new place? Faith didn't know anything about it. Where were the exits? Was it dark in there? Were there hidden corners? Who owned it? What was the clientele like?

Was it safe?

She blinked, swallowed. Caught her breaths coming shorter and faster, her heartbeat racing.

"I forgot, honey. We don't have to go somewhere foreign to you."

Her pulse slowed a bit, her breaths grew fuller. "How about Sean's Pub and Grille?"

"A pub?"

If Faith rolled her eyes any farther, she'd be staring at her brain.

"Well, I'm sure they have a salad or something not fried. Sean's is fine. Are you leaving now?"

"I'm already in my car."

"See you in a few, honey." Her mother disconnected the call before Faith had a chance to hit the button.

She turned the heater down and cracked her window. It was warm for a Pennsylvania March.

Or she was overheating from the stress of dealing with her mother. What had she been thinking, calling her to go out?

She'd been a fool to think her mom would know what she should do about that officer. Most of her life, she'd been closer to her dad. Her twin Hope, for various reasons, had seemed to be her mother's favorite. They'd addressed those issues—and several more—after Hope died, and they'd come a long way. But every now and then, her mother lapsed back into criticize-mode. So not what she needed tonight. She needed compassion, clear-headed thinking.

Wonder which Vanessa Keller was showing up tonight—the one who changed after Hope's death or the one who Faith never seemed to impress?

So far, it looked like she'd be meeting the latter.

Damn it.

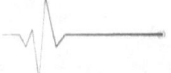

CATHEDRAL LAKE NURSERY HELD THE titles of both largest and best nursery in the area. Her parents had purchased it after Hope died, when her dad was looking for a new focus in his life. He'd since gone back to practicing medicine, but her mother had stayed on to manage the place. She had an affinity for growing plants, an eye for landscape design, and a marketing acumen that rivaled that of any professional firm. She'd grown an already thriving nursery into a dominant force in the landscape market—even starting an online and mail-order segment.

Vanessa Keller was resourceful, no doubt. Maybe she was the person to talk to, after all.

Faith pulled into the parking lot of the nursery and headed inside to find her mom. She was just exiting her office with another employee, likely giving final instructions before she left.

Her mother looked up, smiled at her, and held up one finger.

Yep, definitely giving instructions before leaving.

Faith waved to them and started browsing the store. Indoors they stocked some smaller statuary, books on gardening, seasonal decor, houseplants, and tools and gloves and such. A festive wreath of Easter lilies caught her attention, and she wondered how it would look on the door of her practice. Might be kind of nice to spruce things up for the holidays.

"You ready?"

She jumped when she heard her mother's voice directly behind her, never having heard her approach. After Faith caught her breath, she smiled and turned toward her mom. "How much is this?"

"The markup on that is ridiculous. If people knew how easy it was to make floral decor, I'd never sell another wreath. If you want it, consider it a gift."

"No. I can pay for it. What's it cost?"

"If you insist on paying, pay for the materials. I have twenty-five dollars in it."

"But what are you selling it for?"

Her mother turned and called to the guy at the counter. "Felix?"

"Yes, Miz K."

"Leave a note on my desk to adjust the inventory. I'm giving this wreath to my daughter, and I'll take care of the details tomorrow."

"You got it."

"Let's go, Faith." Her mom scooped up the wreath and headed for the door.

Outside, Faith turned to her. "I can't believe you did that. I'm not destitute. If I want a wreath, I can pay for it myself."

"Can't a mother give her daughter a gift?"

"Not when she thinks her daughter can't afford a little frivolity once in a while."

"The wreath is eighty-nine dollars, ninety-nine cents. Do you really want to cough up ninety bucks for it?"

"You're charging ninety dollars for a wreath?"

"And I can barely keep them on the shelves. Like I said, people just don't realize how easy they are to make."

"I'm not giving you ninety for it. But I will give you twenty-five."

"You can leave the tip tonight and we'll call it even. So, two cars or one?"

"Mom." She hated being handled like that.

"Two cars, it is," her mom said. "No point in backtracking here. We can each just go straight home from the pub."

Well, that settled that. The mighty Vanessa Keller had spoken. God, Faith hated being steamrolled like that. Why had she even asked her mother to go out?

Oh, that's right. Because she needed advice from someone who might have a clue what she should do. And as her father had been in a similar situation before, her mother could draw on their experience and advise her.

Would have been simpler to talk to her dad. Too bad he was likely still busy from the attack.

Just thinking about the event at the basketball arena gave her a chill, caught her breath. Images of the carnage and the aftermath flashed through her mind. She closed her eyes in an attempt to avoid the onslaught of memories, but they only grew more vivid. So she popped her eyes open and looked at her surroundings. Familiar building, familiar lot, familiar cars. Before she succumbed to yet another anxiety attack, she focused on her management techniques.

Her mom rolled down her window. "Faith? What are you waiting for?"

She blinked a few times, startled when her mom spoke to her. She'd been too lost in her thoughts to even realize her mother had gotten in her car, let alone was ready to pull away. "I'm coming. You don't have to wait for me."

"Are you all right?"

Faith chose not to answer and instead got in her car. Her hands shook, her pulse raced. It took all the concentration she could muster, but she managed to calm down. She knew she'd be subjected to the third degree when they got to the restaurant. Dreading the evening in front of her, she drove slowly. By the time she pulled into the parking lot, her breathing had stabilized and she'd calmed down, but her stomach still churned with anxiety. She walked in without waiting for her mother and chose a seat with her back against the wall, where she could see all the windows and exits and not be surprised from behind.

The restaurant hadn't changed since… well, it had never changed in her lifetime. Dim lighting, scarred tables, floor a little too sticky for her liking. But the familiarity didn't breed contempt, it bred comfort. She liked that she had the menu memorized, that the napkin containers on the table would be packed too full to remove only one, that a bottle of hot sauce would be brought to the table no matter what was ordered. More important, she loved knowing just where the restrooms were, just where the bar was, just where a live band would set up on the weekend—and just where she could go to hide or escape in case of emergency.

Vanessa hurried inside, shrugged off her coat, and sat across the table from her. "Again?"

She and her mother may not have been close while she grew up, but the woman could still read her without fail. In some respects it made things easier. In others, it sucked.

"Sorry. I got caught up thinking about last night."

"Dad said it was bad. Worse than anything even the news suggested."

Tears welled in Faith's eyes. "It was awful."

"Jensen said you were… upset before everything went to hell."

Her brother, the traitor. "Mom, I don't want to talk about this."

Her mother reached across the table and grabbed her hand. "Honey. Maybe you should take some time off."

Faith yanked her hand away. "And what good would that do me?"

The waitress walked over and smiled at them, handed each of them a menu. "Welcome to Sean's Pub and Grille. I'm Ashley, and I'll be serving you today. What can I get you to drink?"

"Red wine, please," Vanessa said.

"A cosmo for me."

"Do you really think you should be drinking?" her mom asked.

"And why not?"

Ashley cracked her gum and waited for the finalized drink order with pen in hand and gaze trained on Faith.

Her mom glanced at the waitress then back to Faith. She cocked her head to the side.

Faith glared at her.

"Your medicine." Just because it was whispered—or stage whispered, as it happened—didn't mean the waitress didn't hear her. Didn't mean everyone in the restaurant didn't hear.

"Cosmo," Faith said again. Through clenched teeth.

"Coming right up." Ashley's eyes widened before she walked away. Dashed away, more like it.

"Why would you embarrass me like that?" Faith asked her mother.

"Why are you drinking when your meds clearly state you shouldn't?"

"What do you know about my medication?"

"Only what your father told me when Tod first prescribed them. And thank God someone's talking to me, because Lord knows you haven't been very forthcoming with information."

Faith shook her head. She'd told her dad what medicine she'd taken because she wanted his medical opinion. But she'd never told him she stopped taking it because she didn't want a lecture. She never wanted her mother to know at all. Now she wasn't just a freak in public, she'd become a freak among her own family. "I so don't need this right now."

"I thought we came here to talk."

"We did, but not about this. My health is my business."

Her mom reached for her hand again, but Faith crossed her arms over her chest.

"Your health is my business. You're my daughter. I only want what's best for you."

"What's best for me right now is a drink to take the edge off."

"It's the fact that you have an edge to begin with that concerns me."

"Mom, I didn't ask you here to talk because I'm having trouble with—" She couldn't talk about the attack last night. Or the kidnapping she'd suffered last year. Didn't have the strength to muster the words. Instead, she pressed on. "I have a problem, and I need your advice."

"Another problem? Other than—"

"Yes, Mother." Faith interrupted her before the conversation took a turn to a topic she wanted—needed—to avoid. "It's an 'other than' situation."

"What's going on?"

Ashley returned with their drinks. "Decide on food yet?"

"Sorry," Faith said. "I haven't even looked at the menu." Like she needed to. She knew what she'd order. What she always ordered—a Greek salad and sweet potato fries. But nerves made her blurt out the first thing that came to her mind.

"No rush. I'll be back in a couple of minutes."

Faith's stomach churned. Going out had been a monumentally bad idea. But there was no way her mom would let her leave without discussing something, and she did need a fresh perspective…

"Remember when someone—" she couldn't bear to even say Wade's name aloud "—was stealing meds from the hospital pharmacy, and Dad was under suspicion?"

"Of course." Vanessa sat back in her chair and looked at Faith through hooded eyes.

"I know eventually the truth came out, but before that, how did you and Dad deal with it?"

"What's going on, Faith?"

She hated when her mom had that tone. That you-fucked-up-and-I-need-to-fix-it tone. This situation totally wasn't her fault.

Well, mostly wasn't her fault. Okay, maybe fifty-fifty.

"A cop came to see me today." She fiddled with the napkin dispenser, managed to rip three little pieces off the top napkin before tugging an entire wad free.

"And?"

"And he found drugs at the scene last night."

"So? What's that have to do with you?"

She couldn't meet her mother's gaze. Instead she continued shredding the damaged napkin. "Vials of ketamine. He thinks they came from me. Thinks I'm selling my supply to a dealer in the area. Or maybe he thinks I'm the dealer. I don't really know. I didn't let him get that far into his suspicions."

"Why don't you show him your inventory and prove it's not you?"

"Because the drugs are mine."

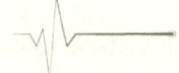

WELL, THAT HAD BEEN ONE of the longest days and nights of Faith's life. Nothing like spending time with her mother to make her feel like the biggest moron on the planet. Of course she knew she'd messed up by not keeping better track of her inventory, by not having a better security system, by not reporting the thefts.

She didn't go to her mother for a lecture, she'd gone for advice.

But there was none to be had. She endured an entire meal's length of "you should have" this and "why didn't you" that, of discussions about irresponsibility and culpability, of questions about her plans and her preparations, before she'd had finally had enough. Not that she'd eaten. Her stomach hurt too much to swallow a bite. By the time the bill came, she was ready to run screaming from her mother. Instead, she had to listen to a second lecture about being organized and prepared when she didn't have the money for the tip because she'd forgotten her purse at work.

"It's not that I need the money, Faith. It's the principle of it all. What if you were here alone? What would you have done then? How am I supposed to feel about the job we did raising you when you're such a mess?"

Every daughter loves it when her mother tells her she's a walking disaster. It was the sprinkles on top of her miserable day sundae.

Vanessa wouldn't let her leave until she promised to stop by for breakfast the following day to talk to her father. Just what she needed—another lecture. What a way to begin a morning.

So she promised, then she beat it out of there as fast as she could. It would have been prudent to drive under the speed limit, given she didn't have ID with her, but she just had to get out of there.

She came to the intersection where turning right would take her home and turning left would take her back to the nursery. Going home made the most sense. She was ninety-nine percent certain she'd left her purse at work. But there was that one-percent chance she'd put it down when she was looking at the wreaths, and she didn't want to have to deal with additional lectures on responsibility from her folks. So she drove to the nursery.

Her parents had given her and Jensen spare keys to the place, just in case, whatever that meant. At the moment, she was thrilled she'd kept it on her keychain rather than in her purse. She'd pop in, check the lost and found and the shelves by the wreaths, and then she'd get on her way. In and out, two minutes tops.

She fairly flew down the road and whipped into the nursery's parking lot, squealing her tires and sliding on the gravel. Thank God her mother didn't see that. Then she didn't even bother to park in a parking space, but rather pulled right up to the door. Good thing her mom didn't see that, either. She'd be racking up the lectures if her mom knew any of what she was doing.

Sometimes breaking the rules was fun. Other times necessary. Often both.

She let herself inside and hurried to the alarm keypad. That was easy enough to remember. They'd chosen Hope's birthday. She'd never forget that. It was her birthday, too.

When the alarm shut off, she looked around. All the leaves from the hanging baskets cast creepy shadows around the room, and the statuary looked like figures ready to pounce at any second. Her pulse quickened, her breaths grew rapid and shallow, her head spun.

Maybe it hadn't been such a good idea to stop by.

"Use your damn techniques, Faith." Her voice echoed in the dark, empty room, which only amped up her fear.

She focused on her breathing, located the exits. Tapped her fingers and hummed to the rhythm. A little time and a lot of effort later, she managed to pull herself together. And a quick search of the premises showed that her purse wasn't there.

All that for nothing.

She reset the alarm, relocked the door, and returned to her car. It took more than one try to get the key in the ignition, her hands trembled so much she nearly dropped it three times. It wasn't until she was half way home that she finally calmed.

God, she really was a mess. Her mom was right.

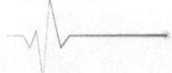

THE NEXT MORNING, AFTER ANOTHER restless night, she got up early, made herself as presentable and professional as possible, and headed to her parents' for breakfast. So what if it was out of her way? Or, to be more precise, in the complete opposite direction? Mom demanded a command performance, and she didn't have the strength to refuse. Besides, maybe her dad would have more than a lecture for her.

And really, sometimes a daughter just needed a hug from her dad.

She walked in the foyer exactly one minute before she was expected. At least she wouldn't get a lecture about being prompt. Scents of coffee and bananas wafted to her from down the hall, and she headed straight for the kitchen.

"Well, look who made it for breakfast." Sylvia, her parents' housekeeper, bustled over to her and wrapped her in a hug, then she held her at arm's length and studied her. "Are you eating? You look like you lost weight. You've got to take better care of yourself. You should stop by for dinner more often."

"Since I moved out, you've had far less work to do. I bet you haven't made one vegan meal in the last month."

"Well, there's where you're wrong. I've got a loaf of vegan banana bread cooling on the counter. Breakfast is served."

Faith squeezed Sylvia's hand and headed for the bread. "It looks divine. I could smell it from the foyer." She poured herself a cup of coffee. "Is it too hot to slice?"

"You sit right down at the table and I'll get it for you."

Yes, it was nice to be taken care of once in a while.

"Where are Mom and Dad?"

Sylvia brought a plate with an enormous slice of banana bread to the table and slid it in front of Faith. "Your father had to go in early. He's backed up."

She didn't have to explain. Faith knew with the blocked roads yesterday and his exhaustion from the emergency the night before that, he had to have fallen behind. "And Mom?"

"She'll be right down, I expect."

Faith took a bite of the warm bread and moaned. It practically melted on her tongue. "Honestly, Syl. You should cater. This is divine."

"I'll give you the recipe."

"I'd never do it justice."

"Then I'll make it for you more often. But you need to stop in more."

"Done."

The doorbell rang, and Sylvia headed for the hallway.

"I'll get it!" Vanessa's voice came from the front of the house.

Faith savored a second bite. She heard her mother speaking to someone, but the voices were muffled and she couldn't make them out. She continued drinking her coffee and eating her breakfast. It almost made up for missing her dad.

"Faith?" her mother said.

She looked up. Vanessa stood under the archway leading into the kitchen, worrying her lip. There was a man behind her, too, hidden by the slant of the hallway.

"Officer Emerson is here. He'd like to talk to you."

Faith's stomach roiled when the officer stepped into the kitchen, Max at his side. Was she not safe anywhere from anything?

"Doctor Keller," he said. "I have a few questions for you."

"I'm going to call Bella," her mom said and left the room.

Bella was an attorney. It frightened Faith to think she needed legal counsel, but it was probably a good idea.

"No need. This won't take long," the officer said. "I just need some clarification on a few things."

"I really shouldn't speak without my lawyer present," Faith said.

"Why?" he asked. "Got something to hide?"

CHAPTER 6

GOD, CARTER HOPED SHE DIDN'T lawyer up. He was ready to haul her down to the station if she tried it. Tony could say what he wanted and argue until he was blue in the face. She was involved in this whole drug mess.

And this was his chance to damn well prove it.

Faith took a long sip of her coffee.

He recognized the stalling tactic for what it was. She might be trying to look calm, but her face had paled, and her hands trembled. It was almost imperceptible, but he noticed.

"I've got nothing to hide. I just don't see why you're harassing me to begin with."

"You might have put me off yesterday, what with Max needing treatment and all, but—"

She got up and approached Max, stooped down to the dog's eye level. "And how are you today, handsome?" She let him sniff her hand before she petted him.

"He's fine. Now, about—"

"Did you schedule his follow up appointment yet? You don't want to wait."

"As a matter of fact, yes. He's going this afternoon."

"If you give me his vet's number, I can arrange to have the aspiration results sent over."

"Fine. Back to my questions."

Carter looked at his dog. Max nuzzled against her hands, clearly enjoying the affection. His K-9 partner needed training on how to behave like a cop around this dog whisperer. He made a mental note to talk to the trainer about it, then he turned his attention back to Faith.

"That's enough." She backed away from Max and took her seat at the table again. "Where were you last night?"

Her mom came back into the room. "Bella's on her way. She said not to say anything until she gets here."

"When?" Faith asked him.

"Faith." Her mother warned her with a brisk tone and stern glare.

"Why don't you just tell me everything you did after you left work. Let me establish a timeline."

"What do you need a timeline for? What am I supposed to be guilty of?"

"Who said you were guilty of anything?" he asked.

"Faith, enough," Mrs. Keller said. "Bella said you shouldn't talk to him."

"I'm happy to take her down to the station if she won't cooperate here."

This time both mother and daughter paled. The housekeeper mumbled something and bustled out of the room. Carter didn't care. His target—or maybe even targets—were right where he wanted them.

"You aren't taking her anywhere!" Mrs. Keller said.

He heard a commotion in the front of the house, then a woman blew into the kitchen. She was dressed to the nines in a business suit that probably cost more than his rent and carried a leather bag that likely cost just as much.

"Officer—" she glanced at his name tag "—Emerson. I'm Bella Perish. I'll be representing Doctor Keller. You know you aren't allowed to question someone who requested legal counsel until her attorney is present."

Perish. She had a reputation. He'd have to be on his toes. "Well, now, that's the thing. She never requested a lawyer."

"That's not my understanding."

"Her mother demanded, but she's not a minor, so that didn't count. And since she didn't ask herself, nor did she object to my questions, I have to believe she consented to the interview."

The hotshot attorney glanced at Faith. Glared, more like it.

"Do you wish to have legal representation during this interview, Faith?" she asked.

Faith nodded.

"Officer. You may proceed."

His jaw ticked, but he continued without delay. "I'll ask again. Where were you last night?"

Faith glanced at her lawyer, who nodded. "I left work, went to the nursery to meet my mom, then we had dinner at Sean's Pub and Grille."

"And what time did you leave after dinner?"

"I don't know. Seven-thirty? Eight? Mom, do you remember?"

Mrs. Keller also looked at the attorney, who again nodded. "We stayed and chatted for quite a while. I think it might have been closer to nine when we left."

Perfect. That lined up with his evidence. "And did you go straight home?"

"Yes," Mrs. Keller said.

"Doctor Keller?" he prompted.

Her eyes grew wide. Whe looked again for her lawyer's advice. The suit nodded, so Faith answered, voice barely above a whisper. "No."

Both women in the room snapped their attention away from him and focused on Faith.

"And where did you go then?"

"Officer Emerson," Miss Perish said, "what relevance do these questions have?"

"I believe I'm asking the questions here."

"Then I'm going to have to insist my client not answer."

"We can go downtown, then."

"Not without a warrant for her arrest. Do you have one?"

He sucked in a deep breath. He didn't, nor would he get one any time soon with Cooper blocking him to protect that family. Not without them admitting their culpability. Best he could hope for now was a warrant for the nursery. Maybe the vet's office. Which he'd be more than happy with. "I'm just doing my job, counselor. Trying to establish a timeline."

"For what?"

Couldn't hurt to tip his hand a little. "There was a disturbance reported at the Cathedral Lake Nursery last night."

"I didn't report anything," Mrs. Keller said.

"No, you didn't. One of the neighbors did. Seems there was some suspicious late night activity there."

"Why wasn't I notified?" Mrs. Keller asked.

"And what does this have to do with Doctor Keller?" Perish said. "I'd think you'd be talking to Missus Keller, as she runs the nursery."

"And we'll get to that. But I'm talking to Doctor Keller because a car matching her description was reported at the scene."

"The Keller family is entitled to visit their property anytime they choose," Perish said.

"She doesn't own any shares in the business. I checked."

"Well, her father and I certainly don't care if our kids come and go at their discretion."

"Makes it easier, doesn't it?" he asked.

"I beg your pardon?" Mrs. Keller said.

"What exactly are you getting at, Officer?"

Even the hot shot lady lawyer seemed frustrated. Good, maybe she'd make a mistake.

"One of our uniforms checked out the nursery last night when the call came in. Didn't see anything suspicious, so he walked the property."

"Without a warrant? Without my client's consent?"

"We were investigating. We didn't violate anyone's rights."

"Well, like I said, our kids can come and go as they please. Even if Faith was there, she has our permission."

Time to drop the *big* bomb. "And whose permission do you have for growing marijuana?"

IT FELT GOOD, DAMN GOOD, to have them scrambling to answer him. They'd requested a moment to confer in private, and as Carter was powerless to stop them, they'd stepped out of the room.

He absently scratched behind Max's ear and glanced at his watch. Another hour before the vet appointment.

His thoughts turned back to the Kellers. No way could he be denied a warrant now, not even with Tony stonewalling him. He all but had Faith Keller on record stating she'd been at the nursery the night before at the time in question. A little more probing, and he'd get her to admit it outright. No way would he miss out on the warrants then.

He felt it as sure as he felt the fur on Max's neck—the Kellers were mixed up in the Cathedral Lake drug business. They may have pinned it on someone else before. Hell, maybe they weren't even involved before. But it was all too coincidental. They were up to their necks in it this time, and he was going to expose them.

The housekeeper came back into the kitchen. "Oh, I'm sorry. It got quiet, so I thought you'd left."

"Nope. Still here. Could be a while still."

"Well, since you're waiting, can I offer you coffee? Banana bread? It's vegan."

Damn. That was too bad. It had smelled really good. "Coffee, please. Black."

She poured him a cup. "Sure I can't get you a slice? It's still slightly warm. Baked it myself. My own recipe."

That coffee was incredible. Sure beat the sludge at the station. Local coffee shops, too. "This is fine, ma'am. And darn good."

She turned toward the counter and busied herself, then walked to the table with a plate. Two thick slices of the bread were on it. "I saw the look of disdain on your face. I never used to like vegan food either. Turns out, I just didn't like the recipes I'd found online. Once I had to start cooking for Faith, I experimented until I found what worked. Even lost a few pounds doing it." She patted her generous belly.

Wonder how plump she was before?

"Trust me. I think this is even better than my regular recipe. One for you, one for your dog. There's no chocolate or anything in it that's bad for him." When he hesitated, she continued. "You don't want to hurt an old lady's feelings, do you?"

No, he didn't. He also didn't want to eat a slice of cardboard. But he sat at the table, planning to take a small bite then give both slices to Max.

He lifted a slice to his lips and took off a small corner. Damn. She didn't lie. It might have been the best banana bread he'd ever eaten. "You're right. It's delicious." He took a large bite, then gave the other slice to his dog.

"Told you." She went to the sink and started washing dishes.

He wolfed down the bread, then carried his dish to the sink. "So, have you worked for the Kellers long?"

She took his plate and submerged it in soapy water. "Since the year after their daughter died. Must be seven, oh, eight years now."

"And she's been vegan since you came here?"

"I think it started when she was in high school. Got a book by that PETA woman and never looked back."

"Newkirk?"

"That's the one." She scrubbed a cup and put it on the drainboard.

"Do you like working here?" He finished his coffee and passed her the cup.

"Love it. You'll never find a nicer family."

"You make them sound like the Brady Bunch."

She chuckled. "No. Nothing so fake as all that. They have their problems, same as everyone. But they've always treated me like family. And they've been through a lot. It takes strength of character to come out the other side of all that and still be okay. Stronger, even."

He wondered if she meant the death of Hope Keller, the hospital investigation into Royce Keller's culpability in her death, or the missing pharmaceuticals in his tenure at the hospital. Maybe a combination? He was about to question her further when the other ladies returned.

"Are you questioning Missus Albertson without her legal counsel present?" Bella Perish asked.

"I wasn't aware you were representing the entire household, Miss Perish."

She put her hands on her hips.

"But to answer your question, no. We were discussing her food."

"And my employment here," the housekeeper said.

Guess she was loyal to them. Wonder why such a suspicious family would have earned her trust? She seemed genuinely sweet and kind. And she could cook! Not that it mattered. Maybe they were paying her for her discretion.

But he didn't take her as the type to be bribed or paid off. He'd have to consider why her opinion of the Kellers was so high.

On the other hand, was every employee of every criminal aware of the illegal activities of their bosses? He thought not.

"Officer Emerson," Perish said, "unless there's anything further, I suggest you leave."

"Anything further? We're just getting started. What about the hidden marijuana growing on the nursery property? What about Doctor Keller's night-time run to the crop?"

"I didn't!" Faith yelled.

"Faith, be quiet," her mother said. "Let Bella handle this."

"No. I'm not going to stand here and be accused and harassed by this… this… this officer of the law when I've done nothing to him. Other than treat his dog."

"One thing has nothing to do with the other," he said. "I'm just doing my job."

"You're on a witch hunt. Yeah, I stopped at the nursery last night. Big deal. I was looking for my purse. That's not a crime. I was in and out of the building in a couple of minutes, and I never walked the grounds. You can look at the surveillance tapes if you won't take my word for it."

"There are tapes?" He looked at Vanessa. The recording could be just the proof he needed.

"Of course we monitor our property. We're not fools." She glanced at Faith.

"Well, I'm going to have to see them."

"Get a warrant, Officer," Perish said.

"I will."

"Until then," Mrs. Keller said, "I'd thank you to leave."

"Very well. Missus Albertson, is it?"

The housekeeper nodded.

"Thank you for the bread and coffee. It was delicious."

She nodded again and turned back to the sink.

He started down the hall, Max at his heels, but stopped and turned around. "One last thing."

Faith sighed. Her mother and her lawyer stared at him.

"Did you ever find your purse?"

Faith blinked. "No. I haven't been to work yet, as you've kept me here and made me late."

"But you think that's where you left it?"

She shrugged. "I don't know where else it could be. I was at the office all day until I met my mother. I didn't leave it at the nursery, so I must have forgotten it at work."

"Weird," he said. "Most women don't go anywhere without a purse."

"Hence the word forgotten."

"Hmm." He nodded to them. "Well, I'll be in touch. Come, Max." Then he rushed out the door. One last stop before he went for those warrants.

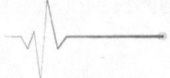

CARTER TURNED INTO THE PARKING lot of Faith Keller's clinic and almost spun out in the gravel. Max whined when he pitched in the car.

"Sorry, buddy. But we're in a hurry."

Four cars sat in the parking lot. He looked them over. None was Faith's. She didn't beat him there. He doubted she could have, but he didn't know if she'd known a short cut. He still wasn't too familiar with all the roads on the outskirts of town.

He got Max out of the car and headed inside. The grumpy black cat was on the counter, glaring and hissing at the other animals—and probably the people—in the room. A young woman clutched a teapot pig to her chest, her back turned to the fearsome cat. A man held the leash of a rather rambunctious Dalmatian who kept lunging at the malcontent feline, only to get yanked back by his master. And an elderly lady stroked an over-plump tabby in her lap.

"Salem, enough," David James said. The cat promptly jumped off the counter and disappeared down a hallway. "Officer Emerson, right? How can I help you?"

Carter and Max walked to the desk. "Busy day here."

"The boss isn't in yet. Appointments are backing up."

"I'm sure she'll be here soon." No need to offer why he knew that. "Can you tell me whether Doctor Keller left a bag or purse here?"

Splotches of color bloomed on his face and neck. "Why would I know that?"

"Just wondered if she left her things behind the desk."

"I'm guessing she keeps her personal belongings in her office."

"You have a key?"

His face flushed darker.

The bell on the door rang, and Carter turned around. "I'm sorry I'm—" Faith rushed inside, but she stopped short when she saw him. "What are you doing here?"

"Just following up on a lead." He looked her over, head to toe. No purse or bag.

She scowled. "Come with me to my office." Then she turned to David. "Start getting our customers into exam rooms. I won't be long."

Carter nodded to her assistant then called Max to attention. They both followed her down the hall.

Once inside her office, she closed the door behind him with a sharp snap. "What do you want? Bella told you I'm not to be questioned without her representation."

"I'm not here to question you. I just wanted to see if you were telling the truth about your bag."

She sighed and ran her hand through her hair. "Do you see me carrying a purse?"

"No. But I don't see one in your office, either."

Faith walked behind her desk, took a key out of her pocket, and fumbled with a lock. He didn't hear a tumbler turn, but she got the drawer open.

Her brows were furrowed when she stood, holding a bag.

"Satisfied?"

He shrugged.

"Well, I'm behind because of you, so if there's nothing else, I'd like to get back to work."

"Nothing now. But I'm sure we'll be seeing each other soon."

"Right. In the meantime, don't let the door hit you on the way out. Or do. I really don't care."

He grinned. She had fire, spunk. An indignant attitude for someone in such trouble.

God help him, but he found that attractive. She wasn't like anyone he'd ever met before. She intrigued him.

He just had to keep reminding himself that she was off limits. And probably headed to prison.

CHAPTER 7

FAITH PUT HER HEAD IN HER hands and rested her elbows on her desk. She couldn't take the stress. There was a better than average chance that she was going to have some kind of meltdown before the day was over.

David popped his head in the door. "You ready? Folks are getting restless."

She never looked up. "I have to make a couple of phone calls, then I'll be out. Can you record weights for all the animals?"

"Sure thing."

"Thanks. Tell everyone I'll be with them shortly."

He left, and she fought to hold back tears. What a mess. All because she'd been careless. It was too much. It was all just too much.

She grabbed her phone and called Tod. He told her he'd stay open for her, to come straight after work. Then she called the service dog breeder and scheduled an appointment for that evening. Anything to feel better, even if she had to potentially compromise her practice. People would just have to accept her new dog, and if they figured out why she had it, so be it.

Finally she sent a text to Bella and told her the cop had been at her clinic. She didn't even have her lab coat on when her phone beeped.

Bella: *u didn't answer any questions, right?*

Faith: *no. just had 2 prove purse was here*

Bella: *didn't have 2 prove anything. stop all communications w/ him*

Faith: *he's a cop. how do I ditch a cop?*

Bella: *tell him 2 go thru me*

Faith: *i'll try. thx*

Too damn hard. She finished donning her coat and headed off to her first client.

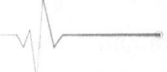

FAITH LOVED TOD. IN A savior kind of way, not an unprofessional way. She thanked her lucky stars—if she had any—that she had him to talk to.

Even if she felt bad that it was almost always after hours.

"I'm sorry to keep you at work so long," she said.

He laughed. "It's not like I have a long commute ahead of me." He led her through his foyer into his office. "Can I get you anything?"

"No, thanks." She was probably keeping him from dinner. "I don't expect to be long. I just needed to see you."

He gestured to the sofa, and she sat across from him. "So what's going on, Faith?"

She needed to talk to him. Had to vent, to rant. Get it all off her chest and out in the open.

But the words wouldn't come. The tears did, though.

She sobbed so hard and so long that he sat beside her on the sofa and offered her a tissue. After she'd settled and mopped up her face, she sank into the cushions. Didn't even have the courage to look at him.

"Feel better?" he asked.

"Yes. No." She sucked in a tremulous breath. "I don't know."

"Talk to me. What's wrong? Are the panic attacks getting worse?"

"You'd have panic attacks, too, if you were headed to prison."

"What?"

"There's this cop who's on a one-man crusade to put me away."

"Why? What did you do?"

"Nothing!" Faith got up and paced the room, tripped on his Aubusson rug, and slammed her knee into the coffee table. She plopped into the chair he'd vacated and let out a string of curses that would horrify Hollywood.

"Are you all right?" He rushed over to her and bent to examine her knee.

"Just another humiliation and pain in a sea of humiliations and pains. I'll survive." She hoped.

Tod walked out of the room and came back a moment later with an ice pack, which he put on her knee.

She flinched from the cold. And how tender her knee was. Probably chipped a bone, just what she needed. She'd be the only woman in jail on crutches. Some Amazon named Bertha with prison tats and body piercings would take advantage of her. Or beat her to within an inch of her life. She'd end up in solitary for her protection, only seeing daylight through the food slot in her door.

"Faith?"

She flinched again, this time from being jarred out of her nightmarish vision. "What am I going to do?"

"Why is this policeman after you?"

"Drugs. He thinks I'm selling drugs."

"Where on earth did he get that idea?"

The ice pack numbed more than her knee. Her hand froze. She shifted in her seat so she could switch hands.

Tod pulled an ottoman over to her, gently lifted her foot onto it, and balanced the ice pack on her knee. Then he rubbed her hands between his to warm them.

She sat back, grateful for the kindness. "He found vials of ketamine at the explosion site."

"So tell him to run the lot numbers and trace them back to the vet who received them. Maybe the vials were stolen from a delivery truck and aren't from a vet's office at all."

"No," Faith said. "They were definitely from a vet."

"And how do you know that?"

"Because they were stolen from my clinic."

He sat on the coffee table, more like his legs gave out than he chose to. "What's that?"

"I've been having trouble in my pharmacy. Vials have gone missing here and there."

"So the police will have a record of the thefts. That's good."

"I never reported them. I was convinced I'd just counted wrong or misplaced them. But the morning after the... incident at the gym, the glass on the medicine cabinet was broken. And I'd been cleaned out."

"Surely you reported that."

She shook her head. "No. I was worried about it, but I was so busy that day. And then the cop showed up."

"He could have investigated while the evidence was fresh. Why didn't you tell him?"

"I was scared! Then I noticed his dog was injured, and I performed a procedure to prove my diagnosis. After that—"

"He let you touch his dog? Officers in charge of K-9s don't do that."

Faith reflected on that for a moment. He was right. Everything she knew about K-9s and their handlers confirmed that. Their care was paramount. Emerson never should have trusted her with his dog.

Maybe he was testing her?

But to risk his dog's life just to observe her, question her? That wasn't right.

That flagrant disregard for the dog's treatment protocols combined with his negligence in Max's care told her all she needed to know about Officer Carter Emerson. He was an unfit animal owner. He didn't even refer to himself as the dog's daddy.

Well, that was her own preference. And he probably considered Max his partner rather than his animal child.

But still, he didn't care for the dog properly. And if he was careless with such a precious life, why would he be anything but careless with his investigation of her and the ketamine?

"Well, he let me. The dog had a sialocele. I drained it and tested the fluid. The cop insisted on watching me the entire time."

"Well, at least he was observing the dog's care."

She shook her head. "No. No, he wasn't. I didn't want him to watch, but he insisted. And he passed out."

Tod took a deep breath and let it out slowly. "Okay, well. Regardless, after all that, you should have reported the break-in. Break-ins. Now it will all look contrived."

She flung her hands in the air. "I know! I was careless and stupid, okay? Nothing my mother hasn't already drilled into me about a hundred times."

"So you spoke with your parents about this?"

"My mother. We had dinner last night. I won't bore you with the details, but I forgot my purse. On the way home from dinner, I stopped at the nursery to look for it. Someone reported a disturbance there, probably because I squealed my tires when I pulled in. The cops investigated and found a grow stash on the property. That Officer Emerson thinks I'm moving ketamine and marijuana and who knows what else through Cathedral Lake, maybe even using the nursery as a front. It's not just my life I've jeopardized. It's my parents' lives, too. And I have no way of proving otherwise."

"Faith—"

"Don't you get it? I'm totally screwed. He questioned me about it this morning. Bella told him he has to go through her and he needs a warrant. And he's going to get them."

"But there's nothing he can find."

"They already found a crop of marijuana. It's only a matter of time before he discovers the ketamine is mine. He's trying to tie it to me. He might already have managed to! With our family history, I don't stand a chance. We're connected to drugs everywhere we turn."

"But Faith, you aren't guilty of anything."

"I don't think that matters."

"Okay. Let's think about this rationally. Start with the marijuana. Did you or your mother plant that crop?"

"Of course not!"

"Doesn't it stand to reason, then, that you aren't guilty of it?"

"But it's on family property."

"Is it? The cops searched in the dark. They didn't have surveying equipment with them. Who's to say that was even Cathedral Lake Nursery property?"

She hadn't considered that. "But what if it is?"

"Then I'd hire a private investigator to look into employees who might have a history of drug possession or distribution."

Hmm. That idea had promise. "But my parents vet all their employees before hiring them."

"Mistakes happen. People get through. Maybe they took a chance on someone who relapsed or was never clean at all. Or someone started growing once they had access to the property. It could be any number of things. Doesn't mean it's your family. It's circumstantial."

"Mom has cameras all over the property. The cop asked for the footage of me from last night. Bella told him to get a warrant, but I'd just as soon give it to him to prove it wasn't me. But maybe the recordings will reveal even more."

"There you go. A little optimism will go a long way."

"But my clinic's pharmacy..." She let her thoughts trail off with her voice.

"Check your cameras. See if you can find the culprit there, too."

"I don't have cameras. Or any security system."

"Faith. What are you doing? You have to protect your clinic. You have to protect yourself. I would think you, of all people..." This time he let his voice trail off.

Her face flamed. She was so damaged. She didn't even react to trauma the way normal people did.

"I'm sorry. That was inappropriate. What I meant—"

"I know what you meant. And you're right. With all the fears I've developed, you'd think I'd be hyper-vigilant about security. But I procrastinated. I didn't want to think about a system because that would mean the threat was real. And I couldn't let it be real. I just couldn't live like that."

He took a deep breath, then he leaned forward and took her hand. "Faith, security is a business necessity, not a crutch. And certainly not a harbinger of doom. It's supposed to offer you peace."

"But if I need a system, that means I need protecting from someone. I can't go through another… another…"

"That's irrational. A security system doesn't protect you. It protects your property. That's why insurance premiums go down when you install them. They're a business decision. No different than a smoke alarm or a carbon dioxide detector. Those things are there because they're practical."

"Those things save lives. I don't want to live in a world where my life is on the line."

He squeezed her hand. "That's not an option. You can develop a disease. Get hit by a bus. Be stuck in a fire. And all those things are more likely than a second kidnapping. Have you been practicing your coping mechanisms?"

She nodded.

"Still won't consider group therapy? Medication?"

She shook her head.

"What about the service dog?"

She sighed and gingerly lowered her foot to the floor. "I'm actually going to look at them now. In fact, I'm very late. I've rescheduled twice because of everything that's going on. Besides, I've kept you from dinner long enough."

"Dinner can wait. I want to be sure you're okay. Are you all right?"

Like she ever would be. She pushed to her feet and smiled at him. "Thanks, Tod."

She left without answering his question.

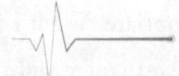

FAITH PULLED INTO THE PARKING lot of Smith's Service Animals. She'd driven an hour to get there—in fog, no less—but no distance was too much for a quality service. And Vonni Smith provided quality.

When Faith was in veterinarian school, Vonni had done a guest lecture. Despite being only a few years older than Faith, Vonni had already become a recognized name in the field. She bred the brightest, most obedient dogs, and six months ago she had started working with miniature horses.

Faith trusted her implicitly.

She scanned the property. It had grown since she'd last visited. The compact office building still connected to a large barn that housed the kennels. But an addition had been built, expanding the barn to twice its original size. There were new fenced in runs and obstacle courses next to the older ones. And there was now a rather large paddock with a miniature horse in it. The animal was tiny and compact, but Faith appreciated its intelligence and strength. She kept her distance and watched a trainer working with it for a while. The horse was learning to walk down a set of stairs rather than a ramp. The trainer and animal made it look so easy, but Faith knew the work that went into such a skill.

"Amazing, isn't it?"

Faith jumped and turned to see Vonni standing behind her. She had her thumbs tucked into the front pockets of her jeans and one booted foot propped on a railroad tie. Her gaze was trained on the paddock even as she spoke. "It's been a while. How've you been?"

"I guess I wouldn't be here if things were okay." Faith toed a stone in the parking lot, unable to meet Vonni's gaze.

"I heard about the abduction. I wanted to call, but I wasn't sure if you'd want to talk about it."

Faith shrugged. "Not so much."

"And since you're not here for a friendly visit or with a client of your own, I'm guessing things aren't any better."

She shook her head and repeated herself in a softer voice. "Not so much." Faith wiped a tear off her cheek. How the hell had she ended up here, in this situation? It wasn't her fault her sister got mixed up with a drug dealer then got herself killed. That Jimmy Salvo sought her out for retribution when the cops tried to put him away. That Bella got shot and she was next. That the basketball game had become a target for a terrorist. That the cops found drugs at the nursery.

None of it was her fault. None of it.

So why was she the one in therapy? Why was she the one afraid to go to unfamiliar places or to crowded venues? Why did she shoulder all the blame and the stress and the fear?

Why was she the one who needed a service animal just to get through the day?

Vonni patted her shoulder. "I think you've made a good choice. These animals are incredible."

"That's why I came to you." Her voice cracked. "You're the best."

"They're the best. I just help them learn a few new skills." She squeezed Faith's shoulder before letting go. "Let's go take a look. I think I have just the animal for you."

She wiped away another tear and followed Vonni through the barn door. Same kennels she'd seen before, but these ones were all empty. They walked through a second set of doors to the new addition. Faith stopped mid-stride, floored by the sight.

It was playtime at Smith's, and the animals frolicked with each other and some of Vonni's staff. Some chased a ball around, others played tug with large woven ropes. A few ran after each other and looked like they played tag, although Faith doubted the possibility. A beautiful dark retriever lapped up water at one of the bowls in the corner. When they walked in, the dog turned and looked at them, then darted through the melee to stand in front of them, greeting them with a lolling tongue and wagging tail.

"Aren't you beautiful?" Faith said. She stooped down and rubbed the dog behind the ears.

"This is Ruby. She's actually the dog I had in mind for you. She's almost two and is fully trained as a psychiatric service dog."

Faith bristled at the term but tamped down her frustration. That was why she was there.

"Just needs some time to bond with a handler," Vonni said.

"Ruby, huh?" She kept petting the dog, who reveled in the attention. "Because she looks red, I'm guessing."

"Actually, no. She came out light like all retrievers do. In her particular litter, all the puppies were given color names. The females were named after jewels and the males after wood."

"Wood?"

"Tree types. The boys were named Alder, Ash, Birch, Chestnut, Hickory, and Tupelo. The girls Ruby, Pearl, and Opal. It was mere chance that Ruby got as dark as she did. And that Pearl stayed fairly light."

"Do you have the whole litter?"

"Not a single one of her siblings left. They were all claimed before they were born."

Faith stood, and the dog sat patiently at her feet. "But not Ruby? What's wrong with her?"

"Not a thing. She was my pick of the litter. I planned on breeding her. When I trained her as a service dog, it was primarily to be certain of her temperament. She was a beauty. She would have borne great pups."

"Planned on? So why didn't you?"

"I think you need her more."

"Vonni, I—"

"Don't object. You need her, and she's basically ready to go. Besides, I'm overworked as it is now that we're working with the minis, and I'm looking for land to open another facility. I don't need to be breeding right now. My hands are full."

"But that's your livelihood."

"No, the training is. I like to breed my own so I know where my stock comes from, but I know a few breeders I trust. I can train their pups until I'm ready to start breeding again."

Faith bit her lip and looked down at Ruby. The dog actually winked at her. She was sold.

"So, how long do I have to travel here for our bonding training?"

"Are you convinced Ruby is the one, or do you want to look at a few others?"

"She's the one."

Ruby's tail thumped against her leg. She giggled. This dog had more personality than some people she knew.

"All right, then. Glad to hear it."

"But the training. How often do I need to come up here, and for how long? Because things are kind of crazy right now, and—"

"About that," Vonni said. "I have a proposition for you. What do you think of me staying in town for a while?"

CHAPTER 8

HE WINCED AGAINST THE TIRADE.

"What did I tell you?" Tony yelled.

Carter was in the middle of a dressing down. A massive one. He was just glad they were at the Square for a coffee break rather than at the precinct. This way, only the random passerby or food truck worker overheard them. Better than the whole squad.

Usually he and Tony got along just fine—he'd looked up to the guy forever—but ever since he started looking into the drugs found at the crime scene, they'd been butting heads. He had to signal Max a few times just during this short, one-sided conversation not to aggress on the detective.

"Why can't you listen?"

If Tony had yelled that phrase at him once in the last ten minutes, he'd yelled it twenty times.

Probably would yell it twenty more if Carter didn't stop him.

Unless Max put a stop to it. And that would be bad. Real bad.

Carter signaled Max to lie down, then he answered the detective. "You told me to stay away from the Kellers."

"But you didn't. I've got the Chief up my ass about this. He's furious!"

"So the Kellers are connected and protected from the top. I can still bring them down."

"Bring them—Carter, Chief isn't pissed because he's friends with the Kellers. He's angry because he also knows they're innocent. What you're doing is a waste of resources. Faith's not involved. None of them is."

"I get it, all right? I looked into their history. I know you originally investigated Royce Keller for the drug thefts at the hospital, and from there the two of you forged a friendship. I know you were involved in saving Faith Keller when she was abducted last year. What I don't know is why you're turning a blind eye to the evidence now. You're more objective than that. That was her ketamine at the gym. And that's their property where the marijuana plants are growing. You have to admit, that's more than coincidence. You'd investigate other people for a lot less."

The detective wiped off a bench in the center of the Square, sat down, and sipped his coffee. When Carter didn't join him, he nodded his head to the seat. When Carter finally sat beside him, Tony slipped off his sunglasses to look the younger cop in the eye. "You don't know them like I do. You're connecting dots to make a straight line, but you can't see half the dots on the page. If you could, you'd know the full picture isn't that she—or any of the Kellers—is guilty."

"Then how do you explain the evidence?"

"It's circumstantial at best. A good attorney will get the marijuana thrown out with the exclusionary rule in about three seconds flat. The cop who found it didn't have a warrant, he wasn't in active pursuit of a suspect, he didn't have owner permission to walk the property, and the plants weren't in plain view. That'll get tossed. Then what do you have?"

"Video from the night the plants were found."

"Inconclusive. Other than Faith coming and going from the building, there's nothing on film. And the timecode shows she couldn't have exited the back, gone to the crop, returned to the building, and left the way she came. Not enough time. Plus, none of the outdoor cameras picked up any activity out back."

"She could have used the building and time as her alibi. She'd know better than anyone how to avoid detection on the cameras."

"Supposition, not evidence."

"I still have the ketamine vials. Lot and batch numbers prove it was from Faith Keller's practice."

"Still circumstantial."

"Not when it's linked to her. Directly."

"You telling me nobody had access to vials but her?"

"Not unless someone broke in."

"Who's to say no one did?"

"She didn't report anything. No security alarms were triggered, no police were called to the clinic before or after hours."

"And it's not possible that she didn't know the vials were missing?"

"Come on, Tony. You think it's more likely that she didn't know she was robbed than that she took the stuff herself?"

"Look, kid. I don't know how the vials got out in public, but I know these people. A random stranger on the street, I'd be suspicious, too. But not the Kellers. Do you really think any one of them would get involved in the same type of illegal activity that cost them Hope's life? Do you honestly believe Faith would sell drugs when it was a drug dealer who kidnapped her last year? If there's a family in this town that hates the drug market more than the Kellers, I don't know who they are."

"What about motive?"

"What about it? She doesn't have one."

"She's a relatively new vet, so she's bound to have a ton in student loans to pay off. And she bought all that land, opened a new practice. That couldn't have been cheap. Money. Her motive is money."

"I haven't looked into the Keller's finances in almost a decade, but I can tell you back then, they had money. They still have a housekeeper, large house, fancy cars. Two businesses bringing in cash. I doubt either Keller kid took out student loans. As for the business, could have been family land. Her parents could have fronted her the money. She could have gotten a good deal on a loan. Woman-owned businesses are always given better rates. I don't think money is your motive."

What did that leave him with? Revenge? Love? Neither of those fit, either.

Carter sipped his iced mocha and looked around the Square. It had rained the day before, and the ground still sported puddles. Gray clouds stretched across the sky, blocking any hope of the sun warming the air and drying the land. Of the twenty or so pedestrians on the street, more than a few carried umbrellas, most wore coats to fight the chill, and all seemed to be in a hurry. Only he and Tony had taken a seat, and he regretted it. He hadn't wiped it like Tony had, and dampness seeped through his uniform pants. It was a miserable day, and it was only beginning.

Tony sighed. "Just think about what I'm telling you, all right? I really need you to turn down the heat on these folks."

"And just let go of the fact that Max found drugs at the gym?"

"No. We work the case. But we start from scratch, with an objective eye."

Seemed to Carter that Tony was the one who wasn't objective, but he could play ball. "Fine. We'll start over. But I can't imagine we'll be led in a different direction."

"Time will tell," Tony said. "Plus, you can help me with the Eli Yavin investigation. The Chief wants this wrapped up ASAP. Says the mayor is on him to close the investigation so the town can move on."

"We all want that." Since the attack at the gym, there had been traffic issues with people going to the site to leave flowers and bears and posters. Someone had organized a vigil for later that evening, and all hands were on deck for that. Yep. It was going to be a long and miserable day. And night.

"I hear Max got injured the other day," Tony said.

"Where'd you hear that?"

"I have my sources. Faith fix him up?"

Carter bristled. "She found the problem, ran a test. I had him at the vet yesterday to confirm her diagnosis."

"And?"

He sighed. "And she was right. His condition was probably caused by injury. Her treatment was just a patch, though. Max needs surgery, although he'll be fine when it's all done."

"When's it scheduled?"

"I have to make the appointment. Our vet doesn't do surgery anymore, but he recommended the best surgeon he knows."

"Hope it's someone beyond reproach. Who is it?"

Carter's jaw clenched before he answered. "Faith Keller."

Tony slipped his sunglasses on and stood. "That must just stick in your craw." He walked away with a smirk on his face.

Carter looked down at Max, who looked up at him. If he didn't know better, he'd swear the dog smirked, too. "Come on, buddy. We've got work to do."

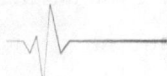

THREE CARS SAT IN THE parking lot at Faith's clinic when Carter pulled in. He got Max out of the car. Despite the miserable weather, the place looked inviting and cheery. A large floral wreath hung on the door, and a new welcome mat lay at the entry. It had a heart on it made entirely from paw prints and across the top was written, "All Species Welcome." He wasn't sure why, but he found that kind of funny.

He still had a smile on his face when he walked inside. No clients waited in the reception area, but the mean black cat was curled up on a chair. When it saw Max, its fur raised and it ran out of the room.

"I'm thinking you should just leave Max here," David said. He sat behind the counter, working on the computer. "He seems to be the only thing Salem is afraid of."

"He doesn't obey you?" Carter walked up to the counter.

David held up both hands. Scratches ran from knuckle to elbow on both arms. "Not so much."

"Well, I can't leave Max, but I'll make you a deal. I'll bring something that smells like him and leave it with you for a deterrent in exchange for some information."

"What kind of information?"

"We have a deal?"

"I thought police were supposed to protect and serve. Not barter."

"You talk to me, and you'll be helping me both protect and serve this town."

David looked down the hall, and Carter's gaze followed. He could hear voices, but they came from behind closed doors.

"You're going to get me in trouble. And I like this job. I need it."

"I won't."

"If Faith comes out and sees you here—"

"If she does, it won't be a problem, because I'm actually making an appointment. We can just chat while you put me in the system."

"Really? You want an appointment?"

"Max needs surgery, and our vet doesn't operate any longer. He recommended Doctor Keller for the procedure. So put us in the system, and while you schedule us, you and I can make small talk."

David's fingers flew over the keys. "Tuesday okay? She only operates on Tuesdays, unless there's an emergency."

"That's fine."

"First thing. You want Max to spend Monday night here before the surgery?"

"Absolutely not."

"Then you'll have to have him here by seven-thirty. And no food or water from midnight on."

"Not a problem."

"All right. So what do you want to know?" David continued typing.

"Have there been any thefts here in the last month?"

"I haven't worked here that long."

"Doesn't mean you don't know the answer."

He kept typing. "Faith didn't mention anything."

Something about his tone told Carter he wasn't totally forthcoming. The semantics game. One he knew well and played often. Fine. Time to get specific. "She didn't say anything to you?"

David shook his head.

"But are you aware of any issues?"

He shrugged and typed some more.

"What have you personally noticed?"

David sighed and looked down the hall again. "Drugs are missing. A lot of them."

"How do you know?"

Max's ears perked, and he turned his head. Carter looked behind him just as a bell tinkled and the door opened. Vanessa Keller stormed into the clinic and marched straight over to Carter.

"I knew you were here when I saw the K-9 patrol unit."

"Were you looking for me?"

She fisted her hands and put them on her hips. "No, I was *not* looking for you. I did, however, call our attorney. We're going to file harassment charges against you."

He noted the aggressive stance and signaled Max to lie down. "I'm not here in an investigative capacity, so I don't think the charge will stick."

"Then what are you doing here, if you're not hounding my daughter?"

Her voice had raised, and Max sat up. Before he could issue another command or answer the question, David spoke up. "Ma'am, if you would please lower your voice. The doctor has someone with her in the back."

"Who are you?" Vanessa scrutinized the new office assistant.

"David. Doctor Keller just hired me."

"David who? You look awfully familiar. Do I know you?"

"I don't believe we've ever met."

She bit her lip and leaned forward to peer at him.

Max shifted his position, and Carter commanded, *"Bleibe!"*

"What? Are you trying to sic your dog on me?" Vanessa's voice grew shrill, and Max bristled again.

Faith and another woman came out of one of the back rooms and hurried down the hall. The other woman held the collar of a beautiful dog with a shiny russet coat. Max rose to his feet, and Carter clenched his leash.

"What is going on out here?" Faith asked. "This is a place of business!"

"Yeah, looks like I disturbed a whole crowd." Carter glanced around the empty seats in the waiting area.

"He tried to get that dog to attack me." Vanessa rushed over to Faith's side.

"No, I didn't. It's a German command. Perfectly innocuous. I'm actually here with the best of intentions. My vet doesn't operate anymore. He recommended you for Max's surgery, and I was here making an appointment."

"Why didn't you just call?" Vanessa asked.

Faith walked over to Max and scratched behind his ear. After he leaned into her fingers to enjoy the rub, she stooped down and probed both sides of his neck. She glanced up at Carter. "Any problems since the aspiration?"

"No. He's been the perfect dog. But he always is, because of his training. He doesn't go off duty when he doesn't feel well, he just works through the discomfort, so changes in his demeanor don't really occur."

"A sensitive owner would notice even slight changes," the other woman said.

Carter looked her up and down. "And you are?"

"An expert in the field."

"Isn't this place just full of people who think they know my dog better than I do?"

"Well," Faith said, "I've already proven I do when I found Max's sialocele. And if I don't impress you, Vonni certainly should. She's even better with animals than I am."

"I wouldn't say that," the woman said. "We just work with them in different ways."

"What is it you do?" Carter asked her.

She glanced at Faith but didn't answer.

Faith rubbed Max on the head and stood. "This is Vonni Smith of Smith's Service Animals."

"Smith's?" Carter asked. "That's where Max came from."

"I know," Vonni said. "I supply the German shepherds to roughly ninety percent of the tri-state police forces."

"He's a great dog. You do the training yourself?"

"A combination of me and my staff. Until it's time to work with specific police commands, then the dogs are turned over to another specialist for their final training. And Missus Keller, don't worry. Many dogs, especially German breeds, are trained to respond to German commands. This officer wasn't trying to hurt you."

"I wouldn't be so sure about that." She glared at Carter.

"Well, Ms. Smith," he said, "you do great work. He's an amazing dog."

"Did you schedule the surgery yet?" Faith asked.

"First thing Tuesday morning."

"Don't let him eat or drink anything after midnight Monday."

"David already said."

"It's a quick procedure. We'll talk more right before I take him in, and then I'll go over after care with you."

"Thanks."

"If that's all, I'll see you Tuesday."

No. That wasn't all. Not by a long shot. But he promised Tony he'd play it cool, so he kept his mouth shut. He and Max walked out.

Before he closed the door, he heard Vanessa say to David, "Are you sure we haven't met?"

The woman was more persistent than a bloodhound. Glad he didn't have to be on that end of an investigation with her.

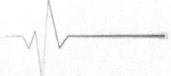

WHEN CARTER PULLED UP TO City Hall, he saw Bella Perish and another man standing in front of the door. Guess Vanessa Keller hadn't been kidding when she said they were filing harassment charges.

Would be just his luck if that was her father with her. Victor Perish had a more formidable reputation than his daughter.

Tony was going to be livid. The Chief would take it out on his ass. He wondered if he'd even have a job when this was all said and done.

No point in prolonging the inevitable. He got out, collected Max, and approached the couple.

"Officer Emerson." Bella Perish was the epitome of professional ice.

"Ms. Perish." He turned toward the gentleman with her. "And you are?"

He crossed his arms over his chest. "Doctor Royce Keller. Faith's father. Do you know why we're here?"

Carter gestured for Max to sit. "Your wife told me she was filing a harassment suit because I was at Faith's clinic when she arrived." He looked at Bella. "You should know, I wasn't there investigating anything." Didn't even blink when he lied. Always best to pepper in some truth so it wasn't noticeable. "I was only scheduling an appointment for Max."

"And you couldn't call?" Keller asked.

"Why does everyone keep asking me that?"

"It's a valid question," Perish said.

"No, I couldn't call. I didn't have her number handy, and I was in the area on patrol. It was faster to drop in than it would have been to look up the number."

"There are plenty of vets in the area. I'm sure the precinct advocates a particular doctor for the K-9 unit, anyway. I suggest you leave my client alone in every capacity. Get your dog treated elsewhere."

"My regular vet recommended her. Max needs surgery, and he felt she was the best vet for the job."

Keller ran a hand through his hair. "Well, we all want what's best for your dog, and Faith is the best. But don't make a habit out of seeing her. She's fragile, and you make things infinitely harder on her."

"Doctor Keller, surely you understand that I'm just doing my job. It's nothing personal."

"Oh, trust me. When you're the subject of a police investigation, it gets very personal."

"If you're referring to your prior experience, things worked out okay in the end, right? And now you have your own practice and a friend and ally on the force."

The precinct door flew open and Tony Cooper stalked down the stairs.

"Speak of the devil," Carter mumbled.

He glared at Carter but addressed the group. "What's going on here?"

"Just a little misunderstanding," Perish said. "And a lot of clarification."

"We're okay, Tony," Keller said.

Tony didn't budge.

"I'm sorry for any confusion this morning," Carter said.

Perish merely harrumphed and walked down the stairs.

Keller shook Tony's hand, then he turned to Carter. "Please. Have a little compassion. Faith isn't involved in anything illegal or immoral or indecent in anyway. She's just a victim. A misunderstood victim. You don't know how difficult that is for a person. Especially for a person like my daughter." And he followed Perish.

"Didn't I tell you to back off?" Tony said.

"I did. I went to the clinic to schedule Max's surgery, and—"

"You went there? Why didn't you just call?"

Long, miserable fucking day.

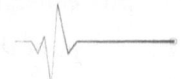

CARTER WRAPPED UP HIS LONG day by beginning a long night. The whole force had to work the Cathedral Lake Terror Attack Vigil at the gym. Tired and cranky, he barely acknowledged the officers who greeted him and Max when he walked up to the staging area.

He caught the tail end of Sergeant Freeman's instructions. "—won't be wearing riot gear. This needs to be a peaceful night. One of healing. Our presence shouldn't be noticed. Stay in the periphery, intervene only if necessary to keep the peace. Get to detractors discreetly so things don't get out of hand. The press is here, and the whole nation is watching. The mayor insists this go off without a hitch. Understood?"

"What kind of protests are we expecting, Sarge?" someone asked.

"We need to be prepared for anything. Hope for the best, plan for the worst."

"We cool?" Tony stood beside him, for once not wearing his sunglasses. Carter figured him for a sunglasses-at-night kind of guy, so perps couldn't see where he looked. Guess he didn't think he needed the edge.

And he was right. The SOB was tough as they came.

"We're tight."

"You know I... I mean, you're a good—" Tony cleared his throat. He sighed and ran his hand through his hair.

Carter didn't think he'd ever see the guy flustered. Should have known this kind of talk would make him uncomfortable, though.

Tony and Carter's brother had been best friends. Inseparable. Mark and Tony, Tony and Mark. Carter couldn't remember his childhood without picturing both of them, and he'd looked up to each almost equally. After high school, they remained inseparable and joined the Army. They served together in Iraq.

But then the ultimate separation—Mark didn't make it back.

Tony moved to Cathedral Lake, but he always kept tabs on the whole Emerson family. That was how Carter ended up a cop four hundred miles from home. He followed in the footsteps of the only brother he had left—Tony Cooper.

They tried to keep things on the professional side. At least, at work they did. But sometimes the past revisited them. Tony saw not a young officer, but a younger brother. And Carter saw not a detective at his precinct, but a hero to look up to.

Fighting about Faith Keller had taken a toll on their relationship. For both of them.

Carter bent down and made an unnecessary adjustment to Max's harness. Then he stood, but didn't meet Tony's gaze. Easiest to just change the subject. "So, what's really going on tonight? What kind of trouble are we expecting?"

"Hard to say." Tony was all business again. Thank God they'd put the awkwardness behind them.

"Coop." One of the detectives walked by and greeted Tony, nodded at Carter. Carter lifted his head in return.

"Sherm," Tony said. Then he continued talking to Carter, but he lowered his voice. "Sherman ran down Eli Yavin's background. Yavin had been an assistant coach with the Cathedral Lake basketball team. When Dillon retired five years ago, instead of promoting Yavin to head coach, they hired out of district. Yavin felt he was discriminated against because he was Jewish. Even toyed with a lawsuit against the school. They settled out of court. Details were sealed, but it looks like part of the deal was that the AD got him a job as an assistant coach at a school on the other side of the city."

"Why would the athletic director help him if he was an anti-Semite? You'd think Yavin would have been grateful."

"The AD isn't prejudiced. He just didn't think Yavin was qualified to run the team. When we questioned him, he said this attack was out of character for Yavin. That the guy was a nice, hard-working man. Or had been. Even the law suit surprised everyone in the district. Because the AD—and the students and the rest of the community—had thought so highly of Yavin before the suit, he tried to help him. And honestly, no legal agreement could force anyone in the district to help the guy find a new job. Based on what Sherman said after talking with the AD, the deal didn't stipulate the school had to help him find a new job or anything. That was all on his own. He just felt bad for the guy."

"So Yavin should have been grateful. Or at least have moved on."

"He did move on. Then he lost his new job due to budget cuts. Reapplied here when Nichols retired last year. But they didn't take him back. Hired Schultz instead."

"And that made him snap?" Carter asked.

"He was convinced Schultz was a Neo-Nazi. That the whole school board was prejudiced. Totally set him off."

"Not really the actions of a 'basically nice guy' then."

"No. No they weren't. Sherman and I are still going through his manifesto. Seems to us the guy was off his rocker. Totally nuts. Fanatical."

"The media never confirmed a manifesto was found."

"We didn't release that we found one. Captain wanted to get through tonight with as little drama as possible."

"Sounds like Yavin was working alone."

"He was," Tony said. "At least, as far as we can tell so far."

"Then there shouldn't be a problem tonight."

"You missed the beginning of Sarge's speech. We've heard rumors that four different groups will be coming to protest tonight."

"Four?"

"One group has been outside the synagogue for over twenty-four hours. They're claiming Yavin was framed."

"What? Why? We caught him in the act."

"They said they've known him all his life, and he was a pacifist. They know about his firing. They think that makes him the perfect scapegoat."

"Scapegoat for who?"

Tony shrugged. "ISIS, I think. They claim this was a terrorist attack—"

"It was a terrorist attack."

"They say it was radical Islamic extremism and the town is trying to hide it, using Yavin as the fall guy."

"There's no proof it was ISIS. Besides, why the hell would a terrorist cell attack here?"

"I don't know. It was a big crowd with media coverage. Lax security. An easy mark for a large head count."

"In Cathedral Lake?"

"It's possible. But unlikely. And given we caught Yavin and not an Islamic terrorist cell, we know that isn't the case. But that's what they're claiming. That's why they're coming to protest. On Yavin's behalf."

"Great." Carter rolled his shoulders, tried to relieve some of the tension building in his body. "Who else is coming?"

"Neo-Nazis. To celebrate. And to cause general mayhem. Their usual MO."

Carter sighed. "Who else?"

"This is what gives me the most concern. A group protesting our government's devolving relationship with Israel. And the corresponding pro-Palestine protestors."

"That's political stuff. This was just a crazy guy at a gym."

"Some people will use any platform to promote their cause. Things between the US and Israel are growing strained. We used to be their staunchest ally. Now we don't give them much support. It's causing a rift in the Middle East that may not be repaired this time. And no one wants to piss of the Israeli military."

"Mossad is coming here?" The thought made his blood frost. "And we're not wearing riot gear?"

"No. Not Mossad. Americans protesting our current foreign policy regarding Israel. People both pro-Israel and pro-Palestine. Things could get messy."

Carter let out a pent up breath with a huff. "Did the mayor call in the National Guard or anything?"

"Nope. All on us."

"And we have four—that we know of—groups coming to protest."

"Yep."

"What the fuck?"

"That's why all hands were called in."

"Hope it's enough."

Tony nodded his head toward the crowd. "Time to take our places. The vigil is about to start."

Carter checked his gear—his earpiece worked, his club was tucked into his belt, and his riot-control shot gun with bean bag rounds was slung over his shoulder—and then he readjusted Max's harness. "See ya later." He turned to walk toward the group he was stationed with.

"Hey," Tony said.

Carter turned around.

"Be careful. And watch your six."

"You, too." He watched Tony fade into the crowd, then he took his place with Max near the western entrance of the facility.

He'd never been to a vigil before. It was kind of beautiful—the hymns, the prayers, the candlelight and camaraderie. Not that he could pay close attention. His focus was trained elsewhere, observing the crowds, searching for trouble. Never looking at one thing for too long in case he missed something somewhere else.

His body buzzed with adrenalin. The pleasing scent of candle wax warred with the stench of cigarette smoke and sweat. Background chatter sometimes drowned out a speaker or refrain. He stayed on his toes.

The pacifist group marched in front of the choir, some holding signs, others holding candles or flowers. They stood, united, and swayed with the music.

Carter continued to scan the crowds.

Then his traveling gaze locked on one woman. Faith Keller.

She looked completely out of place. Nervous. Fidgety. Not one of the mourners, but there with a different purpose. Drugs?

But he'd promised Tony to lay off.

Still, he stared at her. He wasn't actively pursuing a lead. It just fell in his lap. Couldn't hurt to observe and see who she interacted with, what she did.

She was there with that Vonni Smith woman and the dog. But the trainer wasn't holding the leash, Faith was. She continued looking around, her eyes darting from one person to the next, her free hand flitting around her collar. Definitely nervous. But about what?

A noise to his right caught his attention. A group of skinheads marched through the parking lot, headed straight toward Faith and Vonni. They marched with a "White Power" banner decorated with swastikas and the white pride logo. Some carried torches, others raised clenched fists in the air. One of them started a chant, "White Power! White Pride! White Power Worldwide!" Soon the whole group was louder than the religious choir. The pacifists faded into the crowd.

A blue wall of police headed toward the supremacists from the east, and his groups' commander said, "Look alive. We've got trouble. Douse their torches and halt their progress."

Someone near Faith threw a soda can at the leader. He stopped, turned, raised his hand like Braveheart—and the neo-Nazis charged. From out of the melee, pro-Israeli protestors jumped into the fray. Soon pro-Palestine rioters joined them.

"All units! Move in! Move in! Move in!" His earpiece crackled with the same order his group commander barked. Max jumped forward, and Carter ran alongside his fellow officers.

The remaining three protesting factions seemed to be converging right where Faith Keller stood. Her eyes widened, her dog lunged, and the crowds seemed to swallow her.

CHAPTER 9

FAITH'S HEAD THROBBED. SHE FLUTTERED her eyelids open, blinked a few times, then snapped her eyes wide open.

The hospital.

Mom and Dad, Jensen and Bella, Kacee and Vonni sat or stood near her bed, talking quietly among themselves. Ruby sat at Vonni's feet and emitted a soft bark when Faith tried to sit up.

"Faith!" Her mother reached for her hand.

"What happened?" She tried to sit up.

"Ssh. Lie back." Her dad pushed her gently back to the pillow and looked at the monitors.

Monitors! She looked at her hand, where a large IV needle was taped in place. Tubes attached her body to the dreaded monitors. What was wrong with her?

Her body shook with uncontrollable tremors. She panted, her lungs no longer able to expand.

"Faith. Faith!" Jensen yelled at her. "Calm down. You're fine. You're safe."

Her pulse raced. Felt like her heart would pound right out of her chest.

Mom squeezed her hand.

"Breathe, Faith." Bella grabbed her other hand, held onto her fingers, avoiding the needle. "Just breathe. No one's here. No one can get you."

"I'm calling Tod," Dad said.

Faith heard him speaking into the phone but couldn't make out his quiet conversation over the roaring of blood in her ears.

"Darling." Her mom squeezed her hand again.

The tang of hospital antiseptic, air freshener, and sickness assaulted her nose, choked her. The monitors beeped faster, a metronome keeping track of her distress. Air. Why was there no air?

Vonni let go of Ruby's lead and the dog walked to the edge of the bed, put her snout on the mattress, and sniffed.

Faith pulled her hand away from her mom and petted the dog's head. Her fur was soft, silken. Smooth and soothing under her fingers. She pulled her other hand free of Bella and tapped her fingers, drumming the rhythm Tod had taught her on the mattress. She tried to hum with it, but she still labored to breathe.

"Should I get a doctor?" Kacee asked.

Jensen shook his head. "Slow down, Faith."

Ruby nuzzled her hand and snuffled. So warm. So strong.

The band around Faith's lungs eased, and she was able to take one deep breath, then another. Still Ruby kept her head on the bed, right where Faith could reach her.

She pursed her lips and exhaled slowly. Her body had stopped trembling, but it still hurt from tensing her muscles. She rolled her head a little to release the pressure in her neck. "I'm okay. I'm okay." Then she kept repeating it in her head, a tiny mantra that calmed her further.

"Faith," her mom began.

"Dad." She cut her mom off. "Call Tod back. Don't make him leave his practice to come here. I'm fine."

He looked at her for a moment then stepped into the hall, his phone on his ear.

"Can someone please tell me what happened?"

"What do you remember?" Bella asked.

What did she remember? The vigil. She wanted to avoid anything within a twelve-mile radius of that event, but Vonni had talked her into it, telling her they should do a field test with her and Ruby. Faith was thinking dinner, maybe a little shopping. Vonni took her to the most congested area in Cathedral Lake. She'd managed for a while, but then those protesters—

"The vigil. There was a riot." She rubbed her forehead with her free hand. Her fingers brushed up against something.

"Be careful." Her mom took her hand and lowered it to the mattress. "Mind the bandage. You have ten stitches."

Faith gingerly prodded the gauze taped to her head. The spot was tender right under her hairline.

"You were coping beautifully," Vonni said. "Ruby kept you calm, and she kept some space around you, let you breathe."

"But?" Faith asked.

"When the riot broke out, you froze. She tried to pull you to safety, but you were rooted to the spot, and the skinheads advanced so fast. Neither she nor I could get you away in time. They knocked you to the ground."

"I was trampled."

"That's a bit of a stretch," Jensen said. "Ruby stood guard over you until help came."

"Help?"

"That would be me."

Faith looked up and saw Officer Emerson standing in the doorway. He had a black eye and a gash on his cheek. When he walked into the room, he did so with a limp. Max walked next to him. He closed the door and dropped the leash. Then Max approached Ruby and sat right beside her. The two dogs sniffed at each other.

"Are you feeling up to talking?" he asked. "I have a few questions."

FAITH CRINGED AGAINST THE CACOPHONY. Everyone but the dogs had erupted in protest. She could hardly make out the comments.

"Can't you see she's not up to conversation?"

"Why can't you just leave her alone? Leave all of us alone?"

"I'm calling our attorney."

"Dad, Bella's here. She can deal with this scum."

"Enough!" Yelling hurt Faith's head, but so did listening to the vociferous objections. "All right. Everybody out. I'll talk to Officer Emerson. Alone."

"Faith, you should at least have legal counsel present," Bella said.

"Wait outside. If I need you, I'll call for you."

The mutinous looks on everyone's faces would have amused her if the situation weren't so dire. Her visitors shuffled out into the hall, Bella bringing up the rear.

"I'll be right outside the door."

"Thanks."

Bella left the door open when she left, but Officer Emerson closed it behind her. Now it was just the two of them. And the two dogs.

Faith gestured to one of the recently vacated seats. "Why don't you sit? You look like you're about to fall over."

He limped over to the chair and kind of collapsed into it. Then he cleared his throat. "How are you feeling?"

"I'm okay." She played with the corner of her blanket, acutely aware that she was naked underneath the flimsy hospital gown. Made it really awkward to talk to anyone, but especially him. "By the looks of it, better than you."

"I'm not the one in a hospital bed."

"Why do I get the feeling you should be?"

He shrugged and looked around the room. His dark hair was tousled like he'd been running his fingers through it, and his body slouched in the chair. He stifled a yawn.

A brief pang of sympathy for him pierced her heart. Pain and weariness she understood.

"I guess I owe you a thanks," she said. "I don't quite remember what happened, but you got me out of harm's way, so…"

"Just doing my job."

"I thought your job was to harass me about ketamine."

He looked up at her. His blue eyes blazed with an intensity that revealed his exhaustion and frustration. She had to look away.

The silence grew, thick enough to choke on. And she nearly did.

He cleared his throat again. "Are you up to giving a statement?"

"Are you up to taking it? You don't even have a pad and pen."

He lay his head back and closed his eyes. "Coming off a long shift. I'll remember what you say, follow up with you if I have further questions."

"How many cases can you possibly work at once? You're investigating the riot, too?"

"Officers don't investigate. We do leg work for the detectives. I'm one of the officers collecting statements from the victims and witnesses."

"How many officers are taking statements?"

"I don't know. A bunch."

"How many people have you talked to?"

"Who's doing the investigating here?"

"According to you, the detectives. Answer my question. How many people?"

He sighed. "Just you."

Disappointment washed over her. "Are you trying to tie this to the ketamine, too? I wasn't there to push drugs."

He looked up at her. "Why were you there?"

No one had infuriated her so much since Hope. Why did he have to laser-focus on her every action? Why couldn't he just leave her alone.

Or show her another kind of attention. That would be fine, too.

What was wrong with her? The guy was out to get her, she was in a hospital bed, and her mind went straight to the gutter. Maybe she should be medicated.

"Why was anyone there, Officer? I've lived in Cathedral Lake my entire life. A tragedy like this brings people together. And mourning together is quite cathartic."

"You didn't look like you were grieving. You looked nervous."

"So now I grieve wrong, too?" Her voice raised.

Ruby perked her ears up.

Max sat at attention.

"You know, I don't think I'm up to giving a statement. I'm tired, I'm achy, and I'd like to rest. Please leave."

He didn't broach an argument. "Come on, Max." He heaved to his feet, grabbed his dog's lead, and headed for the door. Before he opened it, he turned around. "I hope you feel better soon."

Her thoughts and feelings swirled cyclonically inside her. She couldn't latch on to one long enough to form a reply before he walked out.

CHAPTER 10

CARTER WALKED INTO THE HALLWAY and was immediately accosted by the Keller entourage. He held up his hands to quiet them. "Whoa! One at a time, all right? I can't make sense of any of you if you're talking over each other."

"Why are you harassing my client?" Bella Perish asked.

"I'm not harassing her. I'm doing my job. I needed her statement."

"I called Detective Cooper," Royce said. "He said you were injured tonight and off duty getting treatment. Aren't even here in an official capacity."

Damn it. Like Tony couldn't let one slide. Okay, maybe he was too busy to even think about covering for Carter. God knew there was more than enough work for three full police departments. But more likely Tony didn't want to let it go. He had chosen the Keller family over Carter. Again. That really rankled.

It also made him wonder why his allegiances fell that way.

"Look." He sighed and leaned against the wall. His sprained ankle was killing him, and his head hurt too much for another verbal battle. "I'm just trying to make sense of the evidence I have. I've got ketamine vials at a crime scene that came from Faith's clinic. But she won't explain that to me. I've got a freaking marijuana forest at your nursery, and no one will explain that, either.

The biggest problem I have, though, is a gut feeling that something's off. She's always got wide, frightened eyes. Is constantly scanning the crowd like she's looking for a contact. Shows up places I wouldn't expect her and then bad things happen. I'm just trying to figure all this out, and if she'd cooperate, then maybe we could all move on." He didn't tell them he meant move her on to prison. He'd probably said too much already.

"Your evidence is circumstantial," Perish said. "And there's no reason to suspect any of her appearances at any of the crime scenes is anything more than—"

"Wait," Royce interrupted. "This is all based on her suspicious behavior and your gut feeling?"

"It's a little more complex than that."

"But you said your biggest problem was that she looked nervous."

Carter heaved his body off the wall and looked at him. "Yeah. So? Don't tell me that's not good police work. Gut instinct is how a lot of cases break."

Royce shook his head. "I'm not going to say that. I think there's a lot of merit to intuition."

"Then what?"

"I'm sure Faith has looked nervous. Probably terrified. But not because she was committing a crime."

"Royce," Vanessa said. "That's private. She wouldn't want—"

"She wouldn't *want* to be under investigation. It's time to come clean."

"Dad," Jensen said.

"Officer Emerson," Royce said, "I understand you aren't from Cathedral Lake. What do you really know about our family history over the last decade?"

"I know about Hope, about her getting mixed up with Jimmy Salvo's drug distribution. About Wade Unger accidentally killing her when he tried to scare Salvo. I know Unger and Salvo worked together, but Unger tried to frame you, let you take the fall. I know you intentionally let your clinic be the site of drug drops last year to draw Salvo out. Could have made a lot of contacts that way."

"I didn't, but go on. Anything else?"

"I know *your* little operation last year resulted in your daughter's abduction."

"And my getting shot," Bella Perish said. "Right in front of her."

Carter stared at her until Royce spoke. Then he turned his attention back to him.

"And none of that last bit meant anything to you, Officer?"

"I've been focused on following the drug connections. What do you think I've missed?"

Royce took a deep breath. "Faith has PTSD. She was heartbroken by her twin's murder, but she was flat out traumatized by her abduction and Bella being shot in front of her. Crowds terrify my daughter. She has trouble socializing. Sleeping. Eating. Functioning some days. The slightest trigger can set her off. Like being at a crowded basketball game—"

"Where a terrorist attack occurred," Jensen finished. "She was nearly trampled to death that night, but the first responders needed people on triage, and I forced her to stay and assist. She had to deal with all of that on her own just so she could help the injured. When things calmed down, I personally took her to her therapist in the middle of the night for an emergency session."

Royce put his arm around his son. "Do you have any idea what it's like for us to watch her suffer? She won't take meds for—"

"What?" Vanessa asked.

He turned toward her. "She quit her meds. Didn't like how they made her feel."

"Who told you that?"

"Tod. She put my name on the consent-to-share forms. He told me the day she quit them."

"And you didn't tell me?" Vanessa's voice grew shrill.

"You aren't on the list."

"I'm her mother!"

Vonni cleared her throat. "She's using Ruby as a service animal. I insisted we field test tonight at the vigil. Should have known it was too much, too soon, but I pushed. That's why she—"

"Looked so nervous tonight," Carter finished for her. It all made sense now. PTSD. Panic attacks. Nerves.

The common denominator wasn't the drugs, it was the trauma.

"I'm sorry," he said. "I didn't know."

"You weren't supposed to know," Kacee said.

"No one was." Bella crossed her arms over her chest. "Do you really think victims of violent crimes like to have the details of the event and their reactions to it broadcast to the world? It's a horrible violation of their privacy. It's yet another assault to them."

She would know. She'd been shot.

"I'm truly, truly sorry. I was only trying to do my job. I understand now."

Bella swiped at a tear on her cheek and rushed down the hall.

"Bells!" Jensen called. He shook his head and then ran after her.

"I'll find a way to make this right," Carter said.

"No one can make her life right," Vanessa said. "And by the way, I walked the property where the marijuana was seized."

He looked at her. Tried desperately not to collapse to the floor. His head pounded, his ankle throbbed. His fucking heart hurt for having acted like such a dick.

"It's not my land. It's on the border, but it's someone else's. So maybe you can stop harassing me, too." She walked off after her son and his fiancée.

Kacee tsked him and left with Vanessa.

Vonni shrugged and went into Faith's room. He heard her greet Ruby with a quiet, "Hey, girl," and wondered if Faith had fallen asleep. He hoped so. If anyone needed rest, it was her.

"Don't listen to my wife," Royce said. "I expect you to make this right." He walked into Faith's room, leaving Carter alone and exhausted in the hall.

"Come on, Max. We've got more work to do."

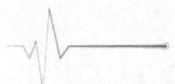

BY THE TIME CARTER GOT home, he was beat. He thought he'd sleep like the dead and review his notes in the morning, but instead he tossed and turned all night. How had he missed all the signs? How had he read her so wrong?

Guess there was a reason he wasn't a detective.

Max whined. Probably had to go out. It was early for him, but maybe he didn't feel well.

Looked like Faith was right about him on that count, too. He wasn't a very intuitive dog owner.

He opened the door, and the dog walked out. Slowly. Was Max ill? Injured? Or just tired? God, what kind of cop was he? Was he going to second guess everything from now on?

He popped a pod in his coffee maker and brewed a single cup. Max had returned before the mug was filled, so he let him in. The poor dog just lay at his feet.

Maybe he should take the day off, or at least get the dog to the vet. No, they both just needed a day off. Not only did Max seem lethargic, Carter also felt drained. His whole body ached, he still limped, and his head wasn't in the game. He had all his sick days left. Time to use one.

He got Max's breakfast before doctoring his coffee with copious amounts of cream and sugar. Then he grabbed his phone, intent on calling them in sick. It rang in his hands before he could dial, startling him. He bobbled it and almost dropped the damn thing. Managed to answer it just before it went to voicemail. "Emerson."

Calls coming in before his shift started were never good. That one was no exception. He ended the call and looked at Max. "Come on, buddy. Going to be another shitty day."

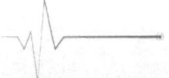

CARTER PULLED INTO THE PARKING lot at Faith's clinic and

surveyed the area. Not a car in sight. He didn't know how Faith had learned her building had been broken into, but she certainly wasn't on site now. Could be her security company notified her of the break-in and she called it in from home. But the company would have called the authorities themselves, so she had to have been on the premises.

Lights blazed inside, the only indication anyone had even been there at this early hour.

Why would she leave before the police got there? Was she trying to hide evidence? Did she steal her own drugs and try to claim a theft?

No. He wouldn't go down that road again. He would investigate the B and E without jumping to conclusions about her. Let the evidence dictate his conclusions, not his gut.

Still, a so-called victim leaving the scene of the crime was suspicious.

Max whined at him. Like he knew Carter's thoughts and disapproved. Or did he agree?

Maybe he should have taken the day off.

"Come on, Max." They headed to the door, the cheerful wreath and cute welcome mat a mockery of the troubles inside. Carter donned gloves and booties, tried the knob and found it unlocked.

A noise in the back echoed through the quiet building. Max's ears perked, and Carter drew his gun. Dispatch didn't say the perp might still be onsite. He crept down the hall toward the noise, tried to ignore the stabbing pain in his ankle as he cleared each room.

All the exam rooms were empty, doors ajar. Same with the OR. The pharmacy wasn't open, but the window allowed him to look inside without opening the door. The cabinet had been broken into. He had no idea what was missing, but no one was in that room.

Another noise cut through the silence. He headed toward Faith's office, the only room he hadn't cleared yet. Light shone from under the door, and more sounds—clinking and scuffling—came from inside. Carter readjusted his grip on his gun, gave a hand signal to Max, and flung the door open. "Freeze!"

Faith screamed and dropped a glass on her desk. It shattered, the amber liquid spilling and spreading over the surface, getting absorbed by random papers littering the top.

"Faith?"

She clutched her chest and panted. "What are you doing, scaring me like that?" She scrambled to clean the mess on her desk and sliced her finger on a broken shard. "Damn it!"

Carter holstered his gun and crossed the room. He took her hand and looked at the cut. It gushed blood, dripped off her finger and mingled with what was—based on the open bottle on her desk—a puddle of expensive bourbon. "Let's get you cleaned up. Then we'll talk."

She glared at him before leading him out of the office and into the OR. There she headed toward the counter, but he stopped her. "Wash that off in the sink. I'll get the supplies."

"You're not the doctor here."

"Maybe not, but you're definitely the patient. Tell me where everything is."

While she scrubbed her hand, she directed him to the antiseptic, gauze, and tape. She patted her cut with paper towels and scowled.

"Hurt?"

"Doesn't feel great." She walked over to him and grabbed a gauze pad.

"I got it," he said. He took the gauze out of her hand and poured some of the antiseptic on the white cloth. Then he lifted her hand higher so he could see it better. It trembled, and she gritted her teeth and looked away. Her skin was soft under his fingers, cool to the touch.

And still dripping like rain from a spout.

Max sidled up to her, nudged her with his head, and looked up expectantly. She petted him with her free hand, and he thumped his tail. "Hello, sweet thing. How are you today, huh? How are you?"

He smiled at their mutual affection. Max was well behaved and safe in social settings, but he had a real fondness for this woman. Dogs were sensitive to things humans missed. Maybe he knew something about her that Carter didn't.

Turning his focus back on her injury, he dabbed the liquid on her finger. She winced and flinched, but he held her hand tight so she couldn't pull away. "You're not one of those doctors who makes a lousy patient, are you?"

She shook her head and peered up at him through thick, lush lashes. He hadn't noticed before, but she had blue eyes. Dark—like the deepest part of the ocean or the twilight sky just before the last rays of the sun disappeared—flecked with bursts of frost and ice and ringed in indigo almost as dark as her pupils. Mesmerizing. But for the shadows under them betraying her discomfort and exhaustion, he could gaze at them for hours.

He grabbed fresh gauze and wrapped her injured finger, securing the bandage with medical tape. "You probably need stitches. Would you like me to call someone to take you to the hospital?"

She huffed with derision. "A hospital? For stitches? I can do them myself."

"We're not talking about your leg or something. It's your finger. You need two hands for something like that."

"It's my left finger, and I'm right-handed. I could stitch myself up just fine, if I needed to, which I don't. And if I couldn't manage, I'd go to my dad or brother. I'm not going to waste time and resources by going to the ER."

"Should I call your dad or brother?"

"Are you trying to get rid of me?"

"I'm trying to take care of you. You've got dark circles under your eyes, so I know you haven't slept. When'd you even leave the hospital? They don't typically discharge people in the middle of the night."

"Not that it's your concern, but I checked myself out after my family left. I hate hospitals, and there was no reason for me to stay."

"You were in the middle of a riot. You have a head injury. Maybe you aren't thinking clearly."

"I'm thinking just fine, Officer. Now, you came here for a reason. Shouldn't we get to it?"

Stubborn. God help the poor sap who ended up with her. "Lead the way."

"When I left the hospital, I didn't have my car, so I called a cab. I was just going to go home, but before the taxi arrived, I started thinking. Given how late it was and how lousy I felt, I figured I'd want the day off tomorrow. Today. Whatever. Anyway, I asked the cabbie to take me here. I planned on getting some paperwork I'm behind on and taking it home. Even told him to wait for me. But when I went inside and saw the pharmacy, I called 9-1-1 then told him he could leave. He offered to wait with me, but I told him to go. He wasn't a witness to anything, and I figured if the cops wanted to talk with him, they could always track him down later. No point in him sitting here, losing fares or not getting to go home and sleep."

"And what time was this?"

"We got here around three-fifteen, I'd guess."

"All right." That fit with the timeline he'd started to construct based on her 9-1-1 call. But he'd follow up with the cabbie later, just to confirm her story. "Then what?"

"I went in my office to do paperwork while I waited. But I couldn't concentrate. So I poured myself a drink. Then you showed up. You know the rest." She lifted her injured hand to the bandage on her head, winced, and lowered her hand. Then she held her head with her good hand.

"Shouldn't be much longer. Let's go to the pharmacy." He followed her down the hall to the closed pharmacy door.

"I haven't gone in yet. I didn't want to touch anything." She took a key out of her pocket.

"Wait." He grabbed her arm. "Try the door first."

She shrugged and turned the knob. The door swung open. "That's odd. I know this door was locked yesterday."

"Does anyone have a key?"

"No. I mean, I keep a spare here at the office, but a person would have to know where to find it in order to use it."

"Where's the spare?"

"My office."

"Okay, we'll check on that in a moment. Let's look inside."

"Wait." She stopped and looked at him. "Now that I think about it, I'm not sure the front door was locked. I don't remember hearing a click when I turned the key."

"Do you have a spare for your front door here, too?"

"No. If I'm already here, I don't need a key. My parents have one, and I have one at my house."

"Hmm. Well, let's put a pin in that and check in here."

He led the way into the pharmacy. It was pretty much what he'd expected. Broken latch on the window, shattered glass door on the medicine cabinet, vials of narcotics gone. He stooped to the floor and picked up a rectangular slab of wood. "What's this?"

"Oh. That's from when I tried to patch the cabinet after the last break-in."

"The last break-in? There's no police report about any break-ins here. How many times have you been hit?"

"I'm not sure. I thought I was misplacing or miscounting inventory for the last few months. But then a few days ago, I came to work and found this room looking, well, looking a lot like this. I patched the cabinet, but I haven't had a chance to get new glass. I guess it's a good thing I didn't. I'd just have to shell out more money for another repair."

"But why haven't you called anything in?" He stared at her, incredulous at her apathy.

"Like I said, I wasn't even aware at first that anything had been stolen."

"What about the big break-in a few days ago?"

"Well, yeah. I was sure then."

"So why didn't you report it? Has your alarm been tripped?"

"My alarm didn't notify the police because I don't have a security system."

"You don't have a—? Faith, every business owner should have a moni-tored system."

She held up a hand. "Stop. I've heard all this and more already."

"Then why don't you have one?"

"I don't know. I just don't. Can we get back to the report?"

Hit a nerve there. He'd revisit that later. "Okay. Why didn't you report the last theft?"

She bit her lip, turned away from him, and spoke in a soft voice. "Would you have reported it if your family history was like mine?"

A "yes" was on the tip of his tongue, but he stopped his retort and thought about it. Seriously pondered her question. Her father had been accused of stealing drugs from the hospital pharmacy. Had undergone public scrutiny for being the drop location for the drug sting last year. More than a few people had questioned his innocence, thinking he'd been caught and had cut a deal in exchange for his freedom, which according to the case file, couldn't be further from the truth. With that kind of family history, he could understand her hesitance to bring another suspicion into the mix. Even if he disagreed with her decision.

"I get your concern. I do. But why report this one?"

She rounded on him, huffed in derision. "You're kidding, right?" Max perked up, walked over to her, and nuzzled her leg. She petted him absently and continued to yell at Carter. "You've been up my ass about the stolen ketamine since the—" She blinked, swallowed. Stooped and hugged the dog. Continued in a muffled voice, her face buried in the scruff of fur at his neck. "Since the attack at the basketball game. You jumped to conclusions about the marijuana they found growing near my parents' nursery. If drugs keep disappearing from here, you'll just trace them back, so I have to report what's happened to establish some credibility."

He sighed. What she said made sense, but what a mess her silence had made. "Let's go check on the key. Then we're going to start over at the beginning. Leave no detail out."

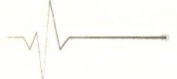

CARTER STOPPED AT THE SQUARE for an iced mocha—two, actually—before heading to the station. His thoughts raced and roiled, giving him a bigger headache than he'd woken with.

He had called CSU around five-thirty and then exhaustively interviewed Faith on every detail she could recall about the weeks of missing inventory, from the first vial that disappeared to the break-in she'd just reported. Crime scene investigators arrived around six, but he didn't leave for another hour after that, making sure he'd left no question unanswered.

At least he didn't have to leave her alone. A whole unit was there and would be processing the scene for a while. Her assistant should be in by then, so she'd have someone with her.

Carter made a mental note to follow up with him, but he already had a clear picture of what had been happening. It gave him chills to consider.

The perp had to have cased the place to know she had no security. He'd been taking small amounts at first to see if she noticed. He would have thought she didn't, because she never reported any thefts to the authorities. A few nights earlier, he'd been rushed or careless and had broken the door to her pharmaceutical case. When she didn't report that, he returned.

The fact that both her pharmacy door and her front door were unlocked told him that the thief hadn't bothered to sneak out the window again, but had walked brazenly out the front door.

She could very well have run right into him, showing up there in the middle of the night like she had done.

He shivered off the chill that crept up his spine. Damn woman was in danger, and she didn't even realize it.

Carter finished his first mocha while he walked from the coffee truck to his car. By the time he and Max walked into the station, he'd downed his second and chucked the cup in the trash by Tony's desk.

Tony glanced in the can then looked up at him. "The extra tall? Tired?"

"It's my second, actually. Third if you count the coffee I had at home. I'm wiped. And it's already been another long fucking day."

"What's up?"

Carter summed up the latest in a series of horrific events surrounding Faith and the stolen drugs. He began with an apology for not listening to

Tony sooner and ended with his theory about the break-ins. "I think she's been targeted specifically because of her lax security and her family's history with stolen pharmaceuticals."

Tony sighed and sat back in his chair. "I see where you're headed with this, and this idea has merit. Two questions, then—who knows about her family's history and who would want to frame her?"

"I didn't live here when everything went down with her dad, but it seems like the whole town knew. Rumor has it that it got a lot of play in the media."

"But so did him getting cleared of all charges."

"Yeah, but once an idea is out there, people always wonder. Casting suspicion in that direction would be simple."

Tony nodded. "True. So who has an axe to grind with the Kellers? Or Faith, specifically? Because it would have been a lot easier to throw Royce under the bus than to make a family association with his daughter."

"You said you know the family. Who has a grudge against any of them?"

"Other than Wade Unger, I can't think of anyone."

"What about Salvo family? Someone looking for retribution since he kidnapped Faith last year?"

"He was the only dirty one in the whole clan. I can't see his parents or anyone going after her."

"Could be a distant cousin. Or a friend. Someone attached but not easy to spot."

"Look into it."

"Got it." He started to leave, but turned back around. "Hey. You might want to tell Royce to convince his daughter to put in a security system. At work and at home. She's leaving herself vulnerable."

"So tell her."

"I did. She won't listen."

"So talk to him yourself."

Carter ran his hand through his hair. "Her family doesn't exactly like me."

"I wonder why."

"He'd listen to you."

"Go mend your fences, Carter."

"You know, sometimes you really suck."

Tony laughed. "Before you go, I could use a second set of eyes and ears."

"Sure, insult me then ask for a favor."

"Hey, you don't want to work on a high profile case, I'll ask another officer for help."

"Don't be such a dick. Of course I want in."

Tony smirked.

"What is it? You stuck on something?"

"Not stuck. Just want another opinion. We've got Yavin's manifesto. I want you to take a look at it. See if you think it really is just him or if there might be a bigger player in the background. We've got a video confession from him, too, that I want you to look at."

"Where's the stuff?"

"I'll email you the files. You can start on them right after you talk to Royce. He should be at work by now. FYI, he likes the apricot and raspberry kolache from the pastry truck in the Square."

Carter sighed and headed for the door.

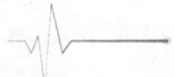

CARTER APPROACHED ROYCE KELLER'S CLINIC with a large pink pastry box filled with kolache. Ttwo dozen—six raspberry, six apricot, six chocolate, and six nut. He also had a bag in his car with a variety for himself.

The clinic looked like the nicest building on the block. There were planter boxes in front of the windows and two large urns flanking the door. He didn't know flowers bloomed in Pennsylvania in early March, but if anyone could make something grow in the cold weather, he supposed it would be someone who owned a nursery. The purple and yellow whatever-they-weres made a cheery welcome in an otherwise dreary month.

He walked in and looked around. The place was packed, and it was still early. A mother read to a moaning child from Highlights. Most of the adults stared vacantly at a television playing a talk show. The man by the door sneezed, and Carter cringed from him and lifted the box in the air. He hurried to the desk. "Could I see Doctor Keller, please?"

"Do you have an appointment?" the receptionist asked, attention riveted on her computer.

"No, but—"

She slid a clipboard full of forms at him through the sliding window and never looked up from her work. "Put your name on the sign-in sheet then fill out these forms. When you bring them back up to me, if you have an insurance card, bring that, too."

She started to close the window, but Carter put his hand out and stopped her. She looked up, a scowl on her face, then she took in his uniform and badge and her mouth dropped into a silent O.

"I don't need an appointment. I only need a moment of his time."

"I'll buzz you in." She gestured to a door to his right, and he grabbed the handle. When the buzzer sounded, he pulled the door open and stepped out of the waiting room into the medical hub. Nurses clustered around computer stations, whispering behind their hands.

Damn it. Carter had wanted to make things better between him and Royce, but instead he'd probably started another round of rumors and gossip. Should have thought to change his clothes first.

The receptionist met him at the door. "If you'll follow me, you can wait in his office. He's with a patient now. Or do you need him immediately?"

Maybe he could do some damage control. "Oh, no. He's not in any trouble. I can wait. I just need to confer with him before I head back to the station."

"Uh-huh." She glanced at Max and then turned and bustled down the hall. "You and the dog can wait in here." She opened the door for him. "He doesn't bite, does he?"

"He's perfectly safe. Unless there's a crime going on."

"I certainly haven't done anything illegal. I can't speak to anyone else in this office, but I'm a law-abiding citizen!" She eyed the dog and stepped away from him.

"Ma'am, I assure you, you're in no danger. No one here is. I'm not here to question Doctor Keller. I'm here to talk to him about—" Well, it was really none of her business what he was doing there. "Could you just let him know I'm here when he's done with his patient?"

She nodded and scurried from the room, closing the door behind her.

"At least we can take a load off while we wait," he said to Max. His ankle still hurt to hold his body weight, and he was bone-weary. He sat across from Royce's chair and Max sat beside him.

Soon the door flew open and Royce Keller entered. He shut the door behind him and didn't even bother taking his seat behind his desk. Instead, he leaned over Carter and spoke with a harsh whisper. "What are you doing here? My entire staff is talking about you, speculating about the reason for your visit. I thought you were going to back off my family."

Max stood and stepped between Royce and Carter.

Carter sighed. "Sir, would you please just sit down? I'm not here to cause any trouble."

"Another mission failed." But Royce walked around his desk and dropped into his chair.

"I brought you these." Carter passed the box across the desk.

Royce looked at him, at the box, and back to him. "What for?"

"Look, I'm making an effort." He opened the box and showed him the delicate cookies. "Truce?"

He looked at the pastry. "What do you want?"

Carter sighed and sat back. "I'm here about Faith."

Royce jumped to his feet. "You leave her alone!"

"Doctor Keller, please." He glanced at the door. "I'm here because I'm worried about her."

"What?" The doctor slumped back in his chair and rubbed his temples.

He looked older than he had just the night before. "What's happened now? I know she left the hospital last night. She should still be there."

"It's not that, although I agree with you. It's about her clinic. Are you aware she's had several break-ins? Vials of ketamine have been stolen."

"Several?"

"Yes. She's only reported the last one, which just happened. I don't know what would possess her to go there in the middle of the night, but she did. And she's lucky she didn't catch the perp in the act."

"She went out to the boonies at night? By herself?"

"That's not all. She doesn't have a security system. I'm concerned for her."

"So you don't think she's stealing and pushing her own drugs?"

Carter was ninety-nine percent sure she wasn't. He just couldn't shake the feeling that he was missing a key component to her case. "No, sir. I don't. But I do think she's in danger. I don't think she was chosen randomly. I think it's personal."

"Personal? Who would want to hurt Faith?"

"I was hoping you could tell me."

He sat back, face slack with shock. Finally he shook his head as if to clear his thoughts. "I don't have any idea."

"Would you think about it? Contact me if anything occurs to you—no matter how small a detail might be, how unlikely your theory. It could be important." Carter slid a cream-colored business card across the desk.

"Of course."

Carter stood, then turned back around. "And make her get a security system. She's vulnerable, and I can't always be around to keep an eye on her."

Royce raised his eyebrows. "If I didn't know better, I'd think you cared about her."

Carter felt a flush rising up the back of his neck. He turned toward the door so his embarrassment didn't show. "I care about this whole town. It's my job."

"Mm-hmm."

He glanced back at Faith's dad.

Royce grinned, glanced in the box, snatched a raspberry pastry, and took a bite. "Damn, but these are good. Thanks."

"Don't mention it." And he and Max left.

He really meant it. He didn't want Royce mentioning his visit to Faith. Or anyone else. Bringing him cookies. Kiss ass. What had he been thinking?

It was Tony's fault. He'd blame him.

Shit—Tony. The files. Man, he was totally spent. Maybe he could take the afternoon off, grab a nap, then review the files at home. Lord knew he needed the break, and he would enjoy thinking about something other than Faith Keller for a while.

CHAPTER 11

FAITH WAS GIVING DAVID FINAL instructions about the following day's calendar when the door opened. She was about to tell the person she was closed, but then she looked up. "Dad! What a nice surprise."

"You would think so, wouldn't you?"

She scrunched her brow. "What?"

"We need to talk."

"Okay. We can go to my office."

"You can stay here, Faith," David said. "I'm headed out, anyway."

Her dad stared at him, and she remembered her manners. "Sorry. Dad, this is my new assistant, David James. David, this is my dad, Doctor Royce Keller."

They shook hands, but David never really managed to look her father in the eye, which was weird, because he was always so friendly and outgoing with her clients. Her dad could be intimidating, though. And he did just insinuate she was in trouble with him. David probably just felt uncomfortable.

Still, she didn't want her dad to think she'd made a bad hire.

"David used to work with Zeke."

"That so?" her dad asked.

"Mm-hmm." David walked toward the hallway, still avoiding her dad.

"Well, if you'll both excuse me. I'm just going to grab my jacket, and I'll be going. Was nice to meet you, sir. Enjoy your evening." He hurried down the hall.

"Friendly guy." Her dad was the king of sarcasm.

"Can you blame him for avoiding you?" She walked around the counter and dropped into one of her cushy chairs. "You didn't exactly make a great impression."

"I don't have to impress anybody."

Faith heard the back door shut and made a mental note to lock it before she left. Like she wouldn't constantly double- and triple-check all the locks from now on before leaving. "It's been a long day, Dad. What do you want?"

"Why'd you check out of the hospital last night?"

She sighed. "Is that why you're here? To check up on me? You could have just called."

"I'm here for a number of reasons, not the least of which is to see how you are." He looked her over. "Want me to look at your head? Check for infection?"

"I already checked it today. It's not red or inflamed. There's no pus or seepage. I don't have a fever. I'm fine." She brushed a lock of hair out of her face.

He grabbed her hand. "What the hell happened here? Your hand wasn't cut last night."

"I cut it today on broken glass."

"From the window of the pharmacy?"

She narrowed her eyes. "Who've you been talking to?"

"Why haven't you been honest with us?"

"I've never lied. You've just never asked if I'd had any thefts."

He jumped to his feet. "And what's that got to do with anything? Most people don't go around asking family members if they've been a victim of a crime. That's information you volunteer."

"I suppose I should say I'm sorry, but I'm not." His face darkened, and she hurried to continue. "I didn't say anything because I didn't want to worry you."

"And look how that strategy worked out."

"Dad, I'm fine."

"You have a gash on your head, Faith, and God knows what's wrong with your finger."

"Neither of which happened because I've had a few break-ins."

"You need to get a security system."

"I have one. Salem."

"The barn cat?"

"He's pretty mean. And there's Ruby."

"The dog Vonni has with her?" He paced the waiting room. "Fat lot of good that does you when the two of you aren't together."

"Vonni has her because I didn't want to leave her in the hospital last night without access to water or the ability to take potty breaks."

"But you didn't stay in the hospital last night."

"That was a spur of the moment decision."

"One that could have gotten you killed."

She stood then, too. "How do you figure?"

"What if you'd arrived a few minutes earlier and caught the guy in the act. A knock on the head would be the least of your worries."

She hadn't considered that. A chill ran down her spine, and she shivered it away.

"Faith, a mean tomcat and an absent dog are not crime deterrents."

"Ruby will be with me wherever I go soon."

"Still doesn't do anything for your clinic. We raised you to be logical, responsible. What are you thinking? You need security here and at home."

He was right. She knew it. But she'd fought it for so long. How could she make him understand?

"Dad, you remember when we lost Hope?"

"Of course."

"You and Mom took Jensen and me to Tod to help us express our feelings."

"I know."

"I told you I went back regularly, but I didn't. I went sporadically, at best. Until last year, after the—" She still had trouble saying it.

"After you were abducted."

"Yes. I know you and Mom still went. I'm pretty sure Jensen even went. But I didn't. I felt like I was admitting a flaw or failure in myself if I needed to use him as a crutch."

"Faith, you know that isn't true."

"Logically, yes. But I can't change my emotions."

"But you've been seeing him since, right?"

"It feels like continuously. But one thing hasn't changed."

He took her hand. "And what's that?"

"I need control and independence to feel safe. Not a machine, not medication. It has to be on my terms."

"What's that have to do with a security system?"

"A system is a reminder to me that I'm not safe. It becomes an electrical crutch telling me I'm in trouble and there's backup waiting."

"What's wrong with backup? Without it, you could be in danger. Grave danger. Did you ever think about that?"

She yanked her hand out of his grip and walked around the room. "Because if I need backup, then I'm really in danger! I can't live in a world where my safety is compromised. I can't function looking over my shoulder every two seconds." The familiar tightness gripped her chest. She panted for breath. Her vision blurred, darkened around the edges.

That scared her even more.

"Faith. Faith! Look at me."

Her gaze darted around the room, landed everywhere but on her father.

"Faith!" He stepped in front of her, took both her hands in his. "Breathe, sweetheart. Slow, deep breaths."

She blinked a few times. Her vision began to clear. Because her dad held her hands, she tapped her toes to the rhythm Tod had taught her. Hummed to herself. Soon her breathing leveled out, the band squeezing the life out of her lessened.

And she burst into tears.

Her father held her, rocked with her. Stroked her hair and murmured in her ear.

She was safe with him.

And she was a basket case when left alone. Hell, she'd just proved she was a basket case even when a family member was in the room with her.

After she'd calmed, she backed out of the embrace. "Oh, I ruined your shirt. I'm so sorry." Mascara and worse was smeared on his chest.

"Don't worry about that. Syl will get it out. Or I'll toss it. I've got plenty more in my closet. What I don't have more of is you."

Tears welled again.

"Faith, I can kind of understand how you feel. But it's time to put your feelings aside and use your head. The system may remind you that you're vulnerable, but without it you're more vulnerable."

She nodded. "I know. Rationally, I know that."

"I'm calling tonight to schedule a system installation for you. Hopefully someone can come tomorrow. Your house and here."

"I don't even know if I can swing the payments, Dad. I've got my mortgage, the loan for this place, a car payment, student loans. And I just hired an assistant. I've got to pay his salary. And benefits. Plus—"

"Hush. I'm paying for it."

"No. I'm an adult. I make my own way."

"Then look at it this way. I'm installing the systems for my peace of mind, so it's my cost to bear. When you get to the point that you appreciate the security, you can take over the monthly monitoring fees."

She worried her lower lip and fought back more tears.

"Let me do this, Faith. I need to do it."

Dread and despair roiled in her stomach, but she nodded.

"Great. Now let's go get some dinner and you can tell me all about your new assistant."

"There's not much to tell."

"Let me be the judge of that. Get your things and let's go."

"I'll be right back."

"And Faith?"

She turned back around.

"Check all your doors and windows before we go."

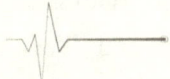

FAITH SAT ACROSS FROM HER father at a little diner on Main Street. He loved their bacon double cheeseburgers. The greasy spoon wasn't exactly known for their vegan choices, so she ordered a salad and grilled veggies.

She hoped they didn't come out of a can.

Dad dipped a fry in mayo and popped it in his mouth.

"That's disgusting."

"I don't criticize your tofurkey. Don't criticize my food."

She picked at her salad and looked toward the kitchen to see what was keeping the rest of her meal.

"So tell me about the new guy."

"David? There's not much to tell."

"Mom said he looked familiar to her, but he dodged the question."

"That's Mom overreacting again. He didn't dodge her question. He just doesn't know her."

"He certainly wasn't very friendly tonight. How is he with clients?"

"Warm and outgoing. I'm telling you, he was just flustered because you bulldozed in all bluster and billow. You embarrassed him. Maybe intimidated him, even."

Their waitress came and slid a plate in front of her. To her surprise, there were heaps of eggplant, zucchini, peppers, mushrooms, and squash, all perfectly grilled.

"Thank you."

"Sure thing, honey. Can get you a bottle of balsamic if you want."

"No, this is perfect. Thanks."

The woman cracked her gum. "I've been telling Marvin to get more healthy things on the menu. Maybe if you come in and order more often, he'll see the potential sales and we can get more choices."

"Like soy burgers or faux chicken patties?" Dad wrinkled his nose.

"I'd actually like those things," Faith said.

"That and more," the waitress said. "I'm a vegetarian, and I can hardly eat anything here. A girl gets tired of the same sad salad or fruit plate."

"I hear you."

"If you need anything else, just flag me down." The waitress made a face at her Dad's burger and walked away.

"Back to my point," Dad said.

So much for a change in subject.

"If you have a man working for you, he should be defending you, not scurrying away at the first sign of trouble."

"I introduced you as my dad. I hardly think that indicates trouble."

"There's something not right with him."

She speared a mushroom with her fork and popped it in her mouth. Mmm. "You think there's something wrong with just about everyone you meet. Especially where it concerns me."

"That's not true." He took a sip of his iced tea. "I like your friends."

"You've never liked a single boy I've brought home."

"That's because you bring home losers."

"Just once, once, I'd like to go out with a guy and not hear you and Jensen tell me all the things that are wrong with him. Too short. Too fat. Too thin. Weird hair. No personality—"

"That one's a deal-breaker. We can't have you subjecting our family to boring holidays."

"You want excitement for Thanksgiving? Invite the grandparents." She laughed at the look of horror that crossed his face.

"You're getting off topic." He finished his burger and wiped his hands and mouth with a paper napkin.

Faith was rather fond of that particular topic. At least, by comparison. If she had to choose between her poor business decisions or her social life, she'd choose the latter. Hands down.

She tucked her head and muttered, "Maybe the next guy I bring home will be a homunculus with a lazy eye and bad breath."

"Oh, I think you can do much better than that."

She looked up to see Officer Emerson standing beside the table. A large grin split his face.

Her face flushed, and she looked at her father. He covered his face with another napkin and smothered a laugh behind it.

"How are you folks this evening?"

He left her speechless. The last time her father had seen him, they'd been yelling outside her hospital room door. Now they were civil? And enjoying a laugh at her expense? What the— "You. It was you."

"It was me who did what?" he asked.

She looked at her father. "I assumed Tony was your source. But it was him." She pointed at the cop/

Dad shrugged. "He had pastry. It's hard to be angry with a man who brings kolache."

"When did he bring you kolache?"

Dad shrugged and took the last bite of his burger.

"That stuff will kill you. Maybe that's what he's trying to do." She scowled at the cop. Traitor. Running to her father behind her back like that. And she thought they'd made some progress when he came to investigate her break-in. He was just taking an end run.

"If he were trying to kill me with pastry, he'd have to bring a lot more than one box. At this rate, I'll be dead in about four decades."

She glared at them both.

"I think I'm going to head out." Dad stood and threw money down on the table. There were enough bills to cover his meal, hers, a generous tip, and still plenty left over for another person to eat.

Her head hurt.

"Carter, why don't you keep Faith company while she finishes her meal. Order something. My treat."

"Carter?" she said. "You're on a first-name basis now?"

"Goodnight, sweetie." He bent down and kissed the top of her head. "I'll let you know when to expect the security installations."

He walked out, leaving her alone with Officer Endless Torment, who promptly slid into her father's vacant seat.

"So, what's good here?"

She doubted he liked salad and a fruit plate.

FAITH SMILED. CARTER EMERSON WAS funny and charming—when he wasn't trying to blame her for the entire drug cartel in Cathedral Lake.

She'd been angry that her father had manipulated them into dining together, but once she relaxed, she enjoyed his company. That Dad seemed to like him spoke volumes, especially after the way the two had met.

Carter cut a morsel off his grilled chicken and tossed it to Max.

"So, are you okay about his surgery tomorrow?"

He tossed the dog another bite. "Can you still do it? You've got to still have a headache, and now your finger is cut."

"Not a problem." Her head almost always hurt, so that was a non-issue. She wiggled her fingers and suppressed a wince. The cut one hurt a bit. But it wasn't her dominant hand, and the procedure was simple.

"Well, my head still hurts," he said. "My whole damn body does. Feels like I was trampled by bulls."

"I was unconscious at the time, but it probably wasn't much different than if you were. I want to thank you again."

"Faith, stop." He reached across the table and grabbed her hand. They both looked at their joined fingers, and he immediately let go. "You've already thanked me. And I told you, I was just doing my job. I didn't do anything special."

"It was special to me. You probably saved my life." This time she reached for his hand and squeezed it. "Let me thank you properly."

"We already had dinner." He smiled, but he didn't pull his hand away. Instead, he turned it over so he could hold her hand, then he rubbed his thumb over her knuckles. "Consider your debt paid."

"Dad paid for this. I'm still on the hook. Maybe I can cook for you."

That time he laughed. "I'm all for healthy food, but I'm not vegan by any means. I like meat."

"Trust me," she said. "You'll like it."

He met her gaze, and she warmed under his attention. He had that black Irish thing going on—black hair, blue eyes, dark complexion. She always loved that combination. Found it striking. And on him? All those features—high cheekbones, aquiline nose, full lips, thick lashes—combined to make one fine-looking man.

Not that she was looking.

"Vegan dinner?" he said.

"I just call it dinner. But yeah."

Carter gazed at her so intently, she swore she felt it. Finally, he said, "Okay. Dinner."

The second he agreed, she regretted it. For all she knew, he still suspected her of selling ketamine and possibly growing marijuana. He was probably just faking charm until he got what he was after—access to her private life. Well, he was in for a surprise. He couldn't find what didn't exist, and God help him if that was his agenda.

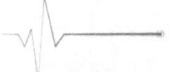

THE SECOND FAITH GOT HOME, she called Kacee.

"Hey! How're you feeling? You out of the hospital yet?"

"I left last night after everyone went home."

"Last night?" Kacee swore a blue streak.

"Kace, not now, okay? I've got a problem."

"You need a ride back to the hospital? I can pick you up in—"

"No. Will you shut up and listen?"

There was a harrumph followed by silence.

"I invited the cop over for dinner."

More silence. Thicker. Harsher. As hostile as silence over the phone could be.

Faith cringed. Now she'd made her best friend angry, too. "Kacee. What am I going to do?"

"Oh, am I allowed to talk now?"

She sighed. Maybe calling her wasn't the best idea. "Yes. Please. What should I do?"

"The cop from the hospital?"

"Yes. Officer Carter Emerson. The one who keeps trying to pin the drugs on me."

"Is he still out to get you?"

"No. Maybe. I don't know. Don't you think it's likely he's just playing nice to get close to me? To find evidence or trip me up?"

"Is he going to find evidence or find out anything he shouldn't?"

"No. Of course not."

"Why'd you ask him to dinner?"

"We were at the diner, and I—"

"You were out with him? On a date?"

"No. Not a date. A random encounter."

"And then you asked him on a date?"

"Dinner at my house isn't a date, either. It's a thank you for saving me."

"Could have done that with words."

Faith sighed.

"You think he's attractive."

"I hardly see where that's relevant."

"So that's a yes."

"Kace, I think I need to cancel. I'm freaking out here."

"I don't see the problem."

Faith squeezed the bridge of her nose. "The problem is I just invited trouble into my life. My home. Do you think I should put this off, or would that look too suspicious?"

"I think you should just have dinner."

"What?"

"The guy is seriously hot. You clearly think so, or you wouldn't have arranged this dinner to begin with. If you're no longer his suspect and he's no longer persona non grata, I think dinner would be good for you."

"Good for me?" Faith's voice fell flat.

"And dessert. Definitely dessert. Tell him you're on the menu."

Faith hung up the phone.

CHAPTER 12

CARTER ABSENTLY STROKED MAX'S HEAD in the parking lot of Faith's practice. He knew the surgery was routine, but he still worried about it. Max was more than a dog or a partner, he was family, even if Carter didn't refer to himself as "daddy" when he talked to him.

Max whimpered. Quiet, short, but still a whimper.

"I know you're probably hungry and thirsty, but you can't have anything yet." When the dog whined louder, Carter hugged his neck. "I'm sorry, buddy. But this afternoon, I'll get you a treat."

He took the dog inside. The door was unlocked and the lights were on, but no one was at the desk. "Hello?"

Faith came out of the back. "Hi." She bent down and petted Max. Then she stood. "David and I were just getting everything ready. Has he had anything to eat or drink?"

"No. We followed all your instructions. But he's hungry."

"We'll get him all fixed up and then he can eat later." She held out her hand for his leash. "Come on, baby. Let's go."

Carter pulled his hand back, out of her reach, keeping her from taking Max's lead. He was probably more apprehensive than Max, who looked up at him the same way Faith looked at him—like he was crazy.

She smiled and lay a hand on his arm. "Max will be fine. Go do whatever it is you do when you don't have him, and I'll call you when he's in recovery."

"You mean I can't stay? I can help you, if—"

"The last time you insisted on being in my OR, you passed out. Neither Max nor I needs the distraction. Besides, you wouldn't ask to assist a human surgeon."

Right. But no human surgeon ever took his dog before.

"Can't I at least stay in the waiting room? Then I can see him the second he wakes up."

"Leave, Carter. He's in good hands. I'll be in touch as soon as I'm done."

He leaned over and petted Max, then he handed her his leash. "As soon as you're done."

She smiled. "I promise."

He watched her take Max to the back, then he left. His vehicle never felt so empty, his chest never so tight.

Partnerless, he headed off to meet Tony.

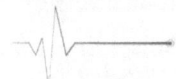

CARTER WALKED THROUGH THE HALLS of Oakland Regional Hospital, thankful to not be going to the ER or a patient's room. Being a cop, trips to the hospital were an occupational necessity—visiting injured comrades, checking on suspects, following up on leads. But to him, hospitals were a step away from death, and death reminded him of his brother.

And he'd been at the hospital too damn many times over the last few days, anyway.

This trip was to talk to Stanford Hammond, one of the muckety-mucks in Hospital Administration. Tony said he used to be an ER doctor and worked his way up. Maybe he'd be a little less business and a little more medical. Because it was his experience that HA folks always played the cover-their-ass card, whether they were potentially in trouble or not.

As Carter walked down the hall, he kept looking for Max at his side. He didn't feel whole without him.

He shrugged off the malaise and approached Tony, who stood waiting for him near the elevators.

"What's wrong?" Tony asked. The guy was too damn observant.

"Max's surgery today. Just a little worried about him."

"He's in good hands, don't worry. Besides, you said it's a simple procedure, right?"

Carter shrugged. Pushed the "up" button to avoid looking at his friend.

Tony clapped him on the back. "It'll be fine." They rode up the elevator in silence. Just before the door opened, he turned to Carter. "You up for this?"

"Yeah. Of course. Why wouldn't I be?" He cleared his throat. His voice had cracked.

Tony raised his eyebrows and stepped off the elevator.

Carter followed him down the hallway, past a series of office doors, to one with Stanford Hammond's name on it. They walked inside and were greeted by a prim receptionist seated behind a very orderly desk in a plush but austere office. "Detective Cooper and Officer Emerson, I presume?"

And efficient. The woman was the very definition of it.

"That's right," Tony said.

"Doctor Hammond is expecting you. Right this way." She took a few brisk steps toward another door and whisked it open.

They walked inside, and the door clicked shut behind them. Stanford Hammond sat behind a large walnut desk talking on the phone. His desk, unlike his assistant's, was rife with folders and piles of papers. The office was decorated in similar hues as hers, just a little more masculine and a lot less spartan. Framed degrees and expensive paintings were hung throughout the room, and shelves lined with books, binders, photos, and mementos took up one entire wall.

Hammond held up one finger, then gestured toward a table in the corner. Royce Keller sat on one of the leather chairs around it and tipped his chin up in greeting. Carter and Tony slipped quietly into two of the other chairs, and they all waited for the administrator to finish his call. A couple of minutes later, he said, "Just deal with it, damn it!" and slammed the receiver down. Then he loosened his wrinkled tie and smoothed it over a rumpled shirt while he crossed the room to join them. "Sorry about that."

"Stanford," Tony shook his hand. "Good to see you again."

"Detective. It's been too long." He turned a steely gaze on Carter.

"This is Officer Carter Emerson. He was one of the first responders at the high school."

Stanford shook his hand, grip brief but firm. "Officer. Pleased to meet you."

"Likewise."

"Let's get on with it, shall we?" Stanford settled into a vacant seat and grabbed a folder off the table in front of him.

"We just need to confirm some of the details from the attack," Tony said.

He opened the folder and scanned its contents. "That night, we treated and released seventy-three victims with minor injuries. Fifty-six more were admitted. Seventeen were DOA or died after admittance. Did tox screens on everyone. Only four people had marijuana in their systems. None had stronger drugs. Thirty-six people had alcohol in their systems. We collected the bullets from all the patients whose wounds weren't pass-throughs, and your CSU already has them."

Carter's mind raced. No narcotics? So the ketamine probably wasn't going to a user, but to a distributer. But the marijuana… that could be from the stuff they found near the Kellers' nursery. Just because it wasn't officially their land didn't mean they didn't grow there. They certainly had the access. And what difference did it make if she moved one drug or two? Or more?

Tony would be pissed that he even considered Faith guilty. Again. And his gut told him she wasn't. But it also told him he was onto something. Something big.

He tuned back into the ongoing conversation.

"What about Yavin?" Tony asked. "Anything noteworthy there?"

"He wasn't drunk or high, if that's what you're asking," Royce said.

"Do I sense a 'but' in there?" Carter asked.

"But he had Creutzfeldt-Jakob disease," Stanford added.

"Never heard of it," Tony said.

"It's pretty rare. It's a degenerative brain disease that usually manifests around age sixty and proves fatal in a year."

"What are the symptoms?" Carter asked.

Royce sighed. "It starts with memory issues and behavioral changes, followed by coordination and vision problems. As the disease progresses, the mind deteriorates. The body succumbs to weakness, muscular spasms, and involuntary movements. Blindness and/or coma may occur shortly before death. It's a terrible, untreatable disease whose only saving grace is that it claims its victims quickly."

"Behavioral changes?" Tony said. "The kind of thing that could make a nice but paranoid guy go off the rails?"

Stanford nodded. "Yeah. Exactly that kind of thing."

"The vision trouble and body control issues could explain why he didn't manage to shoot even more people," Carter said.

"More?" Stanford said. "I think the body count was high enough."

Tony shook his head. "Yavin had an automatic weapon and tons of ammo. And that place was packed. He should have been able to triple the body count. Or more."

Royce's eyebrows shot up. "So you're saying we were lucky it wasn't worse?"

"Yeah. Sounds like it could have been a hell of a lot worse."

"How certain are you that he had that Crust-whatever thing?" Carter asked.

"Creutzfeldt-Jakob," Stanford said. "That's what his medical records indicated. It's hard to diagnose, though. Basically, diagnosis occurs when everything else is ruled out."

"You can do a brain biopsy," Royce said.

"Yeah, but that's dangerous. Yavin's condition was diagnosed by brain degeneration noticed in an MRI. His behavior corroborates it. When the autopsy is done, the ME should be able to confirm it based on a simple brain tissue examination."

"So we suffered a catastrophic terrorist attack because of racial paranoia and a rare brain disease?" Carter asked.

"That's about the gist of it," Stanford said.

"And this had nothing to do with the distribution of drugs?"

Tony shot Carter a warning glance, but it was too late.

"Are you back on that theory again?" Royce asked. "I thought we hashed all that out. And after I bought you dinner and trusted you to see Faith got home safely."

"What's this?" Tony asked.

"Okay, first," Carter said, "you never asked me to see her home. Second, I didn't ask for dinner."

"But you didn't have trouble eating on my dime."

"Yeah, you bought me a burger and I ate with your daughter."

"None of which I would have agreed to if I knew you were still investigating her."

"I wasn't aware she was a minor who needed your approval."

"Let's everybody calm down," Stanford said.

"Calm down! He's after my daughter!"

"This is a place of business, Royce. Not a football field or playground. Indoor voices, please." He glanced at the door and back.

Royce took a deep breath. "Sorry. But still—"

"Before you go off again," Carter said, "you should know that I'm investigating the drugs found at the gym. Drugs that came from your daughter's practice."

"And still—"

"But," he interrupted, "that doesn't mean I'm investigating her. Or anyone in your family. I'm sorry you're caught up in this, but your discomfort doesn't lessen the fact that I have a job to do."

"Royce," Tony said, "you better than anyone know that the truth will come out eventually. Give the kid a chance."

Carter bristled at being called "kid" in front of these men, but he stayed silent. He really hoped the Kellers were innocent, but he knew he couldn't tell anyone—not even Tony—that he still had doubts. Few and far between, but they were there. His greatest hope was that his investigation would clear them all.

"I'm trusting you," Royce said. "Because of Tony. My trust doesn't come easy, and when it's gone, it's difficult to win back. Don't disappoint me."

Carter's phone buzzed with a text. It was from Faith.

Surgery over. Max in recovery. All went well.

"I gotta go." He stood and left the room, never bothering to acknowledge Royce's warning.

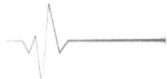

CARTER FASTENED HIS SEATBELT AND his cell rang. "Emerson."

"What the fuck was that all about?"

Should have looked at caller ID before picking up.

"Tony, I don't know what you want from me. The ketamine is my case." He pulled onto the road and headed for Faith's clinic. He needed to see Max, to know he was all right.

"The pot farm isn't. And I thought you were done with the Kellers."

"And I told you I was." He signaled and turned onto the road that would take him out of the town proper and out to her office. "Doctor Keller just jumped to conclusions. You were there. Did I mention anyone in the Keller family being under suspicion?"

Silence on the line.

"You still there?"

"Yeah." Tony didn't sound pissed any longer. More like resigned. *"The Kellers are good people. Good folks stuck in one bad situation after another. Be kind, okay?"*

"Always am."

"No. Not always."

What the hell was that supposed to mean? It was Carter's turn to be quiet while he thought that one over.

"You still there, kid?"

"I'm here."

"You've got me stuck between family and friend. It's an impossible situation. Put this thing to bed. Fast."

Family and friend, huh? Wonder who was which.

Carter thought about his brother and shook his head. He was being immature. He knew who was which. For all intents and purposes, he was the "family." Which made it suck all the more that he was responsible for Tony being caught in the middle.

"I'm not targeting them, Tony. I'm just doing my job." He pulled into the parking lot at the veterinarian clinic. He'd made record time.

"Do it faster, all right? Clear them and move on."

"Sure thing. Gotta go. Max is out of surgery."

"Don't start anything with Faith."

Seriously? "Goodbye, Tony."

Guilt plagued him as he scrambled out of his rig. His gut—and his heart—told him the Kellers were innocent. Even his head was ninety-nine percent on board.

But his gut also said they were somehow connected to the crime. More than just Faith being a victim of pharmaceutical thefts or her parents' nursery butting up against an illegal pot farm.

It felt personal.

Besides, he still hadn't confirmed their allegation that the pot wasn't their property. If it wasn't theirs, it was someone's. And that was his next lead.

He put it all behind him, though. Time to check on his partner.

Carter rushed inside, but the place looked deserted. "Hello?"

Faith popped her head out a doorway. "Be right with you. Finishing with a dressing."

He paced the tiny waiting area, anxious to see his dog. She had barely re-assured him in her text, and he needed to see Max for himself.

She finally came out. "We were just wrapping up our third surgery."

"Three? That's a lot for one morning. You sure you're up for all that?"

"What can I say? I'm not going to let an animal suffer because I don't feel like operating on more than one case a week."

Maybe he wasn't always kind. Or maybe she took what he said wrong. Damn it, now Tony was in his head.

Carter sighed. "I'm sorry. I didn't mean anything by that. But you were injured, and—"

"And what? Too busy selling drugs to do my job?"

"What?"

"My dad texted me."

She definitely took it wrong.

"Guess you've just been being nice to try and uncover dirt on me. Us. Well, guess what? There's no—"

"Faith, that's not what I'm doing. Your dad read the whole thing wrong."

"So you didn't pump him for information about me and my pharmacy?"

"No." God, was everybody punchy today? "I merely mentioned the drug thefts in passing. I wasn't trying to connect them to you. I was trying to deter-mine if they were at all connected to the attack the other day."

She crossed her arms. "And were they?"

"Doesn't look like it."

"Which puts your focus back on me and my family."

He shook his head. "No. It puts me back at square one."

Faith sighed, slumped a little. Her expression softened. "I'm sorry if I—if Dad—jumped to conclusions. It's a touchy subject for us."

"No doubt." He smiled. "Now, can we put this latest argument behind us? I'd like to see Max."

"He's still out. He's in recovery."

"Just let me look at him. I want to see for myself that he's okay."

"You don't trust me?" She crossed her arms again.

"Yes, I do. If I didn't, you wouldn't have done the surgery. I just need to see him."

"Come on." She led him down a hall and into a room he hadn't been in before. Six kennels stacked in rows of two lined one wall. Three of them had animals in them. Max slept in the first one.

He approached and bent down to peer at his partner. It just looked like he was sleeping, not drugged and in post-op care.

"And there were no problems?"

"None. He'll be one-hundred percent in no time."

Relief washed over him, and he turned and hugged her. "Thank you." He spoke into her hair. It smelled like lavender.

"Oh!" she said. After a short but awkward pause, she hugged him back. "You're welcome."

He stepped back, noticed the pungent scent of antiseptic and the fainter odor of manure. Immediately missed the aroma of lavender wafting off her.

"So." He cleared his throat when his voice broke. "We still on for tonight?"

She blushed and looked away. "Sure. Do you like squash?"

"Yeah. It's okay."

"Mushrooms? Artichokes?"

"All good."

"Great. Then let's say you stop by around seven? I'll bring Max with me, if that's okay with you."

All day without his dog? The thought left him feeling hollow. He hadn't expected at that, but he could handle it. "Okay. Thanks." He turned to leave, but spun back around. "Anything I can bring?"

"Nope. I got it covered."

"See you tonight, then." He poked his finger through the wires of the kennel and stroked Max's fur. Then he left.

Out at the car, he called Manuel Rodriguez, the officer he thought was on duty when the pot was found. "Manny? It's Carter."

"Emerson, my man. What's up?"

"You the guy who caught the call the other night to Cathedral Lake Nursery?"

"Yep. Me and Yamamoto were on duty."

"So you found the pot farm."

"Moto noticed first, but yeah."

"You run it down yet? It on Keller property?"

"No. It's its own separate plot of land. Looks like it was purchased by a Frank Anderson, then gifted. Deed is in the name of D. H. Anderson."

"How long did the Andersons own the property?"

"Which time?"

"What?"

"That land, including the land the nursery is on, was first purchased by a D. J. Anderson back in 1907. Seems to have passed down through the family line. During the recession in the late eighties, early nineties, the family lost it. It sat on the market for a long time. Just got purchased last year for twenty thousand."

"Twenty thousand? I thought that parcel was half an acre. That's a lot of cash for a little land."

"The owners of the nursery probably would have snatched it up if they knew it was available," Manny said. "On the other side of it is unusable swampland. The nursery could have made use of the space, but what's some random person going to do with a small chunk of land bordered by a business on one side and a bog on the other?"

"Apparently grow marijuana. You question Anderson?"

"That's the weird part."

"That's the weird part?"

"Yeah. The guy's old. Pretty infirm. Wife, too. Neither of them is going out there and growing anything."

"They got any kids?"

"No family in town."

"So another dead end."

"Looks that way."

"Thanks, Manny."

"Sure. Poker on Thursday?"

"I'll get back to you. Max just had surgery, I need to be sure he's recovering."

"Let us know. Moto's itching to win his money back. Been talking about it all week."

"He can try. He'll fail, but he can try. I'm happy to take his money."

Manny laughed. "Yeah. Guy's got no poker face. Later."

Carter ended the call and sat there thinking. What was an old couple doing with a tiny parcel of land in the middle of nowhere? Nothing. Even if Anderson grabbed that land for sentimental value, he wouldn't—couldn't—do anything with it. And who'd he gift it to?

Who knew that land was even out there? When Carter learned the answer to those questions, he'd be a step closer to putting the puzzle together.

He needed to walk that property. Wouldn't hurt to check out the nursery, either.

Tony would be pissed, but he had to check things out for himself.

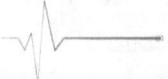

CARTER KNEW IT WAS A shitty thing to do, but he did it, anyway. The key to a successful search was to avoid suspicion by striding right in the front door with confidence, with purpose.

And to have an ulterior motive for being there.

He walked into the Cathedral Lake Nursery and looked for Vanessa. Maybe something in this case would finally go right. He didn't see her anywhere.

So far, so good.

The aisles were wide, large enough for a plant cart to fit through. They didn't provide him with much cover. But he didn't want anything inside, anyway. He walked past a row of small statues—the bent-over gnome with plumber's crack made him chuckle—and ducked under a hanging basket near the houseplants.

"Hi, I'm Kaitlyn. May I help you with something?"

Damn. Almost home. He turned to see who spoke to him. A young woman with a smudge of potting soil on her cheek smiled at him.

"Just browsing, thanks."

"Looking for anything in particular?"

"I have a date tonight. Thought I'd bring her flowers."

She laughed. "You might want to try a florist."

"I kind of wanted something potted. You know, so it won't die in a few days. Something she can keep."

"Well, we've got our houseplants here, but nothing that flowers. If you're looking for blooms, try greenhouses three, five, seven, and eight. Three is all roses, five all lilies. Seven and eight have more original selections, which would be my choice." She smiled.

"Thanks. I think I'll start there."

"Seven and eight are at the end of the path to your right. Three and five are in the middle of the property. If you need help down there, you should be able to find some of our guys in the ornamental tree section. Or let me know if you need something. I'm over there transplanting ferns." She gestured to a potting bench at the end of the aisle.

"Will do. Thanks."

She went back to her plants, and Carter slipped out the back door. The nursery was massive. Trees, shrubs, statuary, a pond, several greenhouses, and more types of plants than he knew existed. Without the clearly marked paths, a guy could get lost there. No wonder that unused plot beside the nursery went unnoticed for so long. It was too tiny next to the expanse of the nursery.

No wonder when it was used, no one noticed that, either.

Carter made his way down to Greenhouse Eight. It bordered the Anderson plot. He walked over there and gave the area a brief glance. He'd never find any clues there, now. All the plants had been removed and the land trampled to hell and back. Shrugging, he stepped inside the greenhouse. Felt like walking into a sauna. Row after row of brightly colored flowers thrived inside, their ruffly petals cupped around deep black or vibrant yellow centers. There was something familiar about the red ones, and he walked over to them to look at their name card.

Poppies.

A whole greenhouse full of poppies—a plant that knocked out all the breathing characters in The Wizard of Oz.

A plant that was illegal because it yielded opium. Heroin. Morphine. Codeine. Fentanyl.

A plant being grown in a greenhouse that bordered the half-acre where they found the marijuana. Seemed like a hell of a lot more than a coincidence.

He pulled his phone out and redialed Manny.

"Yo. You decide about poker?"

"Not yet. This is a business call."

"You chicken?" Yamamoto yelled. He must be on speaker if they both were listening and talking to him.

"No. Busy working."

"We just stopped for coffee," Moto said. *"It's been a slow day."*

"What'd you go and say that for?" Manny said. *"You're going to jinx us."*

Carter rolled his eyes. Partners were often like old married couples. Those two were no exception. "Did either of you do a search of the greenhouse bordering the pot farm?"

"No," Manny said. *"Wasn't included in the warrant or part of search and seizure. Why?"*

"I'm in there now. It's packed full of poppies."

"Okay." He paused for a moment. *"So?"*

"What do you mean, 'So?' Poppies are illegal."

"I don't think so."

Carter clenched his teeth and tried not to swear. A few deep breaths later, he'd calmed enough to talk. "They produce opiates, Manny."

"Remember that huge heroin bust Vice had three years ago?"

"Wasn't here then."

"Right. Well, short version, it depends on the type of poppy. Most are legal."

"How about a longer version?"

Manny sighed. *"You remember the deets, Moto?"*

"Vice seized a shit-ton of of powder and traced it back to a huge poppy farm in Georgia. The owner made a big deal about poppies being legal. And they are. All except for one kind, which the owner didn't have. The case wouldn't have even made it to trial, but someone found an underground grow-house that had the illegal-type of flowers in it. Just one type, man. The rest are legal."

"What type isn't?"

"Do I sound like a botanist to you?" Moto said.

"I'll just Google it." Carter heard the dispatcher's voice crackle tin the background, followed by Yamamoto's indistinct reply. A few seconds later, their siren blared.

"You do that," Manny said. *"We gotta go. Caught a call because Moto had to open his big mouth."*

"Later, guys. And thanks." The "be careful" remained felt but unspoken. Saying it aloud was another jinx. He started to do a web search for poppies on his phone and turned around.

Vanessa Keller, arms crossed over her chest, leaned in the doorway.

"Missus Keller." Wonder how much she heard.

"I thought you were done investigating us."

That answered that question. "I'm not here investigating anything."

"Then what was that call all about?"

"I was just surprised to see poppies. I thought they were illegal." He turned off his phone and then pocketed it.

"The law regarding growing poppies is vague. But the only type in question is the Papaver somniferum, which I don't have anyway. "

"That's pretty much what Officer Yamamoto said."

"So are we off your radar with your drug case?"

"That's right."

"Then why did I see you snooping around my property's border?"

The lady didn't miss a trick. She should be on the force. "Just curious. Had nothing to do with you, though."

"Why are you here, Officer Emerson? What do you want from us?"

"I'm not here on an official capacity. I actually want to buy a plant."

"A plant. Really?"

"Really. I have dinner plans tonight, and I wanted to bring flowers. But cut bouquets die so fast. I thought a plant would be nicer."

She walked a few rows over to a vibrant purple poppy. "Does your friend bake? The Hungarian Blue Breadseed will yield poppy seeds. Of course, the rest of the plant is poisonous, so I don't recommend it for homes with children or pets."

"She has a dog."

"Best to avoid these, then. Let me think." She tapped her finger to her pursed lips. "How romantic does this plant need to be?"

"It's our first date. Not even a date, exactly."

"So not orchids." She kept tapping her finger. "I've got it. Follow me."

He followed her out of the greenhouse, past rows of dormant twigs, past more rows of budding plants, and into another greenhouse that smelled of heaven. It smelled just like Faith.

"Lavender," she said. "It's not overtly sensual, but there's an element of romance to it. Fresh, herby, floral. An unusual yet remarkable choice. It'll grow well indoors or can be transplanted outside."

"Sounds good. I'll take one."

"Let's see." She walked the aisles, looking at the plants. They all looked the same to him, but she clearly saw a difference. "Canary Island is nice. But not great for this climate zone. English smells wonderful, but it doesn't do that well indoors. Here we go—French lavender. The smell isn't quite as pungent, but it'll do well inside or planted outside. I'll give you a card with care instructions."

"Perfect."

She chose a specimen that looked like every other lavender plant in the greenhouse. It had spiky, light purple flowers. At least it was in bloom. He'd feel foolish taking a plant that might never flower.

Who was he kidding? He'd feel ridiculous anyway. It wasn't a date-date. It was just dinner. At least, he thought that was all it was.

Vanessa led him back to the store. She put the plant down on the potting table and walked over to the container section. "Terracotta would be best. The water can evaporate through it."

He shrugged. "Sure."

She chose a pot with a delicate pattern around its rim. "You can get away with a fancier pot. The plant grows upright, so the leaves won't cover any detailing."

"Okay."

A few quick instructions to Kaitlyn, and the girl began transplanting the lavender into the terra cotta pot with the soil additives Vanessa suggested.

"And I think brocade." She opened a cabinet beside the potting bench and searched until she found a patterned purple ribbon woven with gold and copper threads. Somehow she didn't need to measure it, but rather eyeballed the length, cut it, then tied it around the pot and crafted a perfect bow with deft fingers.

His mother's hobby, before his brother died, was working with flowers and creating arrangements and door hangings and stuff like that. She stopped creating anything of beauty—anything at all—on the day she learned of Mark's death, and Carter found he missed it. Missed her and all his family. He wasn't prepared for the wave of nostalgia that crashed over him, didn't want to feel any fondness for the woman in front of him, the woman who—along with her daughter—kept turning up in his investigation. And that she was Faith's mother only made the situation more awkward. But watching Vanessa turn a simple pot and plant into a beautiful gift stabbed him in his gut, reminded him of his mother and happier times, put his current situation on the back burner. He saw her, then, in a different light. Not as a person of interest in a series of drug-related crimes, but as a business owner, as a hobbyist trying to bring beauty into the world. As a mother.

God, when did he become such a girl?

This was all Faith's fault. He didn't refer to himself as "Daddy" from his dog's perspective, he didn't dwell on his family, and he certainly didn't buy flowers for non-dates. She had him all turned around, not thinking clearly. And that needed to stop. Now.

Carter was just about to tell Vanessa he changed his mind about the flowers when she presented him with the pot. The lavender scent was another punch in the gut. It smelled just like Faith, and he had to buy it because he knew she'd love it.

Vanessa led him to the register and tallied his purchases—the plant, the pot, the transplant and soil additives, and the ribbon. She told him the price with a smile on her face.

He tried not to visibly balk. "Do you take American Express?"

After he paid, he took the extravagant plant to his car. His phone vibrated with a text from Faith—Max was awake and alert. Good news, for a change.

Carter was about to turn off his phone when he noticed the results of his Google search.

He didn't know all the different types of poppies the nursery grew, but he'd swear he saw the illegal Papaver somniferum in the greenhouse.

CHAPTER 13

FAITH STIRRED COCONUT MILK INTO her butternut squash soup and inhaled deeply. Nothing like an aromatic soup on a chilly night. She glanced in the oven to check on the mushroom stout pie with potato biscuit topping. The biscuits were golden brown and the stew beneath was thick and bubbly, so she pulled it out to set. Then she tossed her homemade dressing into the salad. The lemon-olive oil mixture over peppery arugula was just the light and fresh dish she needed to balance the other heavy courses.

She'd pulled two large chocolate cupcakes out of the freezer to thaw. Cupcakes were just as easy to make as cake, and as she couldn't—or shouldn't—eat a whole cake by herself, she often made batches of cupcakes and froze all but one or two. They came in handy when company dropped by unexpectedly.

Or when she'd scheduled a date on the spur of the moment.

Not that this was a date. Just dinner and talking. Nothing more.

Why the hell had she asked Carter over, anyway? He wasn't interested in her as anything other than a suspect in a crime. Typical of her. Always into the wrong guys.

Not that she was attracted to Carter Emerson.

God, her lies to herself got weaker every time she told them. If he knew how poorly she fibbed, he'd never suspect her of anything illegal. She just didn't have it in her to break the law, let alone to spin a web of lies to cover her tracks.

She'd just finished setting the table when the doorbell rang. A quick glance in the mirror to make sure her mascara hadn't smeared or her lipstick wasn't on her teeth, and she opened the door. "Hi."

"Hi." Carter pushed a potted plant of lavender at her. "You said you had the food handled, so I figured I'd get you a hostess gift instead."

Faith took the plant and inhaled deeply. Lavender was a favorite of hers, both as a flower and as an herb. It was also her signature scent—she used an Italian lavender bath soap, lavender-scented shampoo and conditioner, and a lavender perfume. She'd switched to lavender after her attack because it was supposed to be a relaxing, calming scent. It comprised her whole beauty regimen, and she still had stress-issues.

Still, she loved the plant, and the pot he'd given her was gorgeous. "Thank you. It's beautiful." She sniffed it again, then stepped aside and opened the door further. "Come on in." She gave him a quick tour of the main part of the house.

"You've got a lovely home."

"Thanks." She looked around at her homey furniture and sparse decor. "It's a little small, and kind of far from work. When the spring thaw is permanent, I'm going to build a new place out near the office. That way I won't be far from the animals I have to keep overnight. And I can get there quickly in an emergency."

"Isn't that kind of far from, well, everybody?"

"I'll enjoy the solitude. Believe me." She led him to the dining room and put the plant in the center of the table. "Everything's ready. I just need to carry it all in."

"Need help?"

"Sure, if you don't mind."

He carried the soup, and she carried the salad. Carter went back for the stew while she opened wine and filled their glasses. When he set the casserole dish down, she handed him one of the goblets. "Care to make a toast?"

"Uh… sure. To the chef." He raised his glass.

She chuckled. "You didn't even taste anything yet. What if you don't like it?"

"You assured me I would."

"*Touché.*" She clinked her glass against his. "To a wonderful meal. And wonderful company."

After they each took a sip, Carter cleared his throat. "Speaking of company, where's Max?"

"He seemed to have an abundance of energy once he came out of the anesthesia. When he got here, he and Ruby kept racing around the house. I took them out back to play."

"Out back?"

"Don't worry. I'm completely fenced in. He's not going anywhere."

"And no problems with the surgery?"

"No." She put her spoon down. "I told you, he's fine. He's alert, playful. He drank and held down water. He'll be ready for food tonight when you take him home."

"Sorry. I was just worried."

"No need to apologize. I bet you missed him today."

"I did. It was weird not being with him, being out on my own." He pushed his soup dish aside and took a bite of the stew. "Everything's delicious, Faith."

"Maybe I'll make a vegan convert out of you after all."

"I don't think I'll ever give up meat. But I could eat like this once a day. Might even help me lose a few extra pounds."

"Doesn't look to me like you've got any weight to lose." Her cheeks flushed when she realized what she'd said.

What the hell was she thinking? Now he'd know she'd been ogling him. Smooth, Faith. Real smooth.

He grinned and took a sip of wine.

At least he let her off the hook.

"So you've been assessing my physique, huh?"

Or not.

Was it possible for her to blush more than she was a moment ago? It felt like her face would soon burst into flames. "What I meant was, police officers need to be fit to do their jobs well. And I know you take your job seriously, so... Well, you must not be out of shape."

He grinned again.

She was a moron. "Let me get these plates out of the way, and I'll bring out dessert."

"I'll help clear."

Guess she wasn't getting a chance to hide her shame in the kitchen.

He stacked the dishes on the counter, and she rinsed them and put them in the dishwasher. The meal was tidied up in just a few minutes, which left her with nothing to do other than be mortified that she'd basically admitted to thinking he was sexy. Lord, keep her from saying or doing anything else that stupid.

She plated the two cupcakes and took them into the dining room. "Want me to make coffee?"

"Sure. Or just milk is fine. I love ice cold milk with chocolate cake."

"I've got ice cold milk. But it's almond milk, not dairy."

"Coffee sounds good."

"Be right back." Thank God she had a moment to compose herself.

Except she didn't. He followed her into the kitchen.

"If you don't mind, I want to go out back and see Max."

"Sure. Door's through the pantry." She pointed to her left.

Carter left, and she got the coffee started. Then she lay her head on the counter. Could she be more embarrassed?

The sound of him clearing his throat again startled her, and she whipped her head up.

"Are you okay?"

"Yeah." So she lied. She sucked at it, so he probably knew, anyway. "Just been a long day."

"I'll get going, then. But I need your help first."

"Oh? With what?"

"Well, uh—Hmm. I don't really know how to say this."

Her heart started to race. "What's wrong?"

"Max and Ruby are... Um, Max is..." He cleared his throat again, then he blushed.

Why would a man blush when talking about two dogs?

Oh. Oh, no.

"Are they...?"

"Oh, yeah. I told him to stop, but like any man, he's laser-focused on what he's doing and isn't going to be dissuaded by me. Any idea how to stop that?"

Based on her humiliation, Faith was certain her cheeks had achieved a new shade of red. "Help yourself to coffee. Eat your cupcake. I'll go deal with it."

Their dinner was a disaster, but at least the dogs had fun. She walked through the pantry and out her back door, certain she'd never see Carter Emerson again.

FAITH SAT AT THE KITCHEN table, drinking her morning coffee and ignoring her berries and granola. She stared at Ruby, who lay contentedly at her feet. The dog looked way too satisfied.

Wonder how many people after a first date could say their dog got lucky but they didn't get so much as a kiss goodbye? Must be some kind of record. She should call the folks at Guinness, but it was just too damn embarrassing.

Her doorbell rang, and Ruby's ears perked up.

"I don't know what you're so excited about. I can assure you, Carter won't be bringing Max back."

Ruby whined and put her head down.

"Unbelievable." Faith walked to the door and opened it without checking her appearance in the foyer mirror. "Mom?"

"Good morning." Her mother breezed into the house.

Faith shut the door and followed her into the kitchen. "Coffee?"

"Yes, thanks." She gave Faith a once-over. "Why aren't you dressed yet? And please tell me you're going to do something with your hair."

It was only seven-thirty. She didn't have to be at the clinic until nine. So she had a lazy morning and was lounging in her jammies. Who cared? Not like anyone important was going to see her.

"Here, Mom. I don't have cream, but I've got almond milk."

Her mother frowned. "Black's fine."

Why did everyone reject the almond milk before even giving it a chance?

Mom looked around the room. "Your kitchen depresses me. Let's take our coffee into the dining room."

"What's wrong with my kitchen?" But Faith followed her around the island as they made their way to the formal dining room.

"You don't even have a single picture on the walls."

"Well, since you hate this house so much, I guess it's a good thing I'm building a new place."

"Which you probably won't bother decorating, either. And it's so far away. I don't know how I feel about you being in the middle of nowhere."

"It's not the middle of nowhere."

"Well, I hope you'll at least decorate it." She turned around in the archway and gestured toward the dining room while she walked backward toward a chair. "This room is as depressing as your kitchen. Blah paint."

"It's beige."

"No cushions on the—" She stopped short when she faced the table. Faith almost ran into her. "Well, what have we here?"

Faith licked coffee off her hand. It had sloshed over the rim of her mug when she tried to avoid bumping into her mother. "What?" Was probably going to blister, damn it.

Her mother took a seat at the head of the table and pointed at the centerpiece. "That's a lovely plant. Is it new?"

"This old thing?" She doubted her mother would appreciate her dating the officer who had suspected them of drug trafficking. "I've had it for weeks. You just never visit."

"I visit you more than you visit me." She stared at her daughter over the rim of her mug. "Where'd you get it?"

"Where'd I—where do you think? The nursery. Kaitlyn repotted it for me."

"And when was that?"

"I don't know. It's a plant, Mom. I didn't know I needed to document its history just to take it home."

"Not a painting on the wall, but you took the time to buy a centerpiece."

"I didn't know that was a crime."

"Funny thing." Her mom put her mug down. "That's brand new ribbon. We just got it Monday."

Faith really needed to practice lying. Her voice grew weaker as she protested. "You must be mistaken. I got it weeks ago."

"Oh, I don't think so. See, I tied this exact ribbon on an identical terracotta pot yesterday. I had to open the wrapping on it before I could use it. It was brand-spanking new. And see this pattern around the pot?" She pointed at the detail around the band. "We only had one pot like this."

"I doubt that. Your inventory is so huge, you probably don't remember what you have multiples of and what's one of a kind."

"Faith, I made up this pot yesterday for Carter Emerson. He said he needed a gift for a date. You want to tell me what you're doing with it?"

The blood drained from Faith's face. Why the hell would Carter shop at her parents' nursery? Of all the places. Of all her rotten luck!

Before she concocted a believable answer, her mother's phone rang.

"Hello... What?... When?... Don't say or do anything. I'll be right there."

"What was that all about?"

"That was Kaitlyn. Apparently your boyfriend is at the nursery again. With a warrant."

FAITH CALLED DAVID AND ASKED him to reschedule all the appointments throughout the rest of the week while Vanessa called Bella and asked her to meet them at the nursery. Her mom wanted to drive—probably to continue her diatribe—and as they streaked down the road toward the nursery, Faith texted her father.

She gripped her seat and cringed when her mom nearly missed the guard rail. "It's not like you to drive so fast." So recklessly. "I don't think I've seen you exceed the speed limit in years."

"I don't think I have. Not since Hope…" She cleared her throat and took another corner at breakneck speed. "I'm just so damn angry. What are you doing, getting involved with that—that *man*? Damn it! He clearly has it out for all of us."

"So this is why you only wanted to take one vehicle? So you could lecture me the whole way there."

"I'm not lecturing you, Faith. I'm asking what you're thinking."

"I'm not 'involved' with him, Mother. We shared a couple of meals. That's it."

"A couple of meals? So he's a liar on top of being a sneak."

"What?"

"He told me it was a first date."

Faith sighed. "If you want to call it a date, then sure, it was. The meal before that was spur of the moment. Dad was there."

"Your father was on your date? He knew and didn't stop it?"

"Mom, it wasn't a date. Dad and I were out. My meal was held up, so Dad finished before me. Carter walked in, we talked for a bit, Dad left, and I stayed and finished my meal while he ate his. Not a date."

"Not a non-date, either, given it led to another one."

"Seriously, you're making too big a deal over this."

She flew into the parking lot and whipped into her reserved spot. "Big deal? He's inside right now with a search warrant, disrupting our lives yet again. I hardly think it's trivial."

"He's just doing his job. He must have found something yesterday when he was here that made him want to follow up."

"I think that's why he was here to begin with." She got out of the car and slammed her door shut. When Faith got out, her mother continued. "To snoop. Not to do something nice for you. And there's nothing suspicious here. This is harassment. It's my livelihood he's impacting now."

Bella pulled into the lot, Jensen right behind her. She parked away from the entrance and strode with purpose across the lot until she reached them. "Have you gone inside yet?"

Vanessa shook her head, and Bella hurried inside.

Jensen walked to his mother and gave her a hug. "Bella will take care of it. Don't worry."

"I'm not worried. I'm furious."

"Okay, then." He hugged Faith. "You okay?"

"She's better than okay," Mom said. "She's dating him."

"You're what?" He turned and gaped at her.

Royce pulled into the lot, parked off to the side, and rushed over to them. "What's going on?"

"Why didn't you tell me you fixed our daughter up with that lunatic cop?"

"What?"

"You left them alone for dinner. Then she had another date with him—"

"It wasn't a date," Faith said.

"—and now he's inside searching for something." She continued like Faith hadn't interrupted. "He's using her, and he's harassing us."

"I thought he was done suspecting us of everything," her dad said.

"Don't you see? It was all a ruse."

Detective Cooper pulled into the lot, got out of his car, and approached them. "Hail, hail, the gang's all here, I see."

"Tony," Royce said, "what the hell is going on?"

He sighed. "Apparently Emerson was here yesterday and found poppies growing on the premises."

"Which I told him were legal."

"Well, the law's fuzzy about the legalities of growing poppies. And your greenhouses are large enough to be concerned about a crop."

"Except I don't grow the questionable one at all. The Papaver somniferum."

"Carter said he saw red poppies with black centers. Isn't that them?"

She flung her hands in the air. "And of course that's the only poppy that's red with a black center. By all means, let's take the word of a cop over a nursery owner. He'd obviously know."

"So you don't have the Papa… whatever?"

She glared at him.

"Tony," Royce said, "you've known us for how long? You know how we feel about drugs. Do you honestly think we'd have anything to do with a crop that had the slightest chance of being used for something illegal?"

"No. No, I don't." He ran his hand through his hair. "This thing has Carter all turned around. He found the drugs at the Yavin scene, and with all the carnage, he's worried drugs were involved. He feels responsible for solving the case."

"To the point that he accuses my family of some heinous crime every couple of days?" Vanessa turned and paced in small circles.

Faith hadn't spoken up during the whole discussion. Carter might feel responsible for solving the crime, but she felt responsible for bringing his attention down on them. Why couldn't he just believe them? What if he found something illegal that her mom simply didn't know was wrong? What if someone planted something there to frame them? The Kellers sure seemed to be targets for someone.

She'd made Carter suspicious when she acted so weird the night of the terrorist attack. Why couldn't she just control her stupid emotions? Would she be the downfall of her whole family? Just because of her trauma? It wasn't fair.

Her chest hurt, and taking in air grew increasingly difficult. She started to pant, to hyperventilate, desperate to inhale even a molecule of air.

Jensen stepped behind her, rubbed her shoulders and neck. "Breathe, sis. Come on. Slow, deep breaths."

She tapped her fingers, focused on her breathing. If only she hadn't rushed out of the house, she'd have Ruby with her—could feel her soft fur, her calm breaths. Her sturdy presence.

Feel safe.

"In and out. Come on, Faith. Calm breaths."

Everyone in the parking lot stared at her as she fought for control. Bella breezed out the door of the nursery and walked straight over to her. "Everything's fine, Faith. Take my hand. Let's walk."

She let Bella lead her away from the center of attention. The way she took charge, the way she rubbed her thumb over her wrist—it soothed Faith.

"It's okay. He didn't find anything. And he feels really bad that he jumped to conclusions. Again. I think he's finally done suspecting you. Any of you."

Faith took a deep breath and looked across the lot. Carter and a few other officers had also exited the building. And here she thought she'd never see the man again. Meanwhile, her mother, God bless her, was in full mama-bear-mode, yelling at him about Papaver somniferum versus Papaver rhoeas and about what his incessant investigating was doing to her daughter.

Shame heated her cheeks, especially when everyone turned to look at her. Of course that was the moment she began to breathe again, right when she wished she'd just pass out and drift into oblivion.

She couldn't hear Carter's response, but the other officers dispersed, so she assumed the worst was over.

"Bella," Faith said, "how do you do it?"

"Do what?"

"Function? We were both abducted, but you were shot, too. Why am I the mess and you're so strong? How do you cope? How can I cope?"

"I'm not saying it's easy, Faith, but I do like to think I'm strong. I'm not going to let the memory of the shooting impact my life. I have too many wonderful things in it right now to let some bad history ruin it."

"But how? I don't want to be afraid anymore."

"Who says I'm not afraid?"

"You're—you're afraid?"

"Of course. Every time I meet a new client, I wonder if he'll get violent. Every time I'm on a back road, I fear breaking down and being attacked. I wake up with nightmares sometimes."

"So how do you put it behind you?"

"By not succumbing to my fears. By facing them. Most of them."

"Most?"

Bella shrugged. "I still haven't been back to the lake since it happened. When I can do that, I'll know I can conquer anything. It used to be such a special place for me and your brother, I hate to lose it permanently. But so far, I haven't been strong enough to go there. Jensen keeps mentioning it as a potential place for us to get married. I don't have the heart to tell him I'm still nervous about being there. I keep hoping I can deal with my fears before we have to make definitive plans, then he'll never know."

"I thought you two told each other everything."

"He has enough on his mind without me adding on. He knows about the nightmares. I don't want to worry him about this, too. Not when it's something I have to deal with. There's nothing he can do about it, so I keep it to myself."

Faith blinked back tears. "At least you have someone who's concerned about you. I don't have anyone to share this with."

"Oh, Faith. Sure you do. You have all of us."

"I know. That's not what I mean. It would be nice to know when I wake up screaming, someone would be there to hold me until I calm down. That if there was a break-in, someone would be there to protect me."

"You can't think that way. You have to be strong enough to deal with it yourself. That's why I haven't told Jensen. Because I need to be the one to deal with it, not him."

Faith sighed.

"Have you been to the lake or the ruins yet?"

She scoffed and shook her head. "No. Just the thought is nearly paralyzing."

"Do you have to hurry back to work?"

"No. I told David to reschedule everything. I didn't know what I'd be dealing with today, so I took the whole day off."

"Why don't I call off and we go together?"

"Go? Go where? The lake?"

"No, Dairy Queen. Yes, the lake. The ruins. Let's get it over with. Then maybe we can both move on."

Icy dread sluiced up her spine, settled like spider feet at the base of her neck. She rolled her head to quash the sensation, but it barely helped. "You want to go back to… to where it happened?"

"I think it's time. Let's help each other through it. Then perhaps we'll both find closure. Maybe then we can both move on."

Faith looked back toward the nursery. Tensions seemed to have eased. At least her mother wasn't yelling any longer.

Her stomach tied in knots so tight, she thought her intestines might burst. But she tried to ignore it. Instead, she squared her shoulders and held her chin high. "I came here with Mom. You'll have to drive."

Bella smiled. "Let's go."

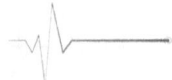

NEITHER SPOKE ON THE DRIVE. Which was fine with Faith. She was too nervous to make idle chit-chat. Why the hell had she agreed to go?

Because she was tired of living like a victim. She needed to take charge.

The closer they got to the lake, the harder it was for Faith to breathe. Invisible bands constricted her lungs, black spots shimmied in front of her, the rush of blood in her ears made hearing even the blaring radio difficult. Which was too bad, because Bella played "The Warrior" on a loop. And Faith could really use that battle cry at the moment.

She tapped her fingers on her thigh to the cadence Tod had taught her. She focused on deep breaths and relaxing her muscles.

Tried to listen carefully to the song. Belt it out, Patty Smyth.

Before she knew it, Bella had stopped the car.

Faith opened her eyes to find them in the parking lot at the lake. She looked at Bella, whose face was as white as her knuckles—she had a death grip on the steering wheel. But her expression was determined.

"You ready to do this?" Bella asked.

No. "Yes."

"All right. Phone off. No distractions."

"Is that really necessary? We can just put them on vibrate."

"So the buzzing interrupts us? No. Phones off. We're on our own."

"Fine." Faith turned her phone off and slipped it into her pocket. She watched Bella do the same. This was crazy. What were they thinking?

"Let's go." Bella opened the door, stepped out, and walked to the trunk, which she opened and bent into.

Faith climbed out of the car and joined Bella near the bumper. "What are you doing?"

She opened a first aid kit and grabbed a flashlight. "You know, it's best to be prepared for any contingency."

It was daylight. Faith wasn't fooled. Bella wanted a weapon.

"You have another?" She wanted one, too, damn it.

"Sorry." Bella took a deep breath. "Let's do this."

It wasn't that chilly for a Pennsylvania March, but it was always colder by the water. Consequently, no one braved the beach that day but them. They were all alone.

At least, Faith prayed they were.

The wind whipping off the water made it all the way to the parking lot and added goosebumps to the ones fear had already caused her to sprout. The bite of the brisk breeze carried with it scents redolent of rotting fall leaves, new spring growth, and clear, cool lake water.

It also carried the ominous sensations of being watched, hunted, subdued.

Sweat beaded on her brow, the gusts off the lake chilling her forehead, an icy palm pressing in toward her brain.

Breath came in ragged gasps, body trembled uncontrollably. Black spots winked in front of her, obscuring all the nature around her.

Bella clutched her hand, her fingers every bit as clammy as Faith's. "Breathe, Faith. We can do this. We have to do this."

Faith hummed under her breath and concentrated on her breathing, on the tune, on the finger-tapping rhythm she patted out with her free hand. Why hadn't she thought to bring Ruby with them?

She inhaled—a slow, deep intake of air, and steeled her resolve. Bella's grip tightened. They looked at each other.

God, Faith so didn't need to see the fear on Bella's face.

"Let's hit the beach first," Faith said. She needed the relative safety of the open space before she braved the confines of the ruins.

"I'm with you," Bella said.

They made their way slowly from the parking lot to the sands at the shore. With each step, Faith's feet grew heavier. Soon she'd be rooted to the spot, paralyzed by fear and dread.

Bella's pace had slowed, too, but she pulled Faith along. Finally they found themselves at the water's edge.

Bella took a deep breath. "This isn't so bad, huh?"

Faith almost blurted out a knee-jerk denial, but she stopped and thought for a moment. It wasn't as bad as she expected. The wind-rippled water lapped gently toward her toes and created a soothing sound. Rustling foliage and soft bird chatter made a beautiful harmony to the melody of the undulating lake. She took a deep breath. The air was crisp, clean. Cleansing. A kind of baptism, infusing her with a sense of peace.

She closed her eyes, content to just exist in the moment. Seconds, minutes, hours—she didn't know, didn't care, how long she stood there. It had been so long, too long, since she'd been able to enjoy the lake, and it was nice to just be for a change. Not frightened, not putting on a brave face for the world.

Just… breathing. More than existing, but actually living. Dare she think it? Content.

She relaxed her grip on Bella's hand, then let go. Standing there, eyes closed. Alone but safe. Free.

God, she hadn't been able to breathe so deeply in months. She stretched her arms out and let the wind whip through her hair. She'd conquered a fear, and she felt power surge in her—she was woman, hear her roar!

A giggle burst from somewhere deep inside, and she looked at Bella.

Bella smiled, and they both started laughing. Deep, belly-clenching, eye-tearing laughs. They held onto each other to keep from falling, and Faith basked in the joy, the freedom of it all.

When their mirth subsided, they again stood on their own. Faith was content to be quiet and look at the water, but Bella broke into her serenity.

"Feels damn good, doesn't it?"

"I haven't breathed this easy in a while. This was far better than I expected."

"Well, that's one hurdle. One to go." Bella looked at the cathedral ruins on top of the hill.

A chill skittered up Faith's back. "Why'd you have to go and mention that? Haven't we done enough for one day?"

"No, we haven't. We need to get this out of the way."

She knew Bella was right, but she didn't have to like it. Faith squared her shoulders and turned toward the hill. "All right. Let's get it over with."

"Just think," Bella said while they trudged along the path, "in a few minutes, we'll be able to put all this behind us."

Faith wasn't so sure. It was one thing to stand on the beach beside someone. Quite another to step inside the room they'd been held captive in. She didn't know if she'd ever be able to move past that terror.

Or ever move on with her life.

The closer she got to the old cathedral, the more she labored to breathe.

She tried to play it off as exertion from the climb, but she knew the signs of yet another impending panic attack.

Focus on breathing. Tap fingers. Hum a cadence.

She stopped outside the ruins. Tod's methods were failing her. What if she died right there?

Teeth clenched, feet rooted to the spot, she trembled and awaited her fate.

"You need to relax." Bella kneaded the tense muscles in her neck.

Faith could barely register the massage and the soothing words, couldn't manage a response at all.

"Come on, Faith. Come back to me. Don't leave me here to deal with this myself."

Bella's fingers and whispered pleas worked a minor miracle. Faith coughed, sucked in a deep breath, and bent over, head to knee, just to avoid blacking out. Once she'd calmed, she stood and looked at her friend. "How? How are you staying so calm?"

"Calm?" She barked a coarse laugh. "Are you crazy? I'm ready to jump out of my skin!"

"But you sound so confident. And you just took care of me. You—"

"The fact that you need me is the only thing keeping me going. Focusing on you is helping me put my fears on hold."

"Well, you're in luck," Faith said, "because I don't see me calming down anytime soon."

They both stood outside the burned husk of a building, arms around each other, trembling and silent. What had they been thinking? They shouldn't have come alone. They shouldn't have come at all! Faith resigned herself to living the rest of her life in fear, and she turned to go back down the hill.

"Where are you going?" Bella's shrill voice stopped her cold.

She turned around. "I can't. I can't do it. How can you? How do you deal with any of this? You were abducted, too. You were shot, for God's sake! You nearly died here."

"That's precisely why I must do it. I lived, damn it. This fear is becoming a figurative death. I'm not going to let my past ruin my present and future. No more. I'm here, alive and well, and it's time I start acting like it."

She was right. Faith knew it, logically. But her heart still raced and rejected the notion.

"What do you say, Faith? Are we going to join the land of the living again? Or are you content to stay trapped in your fears, just like we were imprisoned last year?"

Something in her snapped, and she started yelling. "No, damn it. I'm not content to live like this. It's debilitating. But how do I move past it? How did you? You're never breaking out in sweat and losing your breath and your vision. You never find yourself paralyzed with fear. How? How the hell did you move past it? And how can I? Every sound I hear is a potential threat. Every stranger a possible kidnapper. I don't know what to do!"

Bella took her hands and squeezed. "I haven't moved past it, either. I just manage it better. Most of the time."

"But how?" Tears welled in her eyes and spilled down her cheeks.

"It helps that I'm rarely alone. Even when I am, I keep busy. I throw myself into work. Or wedding plans—you know, reading the magazines and deciding on dress styles and floral arrangements. But pretty soon I'm going to have to start acting on those arrangements, and that includes setting a date and venue. Your brother wants us to get married here, and I owe it to him to try and get over my issues so we can stand on that hill where we met and exchange our vows. And, damn it, I owe it to myself, too. I'm tired of irrational fears. What are the odds of getting abducted twice? It's time I move past this. Come with me."

Faith didn't have a fiancé to rely on, nor did she have an event looming that she needed to conquer her fears for. What she did have, however, was a desire to move on. Maybe she wasn't in the same place Bella was, but for God's sake, she could try. Should try.

Would try.

She sucked in a deep breath and let it out slowly through pursed lips. "We can do this. Let's go in."

Bella squeezed her hands and smiled, then she turned toward the ruins and strode with purpose toward them.

Faith followed her, but with far less conviction. Logic dictated the noises she heard in the trees were the same animals she'd heard down at the beach, but fear overrode reason and convinced her malevolence waited for them, ready to strike. Her breathing quickened, and she hurried to keep pace with Bella.

Inside, they made their way to the inner sanctum, to the place they'd been held. Darkness suffocated Faith, and she lamented not having a flashlight. "Can I turn on my phone, at least? Use the flashlight app?"

"No. I got it." Bella shone the beam around the walls, fixated on a single bullet hole from the night she had been shot. The one projectile that hadn't hit her.

Faith noted the light waver and realized her friend was shaking. She didn't blame her. Sweat beaded on her forehead, and she swiped at it with the back of her hand. She walked to the center of the room and grabbed Bella's hand. Scuffling sounds had followed them in from outside, seemed to bounce off the walls like sinister forces surrounding the two frightened women.

It's just noise. It's just noise. It's just noise.

"It's not so bad, right?" Bella asked, voice weak and echoing in the chamber. She'd moved her hand and shone the flashlight elsewhere on the dank walls. She didn't go anywhere near the bullet hole again.

Eventually the beam of light traveled back to the doorway, illuminating a figure clad in dark clothing.

A scream ripped from the depths of Faith's core. Then all went black.

CHAPTER 14

SO, THAT HAD BEEN EMBARRASSING. Carter hadn't had his ass handed to him like that since he'd gotten into a fight in high school and broken Scott Fulbright's nose.

Never had he been so thoroughly admonished at work. Not even the last time Tony reamed him out.

Not to mention it had been in front of Faith. And about him harassing her family, to boot. Downright humiliating.

That it was Tony who gave him the tongue lashing made it nearly unbearable. Letting him down was like a kick in the nuts. Painful, sickening, and damn hard to recover from.

If his brother was watching from Heaven, he'd let him down, too. Downright unforgivable.

He'd become a cop to honor his brother, to make his family and Tony proud. To bring about real change and make a difference in the world. And since coming to Cathedral Lake, he'd only been on one important case—and he'd fucked it up. Royally.

Tony had given him an ultimatum—back off the Kellers or be thrown off the case. Neither was acceptable. He didn't want a formal reprimand, no one did. But he couldn't stay away from the Keller family. Not now. Not when it was clear they were at the heart of his drug case.

He no longer suspected any of them. Lesson learned, they were great people, totally aboveboard, who just had a shitty hand dealt to them. But he also didn't believe in coincidence. They were far too close to all of his clues to not be connected to the drugs in some way.

Time to be a cop. If the evidence he had wouldn't yield any answers, he'd have to go deeper. Go back to that first case of pharmaceutical thefts. Back to Royce's case.

He was certain the link was out there. And he was going to find it.

CARTER SETTLED INTO THE CONFERENCE room with two boxes he'd hauled up from evidence storage. He began the arduous task of sorting through everything and finding the one needle in a stack of identical needles that would lead him down the right path.

Ten minutes in, and he shook his head in disbelief.

The hospital had suspected Royce Keller of stealing drugs from the onsite pharmacy and selling them on the black market. He'd been the prime suspect because his best friend, Dr. Wade Unger, had framed him. Then Keller had the misfortune of working on his own daughter in the ER—because he hadn't realized it was her—and she died. Not only did he get suspended, but the hospital involved the police. He'd been investigated for both the drug thefts and the murder of his daughter. Beating the second charge was simple enough. Beating the first had proved slightly more difficult.

Keller got suspended and the drug thefts stopped, casting more suspicion on him. He was lucky Tony had caught the case, because he eventually figured it all out. That's how he and Royce had become friends.

"Interesting enough. But where the fuck is the connection?" Carter kept searching through the evidence.

DNA tests. Weren't those fascinating? He made a mental note to talk with Tony about that. He'd never heard of heteropaternal superfecundation before.

Hope's motorcycle accident, the one that landed her in the ER, had claimed more than just her life. The driver of the bike also died. Jimmy Salvo. And a passenger in a different vehicle also died. Paula Haggerty. But what was their connection to all of this?

Hmm. Turns out the accident wasn't an accident at all. Brake line had been tampered with. Carter flipped through the report, looking for more answers. Was stunned when he found them.

"Son of a—"

But before he could process that string of events, a name caught his attention. *Frank Anderson.*

Same damn name associated with the pot farm by the nursery.

He read more of the report. Frank and Sally Anderson were the guardians of Jimmy Salvo. That explained that connection.

But how did it relate to the present day case? The Andersons were old.

Carter knew he was opening himself up to getting another lecture, but he had questions. He took out his phone and called Tony.

Not a good sign—he answered without a greeting. "You make your apologies yet?"

"Not yet, but I promise I will."

"Give me one good reason why I shouldn't just hang up on you right now. Or better yet, report you to the Chief."

"Can you come to the conference room? I'll show you why."

Carter heard a string of curse words before Tony disconnected the call. He was in the doorway in less than thirty seconds.

"What the—are those my old case files?"

"Yeah. I pulled this stuff out of storage."

"Fuck." Tony ran his hand through his hair. "What am I supposed to do with you? You're supposed to be backing off the Kellers, not investigating their closed cases."

"I'm not investigating them. I'm investigating *this.*" Carter handed him the paper listing the Andersons as the guardian for Jimmy Salvo.

Tony dropped into a chair and let out a low whistle. "Shit. I knew that name was familiar, but I'd forgotten all about this."

"What do you make of it?"

He looked up. "Make of what? This case is old news."

"Yeah, but he's clearly connected to my current case."

"Do you know how common the name 'Frank Anderson' is?"

Carter scowled. "You aren't seriously suggesting that these are two different people and the name is just a coincidence?"

"Doesn't matter what I say. You'll believe what you want, anyway."

"Do you believe it?"

Tony sighed. "No. But I don't see a connection, either. The Andersons were old when I conducted my investigation. They'll be ancient now. No way in hell is he growing and selling pot, so he certainly isn't stealing ketamine from veterinarians."

"Maybe he's bankrolling someone who is."

"No way. This guy is as nice as they come. He and his wife are salt-of-the-earth type people. And they couldn't have the money, anyway. Daniel Haggerty sued them for the wrongful death of his wife. They couldn't afford an attorney then, and they lost the suit. Wiped out their savings paying the settlement. In fact, I don't even know if they managed to pay the whole thing off. They've got to be completely broke now."

"Daniel Haggerty. D. H. If Frank Anderson couldn't pay the settlement, maybe he agreed to a partnership with Haggerty. He provides the land and Haggerty does the rest."

"You're grasping at straws."

"That's all I've got."

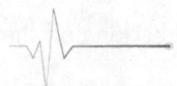

TIME FOR A STEAMING HELPING of humble pie. Carter had been ordered to make amends—in person—to the whole Keller family. Even if Tony hadn't insisted he apologize to all of them, he would have. He owed it to them.

Besides, he couldn't get Faith Keller out of his head, and there was no way he could even consider asking her out when her whole family hated him. Not that he could blame them.

Who was he kidding? A simple apology wasn't going to smooth his way. She's never want to go out with him after he'd accused her so many times.

He ran his hand through his hair and sighed. Maybe if he apologized to Faith first, he could make her understand, win her over. Then she could help pave the way to the good graces of the rest of them.

When he climbed into his rig, Max looked at him like he was the biggest ass. Which he was. Damn, but that dog was perceptive.

And he seemed taken with Faith, too.

Carter petted Max on the head. "I know, buddy, I know. I'm an idiot. Let's go make things right."

He swore the dog smiled.

Once he cleared the town limits, the road to Faith's practice was completely clear. He didn't pass a single vehicle or pedestrian. It sort of bothered him that she spent so much time in such an isolated area. Worried him even more that she planned on building a house out there once winter was definitely done and gone.

Not that he had any right to worry about her and her living arrangements. It was just the cop in him assessing things from a practical safety standpoint.

He pulled into her parking lot and looked around. No cars. Lights out. Just for the hell of it, he climbed out of his rig and peered through the window. No one there. Not even her assistant.

Hmm. She was such a hard worker, he figured her for going in as soon as she left the nursery. Must have decided she wasn't in the frame of mind to work—he couldn't blame her after what he'd put her and her family through—and decided not to open for the day.

Wonder if she could sustain all the closings she'd had lately. Especially if she was about to build a new house.

None of his business.

He headed back to his vehicle. When he got in, Max whined. "Sorry, pal. She's not here."

Max hung his head. Crazy.

A quick drive by Faith's house showed her car in the driveway, but she wasn't home. Probably still with her folks, complaining about him.

Carter swung a wide circle in the lot and headed back toward town. When he got to the nursery, he saw they were open and doing a pretty robust business for a northern March day. But he didn't recognize any of the vehicles as belonging to the Kellers. Strike two.

He could try Royce's practice, or just head to their house. The doctor's office was closer, but he had a feeling he'd just waste his time, so he skipped the commercial district and headed out to the Keller's home. Finally got one right. Three cars sat in the drive, so some of them had to be there.

Faith's car was nowhere to be seen, though.

Carter pulled behind a Chevy Avalanche and climbed out, taking Max with him. At least he'd have a friend with him inside.

If they let him inside.

He knocked on the door, and soon their housekeeper answered. "Officer. Nice to see you again."

What was her name? Cynthia? No, Sylvia. Sylvia Albertson. "Pleasure's mine, Miz Albertson."

She blushed a bit and swung the door open. "Won't you come in?"

"Thank you." He stepped into the familiar foyer and heard muffled conversation coming from the direction of the kitchen. "Mind if I see myself down the hall? I actually want to talk to the whole family."

"Follow me." She bustled down the hallway. "Can I get you anything?"

"No, thanks. I don't expect to be here long."

She stepped into the kitchen. "Officer Emerson for you."

Jensen sat with his parents at their kitchen table. His head snapped up, and he glared at Carter. "What do you want now?"

"Unless you need anything, I'll just be going upstairs to sort laundry." Sylvia didn't wait for an answer. She turned and hurried out of the room.

"Actually, I'm here to apologize." He met all their gazes. Royce looked relatively calm, but Jensen and Vanessa made him understand the expression, "if looks could kill." Max stood at alert.

"I know you think I've been targeting you, but it was never my intention to—" To what? He couldn't say he didn't want to disrupt their lives, because when he believed them guilty, that was precisely what he wanted. Carter shook his head. "I'm just here to make amends. No excuses. I've been a nuisance, and I'm truly sorry for any trouble I've caused."

"Any trouble?" Vanessa's voice sounded shrill. "You think a simple apology can make up for the business we've lost to your interference? Or the sleep we've lost worrying about what you were going to do next?"

"My sister and my fiancée don't need the added stress you've put on them," Jensen said. "They've been through enough already."

"Okay, okay." Royce held up his hands. "Everybody just take a breath."

Vanessa and Jensen looked mutinous, but they stayed silent.

"We know you're just doing your job." Royce glared at Jensen, who looked ready to have another outburst. "And I admire your never-quit spirit. But what I don't understand is why."

"Why, sir?" Guilt warmed his face, but he didn't break eye-contact. He deserved whatever they threw at him.

"Why you're so fixated on my family. Hasn't Tony explained our history? Surely you must understand that we'd never be involved in selling any kind of controlled substance."

"I do." He rubbed the back of his neck and shifted his weight. Max shifted with him. Carter turned his attention to his dog. "Ssh. Sit, Max."

The dog obeyed, but continued to watch the people in the room. Particularly Vanessa and Jensen.

Royce leaned over and pulled out a chair. "You, too. Have a seat."

"Thanks." Carter took his place at Royce's right. Rather than looking across the table at the mutiny twins, he turned to the man beside him. "I'm afraid it's just a case of doing all the right things for all the wrong reasons. Or maybe the other way around."

Jensen scoffed, but he didn't speak.

Carter continued like he didn't notice. "I found drugs at the gym the night of the terrorist attack. A lot. Which were traced back to Faith's office. But she had never reported them missing. That, combined with her nervous behavior at the scene, put her on my radar."

"But we've since explained all of that away," Royce said. "The other night, I thought everything was behind us."

"It was. But as I continued investigating, your family kept creeping into the case. Drugs keep being stolen from Faith's practice. The land beside your nursery had a pot farm on it. Poppies—the opium plant—were found in your greenhouse."

"And I told you they weren't the illegal variety." Vanessa crossed her arms and glared at him.

"My research implied otherwise. I didn't know there were so many different kinds of poppies. When you told me what kind to look out for, I did some research. But I'm not a botanist. I made a mistake when I remembered the one red poppy you grow. I'm profoundly sorry."

"I should think so." She sat back in her seat, but her tone was less hostile.

"Fact is, I believe you. I believe all of you. I know you aren't growing, man-ufacturing, or distributing illegal substances."

"Glad you finally see it our way," Royce said. "Maybe now we can move past all this. For good, this time."

"Well, it's not that easy," Carter said.

"I knew it!" Jensen jumped to his feet. "You're just here to do more covert snooping, aren't you? Well, you aren't going to find anything. We're—"

"That's not why I'm here."

"Jensen," Royce said, "sit down."

He sat, but he continued to glower across the table.

"I truly am here to apologize, but there's something you all should know."

"And what's that?" Vanessa asked.

"I think you're somehow connected to this case."

"You just said you were done suspecting us." This time, Royce's voice held an edge.

"I am. I don't think you're involved in anything illegal. I think you're connected. Someone is making it look like it's you. All the activity has been with Keller property. It's being made to look like you're the ones behind it all. And I'm determined to discover what the connection is and who's doing this."

"You think we're being set up?" Vanessa asked.

Carter nodded. "I do. I haven't figured out who's doing this. Yet. Or why. But I will."

"Are we in danger?" Royce asked.

Talk about a question no one ever wanted to answer. Tell them yes and they panic, tell them no and they're unprepared to defend themselves. He split the difference.

"Until we know who is behind this and why, I'd suggest you be more careful. There's no reason to amend your schedules, but I wouldn't suggest going out alone at night or leaving your doors unlocked. Be prudent."

"What about Bella?" Jensen asked. "She's already been abducted and shot. She doesn't need to be worried about this now, too."

"The issue seems to be directly related to just the Kellers. But as she's engaged to you, she may be pulled into the mix. I'd tell her to be careful."

"I don't want to worry her," Jensen said.

"You also don't want her to get hurt," Vanessa countered. Then she turned her attention back to Carter. "What about Faith? She seems to be the one most involved."

"I ordered security systems for her house and office," Royce said.

"A great first step. Make sure she uses them." Carter looked around the table. "I'm sure you'll all be fine. And now that I understand you're the victims, not the perpetrators, I'll find the connection, and I'll get whoever's responsible for this."

"Have you gone to see Faith yet?" Royce asked. "Maybe I should come with you."

"I stopped at her office, but no one was there."

"Not even her assistant?" Vanessa's eyes had widened, her tone dropped to almost a whisper.

Carter shook his head.

"What?" Jensen said. "No one? But she left with Bella before any of us. They should have been to their offices before we even got here." He took his phone out of his pocket and dialed. "Damn it!" He dialed again. Tried Faith, too. No answers.

They all looked at Carter, but he had no words of reassurance.

"I'm sure it's fine. I'll check her house, and Bella's. They'll turn up."

Jensen's fingers flew across the keypad on his phone. "What's your number, Emerson?"

As soon as Carter gave it to him, he got an alert that he'd received a text. He looked at Jensen and cocked one eyebrow.

"I just sent you addresses for Bella's home, office, and parents' house."

"Thanks. Now, why don't you all just stay by your phones, and I'll get back to you as soon as I know anything."

"But—"

"Jensen, I can't do my job effectively if I have to worry about what you're doing, too. Just let me do what I do best. You know I won't give up until I have answers."

"I guess I do know that."

"Besides, we have no proof that anything is going on. I bet they're just blowing off steam somewhere. Shopping or watching a movie or something."

"Yeah. Yeah, I'm sure that's it." But it sounded more like Royce was trying to convince himself than Jensen.

Carter saw himself out. He put Max in the car, then he joined him. "Where the hell do you think they are?"

Max lowered his head. Damned if his dog wasn't worried, too.

Carter backed out of the driveway and headed toward the first address on the list Jensen had sent him.

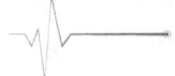

NEITHER BELLA NOR HER CAR were at her home or her office. Carter couldn't even be one hundred percent certain that Faith was with her. No one had seen either of them since they'd left the nursery that morning. But they were together then, so he hoped they still were. One search would be easier than two.

It was a long shot, but he drove out to the Perish estate. Carter didn't let anyone intimidate him, particularly the wealthy and entitled, but even he had to pause in the driveway and take in the opulence of the home and grounds.

These folks definitely lived a different lifestyle than any he was familiar with.

Bella's car wasn't there, either, so he planned on leaving without disturbing the household. No point in worrying them for no reason. He continued around the circular drive, intent on leaving the property, when a barrel-chested man in rolled up shirtsleeves and suspenders ran out the front door and jumped in front of his rig. Carter slammed on the brakes—Max whimpered when he slid off the seat—and narrowly avoided hitting the man. He threw the car in park and jumped out.

"Are you crazy? You can't just jump in front of a moving vehicle. You could have been killed. And you hurt my dog."

"I don't have time for this. It's fortuitous you chose to trespass on my property while turning around."

"I didn't 'trespass' anywhere. I was checking on something. And not finding it, I'm leaving."

"Do you know who I am?"

That he stood in the driveway of the Perish estate didn't matter. He'd know the man on reputation alone. "Victor Perish."

"That's right. My taxes pay your salary, and I need your services."

Ah, *that* old chestnut. If he had a dollar for every time he heard the tax speech, he'd be able to buy Perish's house out from under him. Two times over.

"Mister Perish, I'm in the middle of something right now. If you'd—"

"My daughter is missing, damn it. Again. And after that debacle at the basketball game, I'm not waiting around to see when the police might get here and what they might do about it. You're here now, and I'm coming with you." He walked to the passenger side of Carter's rig, only to back off when Max met his gaze through the window.

"Mister Perish, please."

"I'll ride in the back if I have to! We have to save my daughter!"

Tempting. The renowned and feared Victor Perish in the backseat of a police vehicle? He could probably sell photos across the tri-state area.

But if the Perish family knew Bella was missing, that brought two families into the mix. Probably wasn't something he could keep under wraps any longer.

"Mister Perish, I came out here looking for Bella's car. She and Faith Keller haven't been seen or heard from in a couple of hours. Not since they left Cathedral Lake Nursery this morning. You don't need to climb in my rig to convince me she's incommunicado. I know, and I'm looking for her."

"I'm coming, too."

"No. The best thing you can do is stay here by the phone. If you hear from her, let me know." Carter produced a card and pressed it into his hand. "I'll find her."

"You don't even know where to look!"

"Mister Perish, she hasn't been gone long enough for you to file a report. Or even be concerned yet. There are plenty of places they can be, plenty of things they could be doing. Let me do my job, and stay in touch."

The flush in his cheeks paled as his bluster faded. "Just find my baby girl."

"Don't worry, sir."

Perish strode back into his house, and he'd lost some of the swagger he'd had when he'd barreled out of the house just moments before. Carter couldn't imagine what the Keller and Perish families were going through. They'd suffered through abducted family members before, and now the *same* ones were missing?

It was almost too unbelievable to be true.

He climbed back into his vehicle and looked at Max. "You okay?" He checked his neck and head. All seemed fine, but he wasn't a vet. He'd ask Faith to look at him, but...

Where the hell were they? They couldn't have just disappeared.

He headed back toward town, intent to look for them at one of the food trucks in the Square. As he drove, he called Manny.

"Rodriguez."

"You at the station?"

"Hey, Carter. Yeah, I'm here. About to go off duty, actually. I was just finishing up a report."

"Can you ping a cellphone for me?"

"Sure." Rustling sounds came through the speaker. *"Give me the number."*

Carter relayed Faith's number, then listened to the clacking of keys.

It only took seconds, but it felt like forever.

"Nothing. Phone's off or battery's removed."

He'd called both Faith and Bella, and both calls had gone straight to voice-mail rather than ringing, so he knew it was a long shot. Had to try it anyway, though. "What about this number?" He recited Bella's number, and listened to more clacking.

"Same thing. Sorry. Got a problem?"

Carter sighed. "I fucking hope not."

"I'm going home to grab some shuteye, but if you need something..."

The guy was a true friend. And a damn good cop. "Get some sleep, Manny. And thanks."

He had known based on the lack of ringing that tracking the phones wouldn't work. But other than cruising around, he had no leads. Not even the women's families knew where to look.

Coffee might perk him up and clear his head. He stopped at a food truck in the Square and ordered their tallest and strongest. Tony walked up to him.

"I already apologized, so save the lecture. I don't have time for one, anyway."

"I just thought you might need some help."

"With what?" Carter narrowed his gaze over the rim of his cup.

"Finding Faith and Bella."

"Is there anything you don't know?"

"That's why I'm a detective. I detect things."

Smart ass.

"So, where have you looked? What have you done?"

"Tried to ping their phones. They're off or the batteries have been removed. Checked both places of business. Both individual homes and both family homes. Nada."

"You try Tod Jeffers and Hannah Morgan?"

"Who?"

"Therapists. Jeffers sees Faith. Bella has seen Morgan in the past."

"Are you even supposed to know their medical histories?"

"I'm not just a cop, Carter. I'm a family friend, too. These girls have been through a lot, and Royce confides in me sometimes. Faith first went to see him back when her sister died. He has a long history with the family."

Of course. That's probably how Tony knew they were missing. Royce Keller. Seemed Tony wasn't as omniscient as he wanted people to think.

God, at the moment, he wished he was. Then he could just tell everybody where Faith and Bella were.

"Let's call and see." Tony placed a call, left a voicemail. Placed a second call and had a quick conversation.

"Well?"

"Morgan's receptionist says they haven't heard from Bella and there's no appointment on the books. No answer with Jeffers. I left him a message."

Carter rotated his head to try and work the kinks out of his neck. "Now what? Keep patrolling?"

"Why don't we head over to Jeffers' place?"

"I'll follow you." Carter climbed back in his rig and offered Max a treat from the bag he kept in the car. Felt like it was going to be a long day, might as well give the dog some energy.

It didn't take long to get to another affluent section of town. Instead of mansions like the Perish family, though, was a community of historical brownstones. Tony drove up to a particularly well-appointed one near a park. Carter pulled in behind him.

"Don't see either of their cars," Tony said.

"Faith doesn't have hers. At least, she didn't. Jensen said she rode away with Bella."

"Let's ask the doc if he knows anything."

They approached the door and Tony rang the bell. A few minutes later, a guy who looked like a male model opened the door. Patient? Pool guy?

"Hey, Tod." Tony shook his hand. "This is Officer Emerson."

"Pleasure." The guy extended his hand, and it took Carter a second to respond. Seriously? Faith saw this movie-star wannabe for psychological help? And she started going there years ago? She probably harbored all sorts of fantasies about him.

And now was not the time for jealousy, jackass.

Carter shook his hand and mumbled an unintelligible greeting.

"Have you seen Faith Keller?"

Jeffers stepped onto the stoop and pulled the door closed behind him. He crossed his arms over his chest. "You know I can't discuss clients with you, Tony."

"She's missing. Her and Bella Perish. We're just trying to track them down."

"Missing? For how long?"

"Just a few hours. We lost track of them this morning. Any ideas where they might be?"

"I've been trying to help Faith get past her fears. The next step would be for her to directly seek one out and confront it, but we haven't really dwelled on that much, yet. I'd be surprised if she'd take the initiative."

"So, no ideas?" Carter asked.

"You said she and Bella are together?"

"When last seen," Tony said.

Jeffers patted his lip with one finger. "Together they just might…"

"Might what?" Carter asked.

He put his hands in his pockets. "It's a long shot, but try the beach. They may have decided to face their fears together."

"By going to the beach?" Carter said.

"The lake. That's where they were both abducted. Held in the ruins. If they're together, they may be trying to move past that particular block. Now, if you'll excuse me, I'm with a patient."

"Thanks, Tod," Tony said.

Carter mumbled his appreciation and followed Tony back to their vehicles.

"The lake, then?" Tony said.

"Can't hurt."

"Follow me."

Carter's gut churned on the drive to the lake. The longer Faith was out of reach—he didn't want to think of her as "missing" yet—the more he had cause for alarm. When he pulled into the parking lot at the beach, a flood of relief washed over him.

Bella's car.

He whipped his vehicle into the spot beside hers, jumped out, and rushed to the lake. Nothing but sand, water, and trees as far as he could see. It was quiet, serene.

Kind of reminded him of the Friday the 13th films, which didn't give him a good vibe.

He walked back to the parking lot. Tony had liberated Max from the rig and stood, holding his leash and waiting for Carter.

"No sign of them on the beach."

"Guess we're hiking up to the ruins, then."

Carter took Max's lead and they started up the hill. They were about one hundred yards from the cathedral when a shriek echoed through the trees. He looked at Tony, and they broke into a run.

CHAPTER 15

FAITH LAY ON COLD, HARD earth. She recognized the smell before she managed to flutter her eyelids.

Only reason her eyes opened at all was because something stung her cheek. A slap?

Realization dawned, sudden and swift, and she jumped to her feet, eyes wide and fists clenched.

"Whoa, easy," a male voice said.

Her vision wasn't accustomed to the darkness, and she could only make out shadows. A few flashlight beams bounced around the dark room before landing on her, momentarily blinding her. She didn't want to be the focus of the light—she needed to see who was in there with her.

A deep breath, and she opened her mouth to scream for all she was worth. Fingers clamped over her lips from someone standing in front of her. "Ssh," the same male voice said. She swatted at the hand and tried to bite the fingers, when one of the flashlights trained on the man.

Carter.

Her lungs deflated as the air whooshed out of her in a silent stream.

"It's me. Carter. You calm now?"

She nodded a lie, and he lowered his hand.

Arms wrapped around her, and Bella spoke into her ear. "I was so scared. And then you fainted, and I—"

She tuned out the rest of her friend's babble.

Fainted? She'd passed out? Why?

Again a tidal wave of realization crashed over her. "There was a guy! Someone came down here! I saw him!"

"It was me," another male voice said. "I'm sorry. I didn't mean to scare you."

"Me? Me *who?* Get me out of here!" She fought out of Bella's embrace and stumbled through the dark room until she reached the stairs. Pumping her legs to the brink of exhaustion, she sprinted up the steps and out into the light. Only when she saw familiar faces emerge from the ruins did she start to settle down.

Carter made it out first, and he held his hands up in front of him and walked slowly toward her. "You okay?" Max trotted at his heels and barked once.

He was followed by Bella, Tony, and David.

Faith gulped in air and bent over, resting her elbows on her knees. As her breath regulated, panic gave way to humiliation, and she hung her head, letting her hair cover her face and shield her from intense scrutiny. "What happened?"

"We went into the ruins to try and face our fears," Bella whispered.

"You had turned your phones off," Tony said, "and no one could reach you. No one knew where you were."

"Everyone was really worried." Carter's voice was hard. She knew she must have scared him, scared everybody, but she didn't need his attitude at the moment. Instead of arguing with him, though, she plopped her butt on the ground, tented her legs, and rested her arms and head on her knees.

"I was hiking," David said, "and I heard something in the ruins, so I went exploring. I didn't mean to frighten you, but when you saw me, you screamed and passed out."

"We were on our way to look for you here when we heard you," Carter said.

Faith took a deep breath and looked up at him. His jaw ticked, but he didn't say anything else. She heard the censure in his tone, though.

Bella must have heard it, too, because she put her hand on his arm and spoke softly to him. "Don't. She's had enough of a scare."

He looked down at her hand and then glared at her. "You're telling me to back off? Do you have any idea what problems the two of you have caused? How many people were frantic?"

Faith's scalp tingled as the mortification washed over her.

"We already called your parents," Tony said. "And Bella's. Don't worry. Everyone's just glad you're okay."

"Don't worry? Seriously?" Carter paced, and Max stayed at his side but kept looking back at Bella.

"Carter," Tony began.

"No." He strode back to Faith in five steps and stooped in front of her. "The only reason I knew you were missing was because I came to apologize to you. It seems the two of us keep making the same mistakes, over and over. But mine stem from trying to do my job. Yours are because you're selfish and ignorant. Covering up crimes. Ignoring basic security protocols. Turning off your phone when you didn't even tell people where you'd be. Reckless. Inconsiderate." He stood and headed down the hill, muttering as he walked away. "I don't know why I care so much when you so obviously don't."

"He doesn't mean that, Faith," Bella said. "He was just scared for you."

"He might not have meant to hurt your feelings, but he's not wrong." Tony reached his hand down toward Faith. She grasped it, and he pulled her to her feet. "Bella's right. He was scared. But he's also right about your behavior. You may live on your own now, but that doesn't mean you don't have to account to anyone. Your family, your friends, your coworkers. These folks all care about you. When you aren't forthcoming about your problems and run off and hide from the world, it takes a toll on those you're cutting out."

"I didn't mean to scare anyone." Her cheeks flamed. "We were just trying to get over this hurdle. You don't know what it's like."

"You don't know enough about my history to say that, Faith." He slipped his sunglasses on, making it impossible for her to read his expression. "I'm a detective and a veteran. Suffice it to say I've seen my share of atrocities." Then his tone softened. "I know you're struggling, but use a little common sense, a little consideration. That will save us all a lot of trouble."

"I'm sorry."

"I know." He squeezed her arm and headed down the hill.

"About scaring you," David said after Tony was gone.

Faith waved her hand. "Don't worry about it."

Bella shook his hand. "I guess we should introduce ourselves. Formally. I'm Bella Perish, Faith's soon-to-be sister-in-law."

"Pleasure." Then he cleared his throat and looked around.

Faith recognized the awkward lull in the conversation and tried to save it. "This is my assistant, David James."

Bella smiled. "Why don't I give you two a moment to clear the air? I'll be at the car."

Faith watched her walk down the hill and fought off the icy panic at having to be alone on the path.

"I can walk you down, if you want, before I go."

"Aren't you parked down there, too?"

"No. When you gave me the day off, I decided to go hiking. My car's at the campgrounds a few miles over yonder."

"What are you doing here, then?"

"Told you. Hiking. It's a beautiful day." He headed down the hill.

"David?"

He stopped, turned, and looked at her.

"You never unload your problems on me, but I'm always whining at you about something."

"No, no. Not at all. You've just had more than your fair share to deal with lately."

She joined him on the path and they started walking again. "Well, I'm sorry to dump all my crap on you."

"Really. It's not an issue."

"Who do you talk to when things aren't going your way?"

He sighed and sidestepped a bramble bush. "Used to be my stepbrother, but he died."

"Oh, I'm sorry. You never mentioned—" Faith tripped on a root when she looked at him and struggled to get her footing.

He caught her arm, helped her regain her balance. "Careful."

"Thanks." She scrutinized the path. "So, who do you go to now?"

"What?"

"Since your stepbrother's gone, who's your go-to ear when you need to talk?"

"Hmm." He shrugged. "I guess it's still him. I just throw my thoughts out there and hope he's listening."

"Does it help?"

"Doesn't hurt." They reached the parking lot. "See you at work tomorrow?"

"You bet. And David?"

He turned and looked at her as he backed up the path.

"Sorry I messed up your hike."

"No worries. I was just chatting with Jimbo."

"Your stepbrother?"

He nodded. "I was the only one who called him that. Everyone else called him Jimmy. But to me, he'll always be Jimbo." He sighed.

"James 'Jimbo' James. He must have gotten some grief over that."

David shook his head. His tone grew cold. "He didn't take our last name."

Way to go, Faith. She clearly hit a nerve there. "I'm sorry if I overstepped."

"No, it's fine."

"You know you can talk to me. About anything."

"I'm okay. But thanks. See you Monday." He turned and disappeared into the trees.

Faith sighed and watched him go, then she approached Bella. "Can you take me home now? I've had enough excitement for one day."

"Me, too. And I'm not looking forward to facing my father. He must be beside himself."

"Ugh. My folks, too."

Then they spoke at the same time. "And Jensen."

Faith hugged her while they both laughed. "Long day ahead of us."

"Yep." She broke away and climbed into the car.

When Faith was beside her and they were driving down the road, she said, "Thanks for helping me face my fears today."

"You had a panic attack and fainted."

"Well, I guess I haven't quite mastered the ruins yet. But it was nice being at the lake again."

"It was, wasn't it?" She played "The Warrior" again.

Faith looked out the window and smiled.

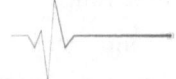

FAITH WAS ONLY HOME LONG enough to shower and change her clothes, then she got in her car. David had a good idea. When she was young, she went to her sister for everything. They'd been inseparable. The years had caused them to drift apart, but when Faith was really upset, Hope had still been the one she turned to. Her advice was almost always spot-on, and she kept secrets better than anyone.

Since the murder, Faith had stopped talking to her. But if David still spoke to his stepbrother, surely she could talk to her sister and not be crazy.

Maybe she should ask Tod if that were true.

No matter. She missed her sister and needed some quality one-on-one time with her. She pulled into the cemetery, drove to Hope's grave, and got out of the car.

They'd chosen a beautiful site to lay her sister to rest. A bench sat under a large tree, its canopy providing dappled light and a break from the harsh sun in the summer months. A poem her sister had written was engraved on one side of the tombstone, a picture of Hope opposite it.

She had been lovely.

And had been taken from them far too soon.

Faith sat on the bench and looked at the flowers her parents had placed at the foot of the stone. Most people used artificial plants, if anything, in the winter, but her mother insisted on bringing fresh flowers weekly. This week, the copper urn—chosen to match the warm-colored granite of the stone—held a bold display in various shades of purple. Tall amethyst calla lilies poked out between clusters of lavender freesia and stalks of periwinkle delphinium. Clouds of white baby's breath filled in the gaps, resulting in a full and lush bouquet.

Hope's favorite color had once been purple, when they were little and liked baby dolls and princesses. She was mostly into black when she died, but Faith had to think she'd like the arrangement, nonetheless.

"Oh, Hope." She sighed. "I miss you."

A gentle breeze blew her hair into her eyes, and she swiped the strands back from her face. When they had fought, and they'd had some doozies, Hope had always fought dirty and pulled her hair. The thought made her smile. It was like her sister was there all over again, only this time teasing her instead of yanking hard on the loose tresses. Tears welled in her eyes, and she blinked them away.

"I don't know where to start."

Again a breeze blew, waving the tree branches and ruffling her hair. She shook her head. She was nuts. Her sister wasn't there, and she certainly wasn't communicating to her through the wind. Tod would have her committed if she mentioned this to him.

"I can't get over losing you," she whispered. "And I can't seem to get past being abducted last year." The wind picked up, shaking the brush around her and blowing a speck of dust into her eye. As if Hope was agitated with her.

She was certifiable.

Faith wiped at her eye and pressed on. "I know it's in the past, Hope. I can't help it. I'm scared it will happen again."

The air fell still. Okay. The silent treatment. She'd endured worse.

"I know it's irrational. But the thought is terrifying. Crippling. I mean, I know Willie Sturgis can't hurt me anymore. Wade is gone, and I don't think he'd hurt me, anyway. At least, not intentionally." She thought about how Wade had inadvertently gotten her sister killed, and she shivered. The wind picked up again. Faith was certain she heard a twig snap, and she looked around, but saw nothing but the long grass undulating under the force of the whipping air.

Should have worn a damn coat.

"In the grand scheme of things, you had it far worse. I may have been terrorized, but you were—" Talking about her sister's death never came easy. Rarely came at all. "You know what happened. I don't need to rehash that."

The brisk gale dissipated. Faith rubbed her arms, anyway.

"I miss you."

Birdsong chirped cheerfully from the trees. First robins of spring. New life. How freaking lovely.

"I really, really miss you." She shook her head, brushed one last tear away, then squared her shoulders.

"I met a guy. You'd like him, I think. Well, I don't know. Maybe not. He's a cop, and you always had that rebellious streak." When the wind picked up, she laughed. "But he makes me miserable, so I'm sure you'd get a kick out of me liking him."

Faith bent and plucked a long weed out of the grass. She picked at it to avoid looking at her sister's headstone.

"I don't think it's going to work out, though. We had dinner, and that was nice, but he keeps investigating me. You don't need to worry about that, though." She waved her hand to dismiss that topic of conversation. Like her sister could push her for more information.

"Anyway, he's mad at me. Apparently I'm reckless and thoughtless and… well, I don't remember everything he said." She sighed. "He was right, though. What I've been doing is so stupid. Why do you let me do these things?"

Hope had always been the more practical of the two of them. At least where Faith was concerned. She was always the voice of reason and steered her sister back onto the proper paths. If only she had approached her own life with the same caution.

"You know, this is your fault. You should be here to tell me what to do." She flung the last bit of weed to the ground. "Why'd you leave me?"

There was another twig-snapping sound, then the cemetery grew still. The wind ceased blowing, and she couldn't even remember what Hope's voice sounded like anymore.

"I'm sorry. I know it wasn't your fault."

The moment was gone, though.

Faith rose to her feet and blew a kiss to the headstone. "I love you."

A gentle wind picked up, coming from the opposite direction, carrying the scent of freesia from the flowers at Hope's grave.

Faith smiled and walked back to her car.

Maybe her sister wasn't so far away that they couldn't communicate.

She'd be back to visit again.

CHAPTER 16

CARTER FELT LIKE SUCH AN asshole.

After he'd left the lake, he'd driven around for a while. He was supposed to be on patrol, anyway. The least he could do is make one round through town.

But one was all he managed. Faith had been on his mind. Her carelessness made him so damn angry. Too bad he didn't have the right to yell at her about it.

Hadn't stopped him, though. He'd laid into her before storming off.

Didn't even have to cool down before he realized how boorish he'd been.

He drove to her house, intent on offering another in a string of apologies when he saw her leave. So he followed her. No qualms about it.

When she drove to the cemetery, he knew why she was there. If he still lived in his hometown, he'd be at his brother's grave marker all the time. Those moments with departed loved ones were precious.

And private.

Didn't stop him from hiding his rig and sneaking up to eavesdrop on her visit, though.

He told himself he just wanted a little insight, a little clarity.

But when she mentioned him to her sister, shame overwhelmed him. Because part of him knew that was why he had really tailed her to her sister's gravesite. He wanted to know if he'd gotten under her skin as far as she'd gotten under his.

And even through his guilt, he had to admit he was glad to know he had affected her. Maybe even more so than she had affected him. Or equally, anyway.

His thoughts ground to a halt when he heard a twig snap. Earlier a similar noise caught his attention, but he chalked the sound up to the wind. That second one, though? There was no mistaking it. That was a snapping twig. Someone was out there with them.

One part of him knew he had no right being suspicious of people at a cemetery. Most likely it was someone visiting a family member, an innocent foot stepping on a dry branch, the noise carrying over the hill to his suspicious ears.

But if he could be in the trees spying, so could someone else. Someone with darker motives than his own.

Which made another part of him, the cop part of him, go on high alert.

While Faith made her way back to her car, he scanned the trees and brush. Just when he was about to give up, he saw a flash of movement.

Someone was out there with them. And he doubted that person was just there to see what Faith was working through.

He slunk through the cemetery, hiding behind trees and shrubs and tombstones, trying to get a look at Faith's stalker. He reached the crest of a slope and looked down toward the road. A car idled there, and someone shut the driver's side door.

Carter knew that car. He'd seen it at Faith's practice.

When the guy pulled away, Carter got a good look at his face though the driver's window.

David James?

Why the hell was Faith's assistant following her? Making sure she was safe, or something far more nefarious?

Carter ran back to his car, batting aside stray stalks of foliage that blocked his way. When he got to his rig, he flung open the door and hopped inside. Max looked up, then out the window.

"We're going after him, buddy."

He drove as fast as he dared, trying to catch up with James without making him aware of his presence. Just when he'd nearly given up, certain he'd lost him, he saw the car turn down the main drive and head to the gate.

How the hell had James gotten on that road? He should have been long gone, not on the other side of the cemetery.

Must have gotten turned around in the huge complex.

Carter was grateful for James' error. It gave him a chance to catch up. Too bad he had a police unit. That would be easy for James to spot in a rear view mirror. So Carter held back and followed his suspect through town. When he entered a lower income section of Cathedral Lake, Carter had to hang back further. He'd definitely be noticed there. And by more than just James.

When he dropped back, James made a left turn. By the time Carter got to the intersection, he'd lost him. He drove around for a while, even stopped and did an address search for the guy. Nothing turned up.

Carter had no idea where James had gone. Must have pulled into a garage somewhere.

But why wasn't he in the system? He had a driver's license, so he should have come up on that database.

But the guy was a ghost. Both physically and digitally.

With no other recourse, Carter headed back to the station. He had some digging to do.

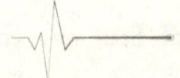

AT THE STATION, CARTER RAN searches in every database he could think of, trying to find anything on David James.

He came up empty.

No driver's license, no known address or aliases, no criminal records. No records of any kind at all.

Damn it, he clearly had a hidden agenda—one that likely involved Faith—

and he worked for her. Was alone with her for God knew how long every day. Didn't she vet him? Check his references? Anything?

Not only could Carter not go to her with another allegation he had no proof of, he probably couldn't talk to her regardless. They'd left things on very bad terms. Well, more precisely, he'd left. Walked right down the hill without giving her a chance to speak on her behalf.

And then followed her. Which is why he stumbled on James' suspicious behavior to begin with. Try explaining that one.

Hey, Faith, after I lost my temper at the cathedral and stormed off, I tailed you to the cemetery. I eavesdropped on you. Yep, I heard everything you said, even the stuff about me. And then I saw your assistant sneaking around, so I investigated him, too. And turned up nothing but questions. I don't suspect you anymore, but I think he's trouble. You might be in danger.

Right. He'd get as far as "Hey, Faith," and she'd either tear him a new one or run screaming from him. Or both. Probably both.

He had no proof the guy was trouble. Just because he couldn't find any record of him didn't mean anything. Could just be he chose to go by a different name. Carter's Uncle Fred's first name was Horace. He went by his middle name, Kyle. His grandfather always went by Ace. When the obituary said Abner Johnson had died, no one knew who that was. The paper had to rerun the announcement with his nickname. Only then did the condolences start pouring in.

His aunt's name was the worst of all. Her birth name was Ima Star Johnson. Ima was a family name, and "Star" was because her parents had a strange sense of humor. Ima Star wasn't too bad until the last name was added, and she suffered her share of teasing growing up. At least she wasn't a boy. But then she had the misfortune of marrying Eric Hooker. She took his last name, because she didn't believe in married women hyphenating or keeping their maiden names. Besides, she'd waited decades to get a new last name. But then she'd become Ima Star Hooker, and that was ten times worse that what she started with. Mom said that was when she started introducing herself by her confirmation name, Grace. But everyone Carter had ever seen around her called her Mimi.

Wonder what her driver's license said—Ima or Grace? Certainly not Mimi.

Maybe it was only his family with these weird issues.

No. He'd seen all sorts of weird naming situations in the short time he'd been a cop. But he'd always been able to determine someone's legal identity. David James posed a new problem. He was clearly not legally David James, but that didn't mean he had an ulterior motive for the name he went by. Or for following Faith to the cemetery. Hell, Carter had followed her, and he didn't wish her harm. On the contrary, he was only looking out for her. And maybe that's all James was doing, too. After all, he'd been the one to scare her at the ruins. He might have just wanted to be certain she was all right.

But Carter's gut said that wasn't it. Something was up with that guy. He just couldn't go to Faith or any of the Kellers until he knew more.

Maybe he was connected to Daniel Haggerty!

Carter grew excited and dove into his research. That would answer so many questions.

But more bad news. Haggerty had left town after his wife died. More to the point, he was probably too old to be farming pot, too.

Another dead end.

Out of ideas, he did what he always did when he was stuck—he called Tony.

"Cooper."

"Hey, Tony. I've got a problem I can't solve, and I could use a fresh opinion."

"I'm about to grab a late lunch. Want to come?"

Carter looked at Max. They had an afternoon presentation at the local junior high about the K-9 unit. Kids usually treated him like a narc until he explained Max only sniffed out explosives. K-9 officers couldn't do both. There was too great a risk of the dog signaling one issue when it was the other, resulting in dangers, injuries, or deaths. Carter and Max most often worked at the airport or checked out bomb threats, and upon hearing that, the students grew fascinated. It simultaneously discouraged him that so many kids still thought drugs were cool and heartened him that so many had such patriotism. Mark would have been proud.

But time was short. "Can I meet you somewhere? I'm supposed to be at a school assembly in about forty-five minutes."

"Just going to the Square. I'll grab us a table in the park. See you there."

Lunch was winding down, so the congestion and crowds had abated. Carter walked right up to the window at Neil's on Wheels, one of his favorite sandwich places. He got a loaded cheesesteak twelve-inch for himself, side of fried mushrooms and a large drink. For Max, he ordered a plain grilled chicken breast, no bun or toppings. Poor guy salivated just smelling all the aromas in the Square. Hadn't had a large appetite since his surgery. It was good to see him hungry again.

Carter sat across from Tony and broke the chicken into bite-sized pieces while he waited for his food to cool off.

"Food like that'll kill ya." Tony had a container in front of him with seaweed salad, some pieces of sashimi, and a riceless sushi roll.

"Does that even fill you up?"

"Not only is it satisfying, I'm not tired forty minutes later, and I'm not hungry again until dinner." He dipped one of the roll slices in a mix of wasabi and soy sauce, and deftly raised the chopsticks to his mouth. "And I don't gain weight from all that sugar."

Carter looked down. "What sugar? I didn't get dessert. And this is unsweetened tea."

"The bread is all carbs. Batter on the mushrooms, too. Simple sugars. Terrible for you."

Sometimes Tony took the surrogate big brother thing too far.

"I'm healthy enough, thanks."

"What's 'healthy enough' mean?" He took a bite of the stringy seaweed. "You can never be too healthy. Isn't your physical coming up?"

Carter grimaced and tossed Max a piece of chicken. "Is there anything you don't miss? I can keep my own schedule, thanks."

Tony shrugged and took a bite of seaweed.

"I need to talk to you about something I discovered today. And you're probably not going to like it." He took a big bite of his sandwich. Damn, but he swore it was better than any he'd ever had in Philly.

"What did you do?"

Carter filled him in on everything. The Haggerty lead fizzling out. The argument at the ruins—not that he needed to remind him of that—and him subsequently following her later. Seeing James out there, tailing and losing him. Finally, he explained his thoughts about James' identity.

"So, you see, if I go to Faith with my suspicions now, she won't listen to me. She might not even talk to me. And I think she's in trouble."

Tony pushed his container away from him and leaned on the table, staring at Carter. "Let me get this straight. Not only did you tell her off when she was in the middle of a panic attack—dick move, by the way—but then you followed her and eavesdropped on her private thoughts?"

"Well, that's the negative version of things."

"And there's a positive version?"

He threw more food to Max and then pushed his own sandwich away. "Look, I know there are a thousand reasons why I can't find any record of a David James in Cathedral Lake. But something in my gut tells me it's wrong."

"Are you sure that isn't guilt tearing up your insides?"

"Give it a rest, all right? I know her family means a lot to you. But I care about them, too."

Tony's brows popped up and he smiled. "That so? Or maybe you mean you care about one particular Keller."

Carter's cheeks burned, and he looked away. "I'm telling you, this doesn't feel right."

Tony wiped his mouth and stood up. "I'll do a little digging."

"I've dug deep. There's nothing."

"Then let me talk to Royce. Maybe Faith will be a little more receptive of the message coming from her father than from you."

"But what message?"

"Let me feel Royce out. I don't want him to worry needlessly, but I don't want Faith unprotected, either."

Carter threw the last piece of chicken to Max, then he gathered his lunch and put it back in the bag. "Thanks, man. Let me know if I need to do something else."

"I think you've done enough."

He sighed and took Max to the car. Time for the school assembly, and they still had a ten minute drive ahead of them.

CHAPTER 17

FAITH MOVED HER SPOON THROUGH the bowl of gazpacho, her movements listless, her appetite nonexistent.

Talking with her sister had buoyed her spirits.

And seeing her family had sunk them again.

She leaned down and patted Ruby on the head. Her fur felt soft in her fingers, and the dog's contented snuffle at the attention made her feel better. Marginally, at least.

Nothing could stop the verbal vomit her family spewed all over her. Just exactly what she didn't need at the moment. And as the voices raised, it grew impossible to tune them out.

Irresponsible.

Foolhardy.

Inconsiderate.

Just some of the highlights. Or lowlights, as it were. She refused to sink to their level and engage in an argument. Regretted even showing up at all, but since she had, she would take the high road.

"After we just got done talking about safety and security," Dad said, "the first thing you do is go running off on some asinine notion."

Score one point for not replying.

"There we were, dealing with yet another invasion of privacy—from your boyfriend—and you just disappear."

"He's not my boyfriend." Lose a point for engaging, but gain one for not shouting. She took a deliberate bite of gazpacho, took her time chewing the two chunks of chopped vegetables Sylvia had garnished it with. It was just a smidge spicy, but the cold soup was still refreshing.

Yet it did nothing to cool her temper.

"You took my fiancée on your fool's errand. What if it hadn't been your assistant at the lake, but some crazy freak? She could have been killed. You could have been killed. Or worse!" Jensen tossed his sandwich on his plate and glared at her across the table.

And she reached her limit. Game over. "Worse? What's worse than dying? Which didn't happen, by the way."

"There are plenty of things someone can do to you before killing you. Assault. Rape. Torture."

The thoughts weren't new to her. They were the primary reasons she had issues in social scenes and foreign spaces. Still, hearing her brother speak them aloud skittered an icy trail up her spine, tingling her scalp.

She shook off the chill and tossed her spoon onto the table. "Give me a break. All of you. Seriously. This isn't about security systems or Carter Emerson. Or about me convincing Bella to go to the lake and not telling anyone where we were going. And by the way, it wasn't my idea to do that, anyway. It was hers."

"What?"

Okay, so she just threw her friend under Jensen's speeding bus, which wasn't really her intent, but she was tired of the yelling and the blame, and she'd ramped up her velocity, as well.

"That's right. It was her plan, not mine. And she did it for you."

"For me? What the hell are you talking about?"

"That's between the two of you. Ask her if you're curious. But as for this ambush, don't kid yourselves. I know why we're really here and what this is all about, and I'm sick of it."

The doorbell rang. Sylvia called out from elsewhere in the house. "I'll get it!"

Faith had forgotten someone else was there, or maybe she would have kept the volume to a minimum.

Or not. Her stresses had built up too much, and it was either release the pressure or explode. And now that she'd started, she doubted she'd stop until she said everything she'd been holding in.

Her mother crossed her arms. "Do tell, Faith. What do you think this is about, if not you?"

"Oh, I know it's about me. But not about me putting Bella in harm's way, or my safety, or my choice in men. I'm not the one in charge of what Bella does. I've accepted all the security measures you've forced on me, regardless of my feelings about them. And I can date whomever I damn well please. It's about you—all of you—trying to control me. I'm not a little girl anymore."

"Then maybe you should stop acting like one," her father said.

"Maybe I should—"

"Excuse me," Sylvia interrupted. "Officer Emerson is here to speak with you... again."

She closed her eyes, took a deep breath. This time the chill crept over her whole body, a fast, free-falling avalanche of dread and humiliation that landed in her gut and buried any momentum she'd had to her argument. It smothered her words before she could speak them, her thoughts before they'd fully formed. Only one sentence survived—

Please don't let him have heard that.

Faith slowly spun around and opened her eyes. Carter stood slightly behind Sylvia, but he towered over the short housekeeper, giving him a clear view of the room. Which meant he had probably heard everything. Or at least, enough. She met his gaze, and it burned right through her frosty shame, heating her from the inside until her cheeks flamed.

She swore the corners of his mouth twitched.

"I feel like I'm making a habit of this, but I wanted to stop by and apologize for today."

"For which part?" her mother asked. "The invasion of our privacy? The public humiliation? Your involvement with our daughter?"

"Well, actually, for everything that's caused you any inconvenience."

Wonder where Faith fell on the inconvenience scale? She loathed noncommittal answers. Hated receiving them as much as she enjoyed giving them. Seemed she'd met her match on that one.

"That's rather vague, don't you think?" Mom said.

Huh. Who would have thought they'd be on the same page about anything regarding Carter?

"Missus Keller, please believe me—again—when I tell you I never meant to cause any trouble for you or anyone in your family. I was only doing my job to the best of my ability, and it seems it's been a direct conflict with you since I started. I can only apologize for the results of my actions, and not the actions themselves."

"Well, isn't that nice?" Jensen said. "That's basically a convenient loophole for you, isn't it? You're sorry we got the shaft, but your actions were justified because you were doing your job. Fucking marvelous."

"Mister Keller—"

"That's *Doctor* Keller."

Carter sighed. "Again, my apologies. *Doctor* Keller."

"Another vague reply. Were you forced to come here?"

"Jensen." Faith tipped her head and widened her eyes.

"He has a right to some answers," her dad said. "We all do. I think I've been more than understanding about all this. But you aren't just questioning us in the privacy of our home. You've been to both my practice and my wife's business. You can affect our livelihood with your interference. It's not just about your job any longer."

"Not to mention Faith," Mom said.

"Knock it off. Stop talking about me like I'm not even in the room, or like I'm incapable of making my own decisions. That's what started this whole thing to begin with!" She threw her hands in the air. "You know, Dad, this isn't all that different from when Tony investigated you. And the two of you ended up friends. Carter's just doing his job. Sure, it's been a royal pain in the ass to be under suspicion so much, but he's a cop. Don't you get that? It's his job to protect and serve. It says so right on his car. Cut him some slack."

"Slack?" This time Jensen shot her the dirty look. "We've been more than patient with him. Tony backed off Dad a lot faster than Emerson's left us alone. Hell, as of this morning, he hasn't left us alone yet."

"Enough." She sighed and closed her eyes again. Then she took a deep breath, opened her eyes, and looked at each of her family members. "I've had enough. Carter's the one who tracked me down at the cathedral, not you. Not any of you."

"He wouldn't have had to find you if you had been responsible and told us where you were going."

"You know what, Dad? That's an excuse. You, Mom, Jensen—you all go places without checking in with me. Why am I the exception?"

But this time, no one answered her. Maybe she'd finally gotten through to them. Or maybe she'd just stumped them, and they were all looking for an answer. Either way, she'd take the momentary victory and leave on a high note.

"I'm sorry you're angry. With me, with Carter, with the situation. With whatever. But it is what it is, and I'm tired of worrying about it. You're the ones with the problem, not me. So you'll have to find a way to deal with it." She turned to Carter. "On behalf of my family, apology accepted. I hope we can move forward peacefully from here."

He blinked a few times. Maybe she'd stunned him into silence, too. Then he said, "I'm glad to hear you say that, because I've already apologized to your family. I really came here to apologize to you."

"Oh." Well, then. Wonder what to make of *that*. "Well, like I said, apology accepted."

A quick glance at each of her family members, then he met her gaze and smiled.

"Great. Now, I need to cool down and I'm taking a walk. Care to join me?"
Carter smiled. "Sure."

"Wonderful. Let's go." She didn't say goodbye, didn't even look back. "Ruby. Come."

The dog bounded to her feet and trotted after his mistress.

For the first time in a long time, Faith felt like she was in control of everything. And she liked that feeling. She walked out into the brisk night air with a smile on her face.

WHEN THEY WALKED OUTSIDE, RUBY tugged at her leash so hard, Faith almost lost her grip on it. Then she saw what had excited her dog— Max was waiting beside Carter's car. And he trembled and thumped his tail.

Guess he was happy to see Ruby, too. And despite his obvious pleasure, he managed to stay where Carter had left him. Good dog. Better behaved than even her service animal. Of course, he'd have to be well trained to be on the force. She'd have to talk to Vonni about Ruby's lack of discipline where Max was concerned.

"Looks like they're happy to see each other," Carter said.

"Seems so." She led Ruby over to him, and the two sniffed each other and frolicked a bit.

"I'm happy to see you, too." Carter met her gaze. "I wanted to talk to you in private."

"Oh? What about?" Please let it be about another date and not their dogs or her family.

He took control of Max and started walking down the driveway. Faith and Ruby followed, and soon they walked side-by-side in an awkward silence. She regretted not stopping in the foyer for her jacket, and rubbed her arm with her free hand.

"You cold?"

"Chilly. It was warmer when the sun was out."

"Here." He slipped out of his jacket.

"No, I couldn't. Then you'll be cold."

"I'm fine."

He helped her put it on. It was large on her, warm from his body heat, and smelled like him—a natural, masculine scent of oud, rosewood, amber, and spices. She closed her eyes an inhaled deeply. Felt like coming home—not the home she was currently stuck with, but the home that welcomed a person, embraced them, took care of them.

What home was supposed to be.

They continued walking, this time in a comfortable, companionable silence.

Finally he spoke. "What can you tell me about David? What do you really know about him?"

And there went that feeling of camaraderie and welcome.

She shrugged inside his jacket, her shoulders barely moving the oversized garment. "Not much."

He shot her a familiar look—one her family gave her constantly, filled with censure, disbelief, and disappointment. Even his toasty coat couldn't warm the chill that washed over her.

"We aren't friends. We're work associates. Nothing more."

"You hired a guy you know nothing about?"

"I know enough."

"Such as?"

She stopped walking and tugged at Ruby's leash. "Why all the questions?"

He stood beside her, and Max heeled. "I'm just wondering about him. Seems awfully convenient that he showed up at the same desolate area you happened to be visiting."

"Actually, it was convenient. He helped calm me after my scare."

"He was your scare."

"I'd ask you if my family put you up to this line of questioning, but I know they didn't. So that makes me wonder why you're asking about David."

"I'm just following all the leads. Dotting I's, crossing T's. That sort of thing."

How disappointing. She had basically professed her interest in dating him when they stood in her parents' kitchen, reveled in him wanting to spend time alone with her. And instead of him returning her feelings—like she thought he did—he basically told her she was just a job to him.

Screw disappointing. It was humiliating.

She started walking again, at a much faster pace than their earlier stroll. "Look, he used to work for an old friend. Zeke Jones, over at the shelter. If David's good enough for Zeke, he's good enough for me."

"And you talked to Doctor Jones before you hired him?"

Faith didn't answer.

"Tell me you've at least checked his references."

She couldn't do that. Because she hadn't. Instead, she said, "I've come to trust David. He's been a godsend."

"Right. He's a virtual paragon of society."

Again she stopped in her tracks. "Is there something you aren't telling me? Or is this jealousy rearing its ugly head?"

"Jealousy? What do I have to be jealous about?"

Clearly nothing. Shame stained her cheeks, and she wheeled around and headed back toward her parents' house. She yelled so he could hear her as she stormed off. "Unless you have useful information for me—proof of whatever allegation you come up with next—just steer clear, okay? Please leave me alone."

"Faith. Faith, wait!"

But she didn't. And he didn't follow. Which was fine by her. Ruby looked back a few times, but she pulled her along, and soon they walked at a vigorous clip toward her family's house. Couldn't have read the situation more wrong if she'd tried to. Carter wasn't interested in her. He was interested in David, for whatever reason.

And she was mortified that Carter knew she liked him, when he obviously didn't feel the same. At least she'd never have to see him again. There was that.

If only she'd checked with Zeke, she could have thrown her proof back in his face, left with a modicum of dignity. Instead, she was once again caught having made a mistake.

Maybe her family was right and she was immature and naive.

Damn it all to hell. Now she'd have to check David's references. Ugh. She didn't even know where he'd filed his paperwork.

Well, at least she could call Zeke. That would set her fears to rest. And shut everyone else up.

First thing in the morning, she'd make the call. Until then, she needed to blow off some steam. She pulled her phone out of her pocket and sent a text. The reply came almost immediately, and plans were set for the rest of the night.

When she started to put her phone back in her pocket, she realized she still wore Carter's jacket.

Crap on a cracker, she'd have to face him again. Or she could just leave it at the station for him. Yeah, that's what she'd do.

She hurried back to her car and headed home. Hopefully the night would go better than the rest of the day had.

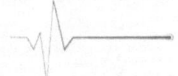

RUBY'S EARS PERKED UP WHEN the doorbell rang, and Faith rushed to answer it. She flung the door open, then her eyes widened. Not the visitor she was expecting.

"Mom? What are you doing here?"

Her mother breezed past her and peered into the living room, tilted her head like she was listening for sounds from another part of the house.

"Carter isn't here, if that's what you're wondering."

"I wouldn't have to wonder anything if you'd answer your damn phone."

Faith bit back a sigh. "What do you want, Mother?"

"We weren't done talking when you stormed off with… him."

"I was done."

"Faith, please."

"Please *what?*"

Mom walked into the living room and sat daintily on a wooden rocker. She looked around. "I can't believe you haven't decorated this place yet."

"Again with that? Why would I bother when I won't be here much longer?"

"So you're still determined to move out to the sticks?"

"It's not the sticks. It's where my practice is. It's secluded and peaceful, and it's convenient for me."

"Secluded and peaceful are just other words for the sticks."

"Is this what you came here for? To question my judgment about home decor and living arrangements? Or is it about the money the house will cost? Honestly, I can't keep track of all the things I do wrong in your eyes."

Mom sat back and pushed with her toe, rocking the chair. "I'm not trying to be critical. I'm just concerned."

"About absolutely everything. My love life. My diet. Where I go. What I do. Who I'm with. God, does it ever stop?"

"You're my daughter, Faith. My concern will never stop."

"Then you might want to learn to keep it to yourself. I'm fine, and I don't need your help."

"You aren't fine. You're a mess! You're having panic attacks in public. You've gone off your medication. You disappear in the middle of the day. You don't answer our calls. Of course I'm worried. You need help. Let us help you."

Faith shook her head. "For hours this evening, I listened to you and Dad and even Jensen yell at and lecture and rebuke me."

"You argued back."

"Don't interrupt."

Her mother gasped, but then she set her jaw and gestured for her to continue.

"I only argued back when my patience snapped. I tried to stay calm, but you guys kept pushing and nagging. But what you didn't do? You didn't ask me what happened."

"When Officer Emerson found you, he called Tony, who called and told us what happened."

"That's geography." Faith waved her hand. "I'm talking about what happened. To me."

"Were you hurt? You didn't say—"

"Mom, stop."

Again her mother snapped her mouth closed.

"I've been a mess since Hope died. A total wreck since my abduction. I couldn't bear to say the word let alone think about it. Then Bella and I talked, and I realized I wasn't the only one crippled by fear. She just hid it better. And together we went to face our demons. Do you realize neither of us had been to the lake since the night she was shot?"

"Well, I hadn't really thought about it. Like I said, you never report to us and tell us where you're going."

Faith sighed. "Does Jensen call you ten times a day to tell you when he's going to work or to the store? To dinner or a movie?"

"Of course not."

"Then why do you think I have to?"

"We just want to know you're safe."

"I am. And you know what? Today, at the lake? That was the first time in months that I could breathe. And it wasn't because you or Dad or Jensen knew where I was and who I was with and what I was doing. It was because I took control. I took charge of my life and I managed to conquer a fear."

"Tony said you were hysterical when they found you."

"I was frightened by a series of unfortunate circumstances. But before the cathedral, when we were at the water? I felt free. For the first time in months, in years, I was relaxed. Calm. And I did that. On my own. Without reporting to you or installing cameras and alarms. Just by taking a drive with a friend and standing in an open, unprotected space. That might not mean anything to you, but to me? That's amazing."

Her mother rose, crossed the room, and embraced her. "Of course it's amazing. I'm sorry we didn't ask sooner. I'm proud of you."

"*But?*"

Mom sighed. "But I'm still concerned. What about what happened at the cathedral?"

She stepped away from her mom. "David startled me."

"About David."

Faith turned away and paced in the small room. Ruby walked around her feet, and she finally had to stand still so she didn't trip over her dog. She turned and faced her mother. "What about him? This is the second time today someone's had an issue with him."

"Oh? Who else?"

"What are you getting at, Mother?" Faith asked. "Why does everybody keep asking me that?"

"Maybe because he dropped out of thin air. You met him the night of the terrorist attack. Hired him out of the blue. He shows up at the ruins and scares you nearly to death. I think my concern is justified."

"He's a nice guy. A good worker. What else is there to know?"

"Where did he come from, Faith? What do you really know about him? Because there's something familiar about him. I can't put my finger on it, but I know we know him from somewhere."

"Maybe he has one of those faces. Or maybe you're just paranoid."

"Did you check his references?"

Faith didn't answer.

"Tell me you checked his references."

Again, she said nothing.

"For the love of—Did you even get references from him?"

"Yes, Mother. Impeccable ones."

"What are they?"

"You need to go now. I'm expecting company."

"Who?"

"None of your business." She walked into the foyer.

Her mother followed. "Is that cop coming over?"

"Goodnight, Mother."

"So you won't admit you screwed up, won't tell me who's coming over. And now you're throwing me out?"

Faith opened the door. "That about sums it up."

"And you wonder why we think you're immature."

"I'm rising to the level you've established for me. Stop treating me like a helpless simpleton."

"Then stop acting like one."

"Now you sound like Dad. What a wonderful united front. Glad to see you two finally agree about something. I remember years where you couldn't even agree on what to eat for dinner."

Her mom walked onto the porch and turned back around. "That's a low blow. And far in the past. We've worked through our problems. Maybe it's time you do the same. That's what a responsible, mature adult would do." And she walked to her car, leaving Faith in the doorway, speechless. She stood there until her phone rang.

Faith dashed through the house and picked up the handset right before the call went to voicemail. "Hello?"

"*Faith? Thank God.*" Kacee let out a long, audible sigh. "*I thought something happened to you.*"

"Why would anything have happened to me?"

"*Well, the phone rang for so long, and—*"

"You're the one twenty minutes late, but you're worrying about me?" Incredulity warred with concern for her friend.

"*Sorry. After what happened to you today, I'm just a little on edge.*"

"Nothing happened to me today! And what do you know about it, anyway?"

"*Your parents called looking for you. Then they called me when you were found. We were all worried sick.*"

Faith rolled her eyes and took a deep breath. Counting to ten did not calm her temper. Complete waste of time. "I was going to tell you all about it tonight. Which brings me back to my question—where the hell are you? You're late."

"*That's why I'm calling. I have a flat.*"

"Do you know how to change it? Want me to come help?"

"*No.*"

"No—you don't know how to change it, or no—you don't want my help?"

"*Either. Or both.*"

"Kacee—"

"*I called the auto club.*"

"I can't believe your dad never taught you how to change a tire."

"*He did, but—*"

"Then why'd you call the auto club?"

"*Would you just shut up and listen to me for a minute?*"

Faith was tired of being told to shut up and listen to other people, but she did as her friend asked.

"*I misspoke. I don't have 'a' flat. I have multiple flats. Every tire I have was slashed.*"

"What? Where are you?"

"*Is anyone with you? Are you safe?*"

"My mom just left, but I'm fine. Why would you think otherwise?"

"*Because no one has ever been after me.*"

"And no one's after me now. Besides, if I was in danger, why would anyone slash your tires?"

"*So I couldn't get to you to help.*"

"No offense, Kacee, but if I were in trouble, I wouldn't call you. I'd call my dad, Jensen. Tony." Carter.

Nope. No way. He was off limits now.

"*I just freaked a little.*"

"Don't you think it's more likely that one of your disgruntled charges did that to you out of revenge?"

"*Huh. That's never happened before, but it makes sense. There are a few who didn't like my testimonies in court. Lost custody. Maybe it was one of them…*" Her voice trailed off.

"Well, I'm sorry we aren't going to get a gab session in tonight. Maybe next weekend. Unless you want me to come pick you up?"

"I don't need a ride. I'm at home. The tires were slashed in my driveway."

"You better call the police. That means someone who hates you knows where you live." Fear for her friend trickled down her spine.

"Raincheck, Faith? I better call 9-1-1. And then my boss."

"Be safe. And if you need me, call, okay?"

"You, too. Night."

"Good night."

Poor Kacee. She must be scared out of her mind to be the target of such an attack. Faith was certainly scared for her.

Or was her friend's first instinct right? Was she targeted just to leave Faith alone and unprotected?

Ridiculous.

She shook off the feeling.

No one knew she'd called Kacee, or that they had plans. It's not like her phone was bugged or she was under surveillance. Besides, who would be after her?

Isn't that what Tod always told her when she freaked out. To be the target of a nefarious plan, she had to first do something to antagonize someone. And other than her family, she never caused problems for anyone. No, this had to be an Occam's Razor moment. The simplest answer was the most likely. Kacee's job as a social worker put her in constant contact with some less-than-desirable characters. Deadbeat parents. Ex-cons. She had obviously angered someone, and that person had retaliated.

Still, Faith locked the door handle and the deadbolt, then she went around checking all the other locks in the house.

Finally, she set her new alarm.

She hated to admit it, but she was grateful her father had insisted on it. All the bravado she'd found at the lake had long since vanished, and her earlier arguments against a security system made little sense to her.

Alarm or not—reality or not—she felt like a target. And thank God for the extra protection.

She walked to her bedroom, Ruby close to her heels. Noises from outside seemed to be encroaching on her. Every animal call, every rustling of foliage, every vehicle passing by set her teeth on edge. Only her dog's calm demeanor kept her from running screaming from the house.

When the thunder and lightning started and the rain pelted her window, she pulled the covers over her head.

Maybe she'd look into buying a gun.

That thought gave her a lot to think about as sleep eluded her.

CHAPTER 18

WHEN THE SUN CRACKED OVER the horizon and cut a swath of pale light through Carter's blinds, he swore. He'd spent a restless night, and he wasn't even sure why. All he knew was he had managed to piss off Faith—again.

Maybe she wasn't worth the aggravation. Of course, she was anything but boring, and boring was just another kind of aggravation. Faith, for all the reasons she drove him nuts, kept things interesting.

Not that they had a "thing" to keep interesting. He'd never gotten to explore a relationship with her because he kept driving her off.

Damn. She still had his jacket. He'd bet his last dollar the rain had brought in another cold front. Would spring never get here? Then he wouldn't even need a coat. Or be forced to lend one to someone who would storm off in it.

He shook his head. Sounded like a fucking fourth grader, whining about a girl and making an excuse about why she doesn't like him.

Man, he was a pussy.

He stepped into a pair of boxers and headed downstairs. Walking around indoors naked was one thing, but opening the door was quite another. He'd learned his lesson when he'd let Max out one morning only to find a neighbor in his back yard. Her grill cover had blown over the privacy hedge during one of Cathedral Lake's famous storms. And what he wouldn't have given that day to wrap himself up in that damn sheet of canvas.

The woman still ogled him every time he saw her. Which was almost every morning and every evening. She had even cut the hedge back a bit so she could more easily see into his yard.

He shook his head, walked into the kitchen, and let Max out. Wouldn't you know it, she was on her porch and staring in his direction. Of course she was. She'd memorized his schedule and adapted hers to try and see him.

She smiled and waved. Predictable.

Wasn't she married? Carter muttered a curse and returned her greeting with a half-hearted head bob. Then he went inside and got out a coffee pod.

Maybe he'd install a doggie door so he didn't have to step onto his back porch again.

Dodging his nosy neighbor had become a morning routine. Tedious. Boring. He supposed she was attractive, but he didn't even let himself think about her like that. Married women were totally off limits. And attractive or not, she didn't interest him, anyway.

Not like the completely unpredictable and utterly infuriating Faith Keller.

Annnnnd he was back to thinking about her. Again.

Usually days off were for sleeping in, running errands, and maybe hanging out with the guys. Today would be different.

He needed answers, and it was time he got them.

Max returned to the door, and Carter let him in. Didn't even glance in Mrs. So-and-So's direction. Maybe he should move. Maybe Faith had the right idea about building a house outside of the city limits.

He grabbed the cup of coffee he'd just brewed and took a sip. It was going to take a lot more than one cup to perk him up after the night he'd had, but he was a man on a mission, and lack of caffeine wasn't going to stop him. He downed the hot liquid in five scalding gulps and headed for the shower.

Could always grab a cup at the Square on his way to the shelter.

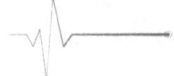

CARTER MADE SHORT WORK OF getting ready and headed out. A quick stop for a second cup of coffee, and he was back on the road. He arrived at the shelter just as a man unlocked the door for the day and flipped over the sign so it read OPEN. He and Max walked in, and the man greeted them warmly.

"So nice to see such a hale and hearty specimen for a change." He petted Max then shook Carter's hand. "Zeke Jones. I'm in charge here. What can I do for you today? Looking for a sibling for your dog? We've got some energetic mixed breeds in the back, and at least two of them have some shepherd in their genes."

Carter smiled. "No, Max doesn't need a friend. He's my partner."

The vet gave him a strange look, and Carter realized what he'd said. He shook his head. "No. Not that kind of partner. I'm Officer Carter Emerson, and this is Max. He's with the K-9 unit."

Dr. Jones laughed. "Sorry for the misunderstanding. But there are some real weirdos out there these days. I mean, I'm tolerant of all kinds of alternative lifestyles, but that's crossing the line."

Amen to that. "Doc, I was wondering if you could give me a little information on a former employee of yours."

"If I can, sure. Who?"

"David James."

"James?" The vet tapped his chin. "I don't know a James. Don't think I've ever even had a David work here before."

"Are you sure? Maybe he was a volunteer? Or an intern?"

"No. No, I don't think so." He looked at the front desk. "Let me boot the computer up and search employment records. You know what they say—the mind is the second thing to go."

Carter smiled and waited for the vet to look through his files. Seemed like a genuinely nice guy. Wasn't hiding anything. Was forthcoming and direct. If David James had worked there, Dr. Jones would tell him.

And if he didn't, he'd tell him that, too.

He didn't worry about the vet lying to him or covering for James. His gut told him the guy just wanted to help.

His gut also told him James was a threat to Faith.

Dr. Jones all but confirmed it. "Sorry. No record of anyone by that name worked here, volunteer or otherwise. Is the shelter in any danger from this guy?"

"No. You don't need to worry."

"Okay, then. Anything else I can do for you?"

A woman and man walked in, each holding a hand of a young girl.

"Thanks, Doc. But I'm good. You can take care of these folks."

"I want a doggie!" the little girl said.

"Then let's see what we can do for you." The vet led them to the back of the shelter, and Carter stepped out the door to the parking lot.

"Time to do a little investigating, Max." He settled his dog in the front seat, then he got behind the wheel and pulled out.

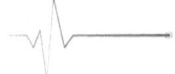

CARTER PULLED INTO THE PARKING lot at Faith's practice, and he was relieved to find it empty. It would give him the time and freedom to snoop around without having to make up an excuse.

Rain started to fall when he put his car in park. Cold, miserable day. Especially without a jacket. The rain was going to make things more difficult. He grabbed a latent print kit out of his bag of supplies. If he could get a clean print off the door handle—granted, a long shot in a public place—or maybe off the window sill outside the pharmacy area, he might get lucky tracking down James' real ID. If the guy was in AFIS…

Before he got out of the vehicle, movement near the barn caught his attention. He watched a hooded figure sneak across the field and disappear around the side of the clinic. Right where the pharmacy window would be.

Carter grabbed his spare weapon from the glove box, checked his ammo, then opened his door and had Max follow him out the driver's side. He left the door open so the suspect didn't hear it close, even though that meant his seat would be soaked. He used hand signals to communicate to his partner, and they made their way to the side of the building. At least the falling rain would mask the sound of their approach

Max rounded the corner a step before he did, and he leapt. When his body was fully extended in the air, a shot rang out. The dog yelped and collapsed on the ground.

Carter rushed to his side in time to see a person running toward the back of the building. *"Freeze!"*

The perp fired a shot without looking back. It missed high and wide, and Carter returned fire as he pursued. His shot either just missed the guy or grazed him.

By the time Carter rounded the corner of the building, the perp was out of sight. He rushed back to Max's side. "Stay with me, buddy."

His partner whimpered, rolled his eyes, and passed out.

Carter whipped his phone out of his pocket and called Faith. "Please pick up. Please. *Please.*" Just as he was about to hang up and call Max's regular vet, a car pulled into the parking lot. He looked up in time to see Faith get out of her car.

"Faith! Thank God!"

"What are you doing here? Are you trying to sneak in the back? Unless you have a warrant, that's—"

"Faith, no. We need to get inside. Please, help me. Max has been shot."

CHAPTER 19

FAITH THANKED GOD FOR MUSCLE memory, because her thoughts reeled, and she slipped into auto-mode. She needed to save that beautiful animal.

She got Ruby settled in her office so they wouldn't be disturbed. Then she texted David, but she had no idea if he'd get the message. And this was so important, she'd really prefer to have help with the surgery. Normally a cop could be counted on to assist in an emergency, but not when the animal was his partner. Wasn't a good idea for an owner to work on a pet. It was like a doctor working on a family member. And especially not Carter, who had already proven he didn't have the stomach for it.

They'd carried Max to an exam room, and she shaved and prepped him. "Help me get him to the OR."

"Why didn't we just take him there to begin with?" Carter helped her transfer Max to a room across the hall. They placed him carefully on a steel table covered with a pad.

"Couldn't risk the hair or other germs infecting him. This room is sterile. Exam One isn't."

She put blankets over his lower body to help keep his temperature from dropping. Then she prepped the OR as fast as she could, praying David would reply or just show up.

No such luck. Time was of the essence, and she couldn't wait.

"All right. I haven't heard from David, so I guess I'm going in alone. Go wait in reception."

"Do you need help? I can help."

No he couldn't. He'd pass out and she'd have a tougher time of things. She hooked Max up to monitors and scrubbed up. "I'm going to anesthetize him. You can stay with him until he's out, just to comfort him. It won't be long. Then you have to go."

"I want to stay. You need an assistant, anyway."

"I don't have time to argue. I can't deal with you fainting while I'm extracting this bullet." She inserted an IV and administered an analgesic and a sedative. A quick glance at Carter told her all she needed to know—pale face, clenched jaw, closed eyes. "Just go now. Before you collapse."

"No. I'm staying. He needs me. You might need me."

"Carter!"

"You don't have time to argue, Doc. Fix my dog."

She sighed. "Help me dress." She directed him to her surgical gown, and he held it for her then tied it in the back. She scrubbed her hands again, and he helped her put on two sets of gloves. Then she got to work inserting an intravenous catheter into the dog, necessary in case emergency medication was needed and Max's blood pressure had dropped. Carter, still white-faced, stood at Max's head, stroking his fur and whispering to him. At least he hadn't passed out. Yet. She started inducement and checked her monitors.

"His eyes are closing." Carter sounded alarmed.

"He'll be out in a minute. Then I'll control the anesthesia with gas. He won't feel a thing. These monitors will keep track of everything. I'm in good shape here. You should go."

"I told you I'm staying."

Only minutes had passed since she found them in crisis outside, but it felt like a lifetime. And she hadn't even opened Max up yet. No time to keep arguing with Carter. Whatever happened from that moment forward, her focus had to be fixated on her patient.

When the dog was out, she intubated him and checked the monitors. His blood pressure held. So far, so good, but she really wished she had a technologist there to keep an eye on things. David wasn't certified, but he was better than a novice.

"Here we go." And she opened him up.

After she'd lavaged the area, she was able to assess the damage. Thank God no vital organs were hit. He'd be sore for a while, but he should make a full recovery.

She extracted the bullet, debrided a small amount of damaged tissue, and prepared to close.

"Uh, Faith?"

The monitors began beeping. Max's blood pressure plummeted.

"Damn it!"

"What's happening?"

"He's in v-fib. Flip that switch." She began CPR while directing Carter on starting and charging the defibrillator. "Turn the knob to four hundred joules."

When she heard the tone signaling the machine was ready, she moved into position and grabbed the paddles. Carter was petting Max's head. "Stand clear." Carter didn't move. "Clear!" He stepped back, and she shocked Max.

No change.

She put the paddles down, prepped an epinephrine injection, and administered it. Because she now stood closer to the machine, she upped the charge herself. *"Clear."*

Carter was already far from the table. She shocked Max again.

That time, it worked. "Sinus rhythm."

"What's that mean?" Carter's eyes were wide, his voice weak.

"His heart is beating correctly again." She prepped another injection.

"And what's that?"

"Lidocaine. It should prevent another cardiac event."

"So he's okay now?"

She injected the lidocaine and looked up at Carter. "I think he's going to be fine. But I'll need to monitor him. Let's get him closed and into recovery."

He nodded his head and stepped back to the table.

"Help me get the top set off gloves off. I don't want to risk infection, since I touched the machine."

Credit where it's due, he didn't even blanch when he touched the bloody gloves and pulled them off, taking care to only remove the top set and not touch the second, sterile ones.

"Good idea, double-gloving."

"Something I learned in school, for emergencies. In case you have to touch something mid-procedure. It deadens the tactile sensation a bit, but it's worth it if it can prevent an infection."

He took a deep breath. "What else can I do?"

"Just keep an eye on the machines. Let me know if you see something change before I hear it. I'll finish up."

"Okay."

She stitched the inner tissue with absorbable sutures then stapled his incision closed. Once the surgery concluded, she switched the gas to straight oxygen to flush his system. Soon his protective reflexes reestablished, and he started to gag on the intubation tube, which she promptly removed.

Carter stayed silent while Max came out of anesthesia, but Faith felt his gaze on her every movement. She didn't stop to explain her actions, though, because she still wasn't convinced he wasn't going to pass out. She tried to get anything bloody away from his line of sight as quickly as possible. She tossed her gloves, stripped out of her gown, and began to clean the OR.

After about fifteen minutes, Max opened his eyes and fidgeted on the table.

"He's coming out of it now. Hold him. I don't want him thrashing or sitting up just yet."

Carter stepped over to the table and stood by Max's head so his dog could see him. Carter's presence seemed to soothe him, and he settled right down, seemingly content to let his owner pet him and whisper to him.

When she was satisfied Max was alert enough not to fall off the table, she allowed him to sit up.

"He didn't even whimper," Carter said.

"That's the pain meds. Let's get him to post-op."

Carter helped her move Max carefully to a large kennel in a different room. She was still worried about disturbing his incision site as well as the condition of his heart, so she planned on monitoring him overnight.

"Let's let him rest." She liberated Ruby from her office and let her out to relieve herself. Then she led Carter to the lounge and offered him a bottled water. Also grabbed one for herself. She was tired and a bit dehydrated, and the cool liquid did a lot to refresh her.

She grabbed a can of mixed nuts and put them on the table, then brought Ruby back in. The lovable dog sat at her feet. Faith reached for a handful of nuts, tossed a few to Ruby, and ate the rest. She and Carter continued to munch on the snack in silence.

"How does this anesthesia-thing work? He still seems out of it."

"He'll be lethargic for a while. And when the pain meds wear off, he'll have some discomfort. I'll keep an eye on him. If you're tired, you can go."

"I can't take him with me today?"

"We were lucky this wasn't as invasive a procedure as it could have been. Hard to believe, but not a single organ was hit. His recovery should be quick. He can probably go home tomorrow, provided you follow the post-op regimen I give you. But I want him here for the next twenty-four hours, at least. Just to be sure everything's okay."

"So he's in danger still?"

"I think he's going to be fine. But I want to keep him under observation, just to be sure there are no complications."

"How does that work? You have cameras here and you forward the monitor outputs to your computer, or something?"

"Actually, that's exactly how it usually works. But I'm not going home. I'm staying here tonight."

"You are worried about him."

Faith sighed. "Yes. All right? Yes, I'm worried. I've never done emergency surgery without an assistant before, and I want to be sure he's okay. But I really do think he'll be fine. This is more about my insecurities than his medical condition."

"I'm staying, too."

"You really don't have to do that."

"I insist."

"You don't trust me here alone with your dog? After I just saved his life?" Anger burned through her exhaustion, and incredulous, she nearly vibrated as she got ready to deliver one hell of a tongue-lashing.

"Of course I do. Implicitly."

"Then what's your problem?"

Carter shoved his chair back and paced in the small room. He looked at her, started to speak, then stopped. He paced again, and ran his hand through his hair.

"What is it? You're scaring me."

"I'm not leaving you alone out here."

"You're worried about my safety? Don't be ridiculous."

"Faith, Max wasn't shot in the field."

"What?"

"He was shot here. On your property. Someone was trying to break into the clinic. Someone with a gun. And he wasn't afraid to use it. You're in danger."

"I CAN'T DEAL WITH THIS right now." Faith put her head down on the table.

"Well, I'm not going anywhere."

"Do you like gluten-free pizza?"

"I like pizza."

She lifted her head and took out her phone. "What toppings?"

"Sausage, peppers, onions. Heavy sauce."

"Ugh." She typed into her phone for a bit, then put it down on the table. "Scuderi's delivers out here. We can have a late lunch. Or early dinner. They have a really good gluten-free crust, and they offer soy cheese."

"Is that what we're getting?"

She laughed at his expression. "That's what I'm getting. I ordered you your chemical-laden, gluten-rich, heart attack-inducing choice."

"Perfect." He grabbed another water and joined her at the table. "So can we discuss this now?"

"No. Not until I eat. I can't handle more stress on an empty stomach."

"Most people get queasy when they're worried or angry."

"Not me. I stress-eat. Always have."

"You must not be troubled often, then."

"I live in an almost constant state of stress, which is why I'm always snacking on something. I've got granola in my purse right now."

"The way you talk, you should weigh seven hundred pounds."

"It's the vegan lifestyle. Or maybe I just have a good metabolism."

"Whatever the cause, it's working for you."

She smiled, completely at a loss. Was that flirting? Or was she reading him wrong? It had been so long since she had even been interested in a guy, let alone dated one. Her social skills were rusty.

Too bad Kacee wasn't there. She'd know how to read the situation.

If Faith didn't know better, she'd swear he blushed. But it was probably just his coloring returning to normal after witnessing the surgery.

He cleared his throat. "So, when's the pizza due?"

"Another fifteen minutes, probably."

At the sound of tires crunching gravel, they both looked up. "Or now," Carter said.

She pushed to her feet, but he waved her off. "I got it."

He was gone far longer than she expected. Just as she was about to go check on him, he returned. Without food. "Where's the pizza?"

"Wasn't the delivery guy."

"Then who was it?"

David stepped into the room. His hair was soaked, his coloring seemed off, and his arm was in a poorly-fashioned sling over a black slicker. "Sorry. I just got your text. I was out for a hike."

"In the rain? And what happened to your arm?"

Ruby perked up, but Faith made her heel.

"It wasn't raining when I left. But I got caught in the storm, then I fell and hurt my arm. By the time I got back from my hike and saw your message, I was worried you would be elbows-deep in surgery. So I rushed right over."

"And how were you going to be of any help with your arm like that?" Carter stared hard at him, his kind demeanor from earlier totally gone. He was in uber-suspicious cop-mode.

She hated that part of him. Even though she respected what he did for a living, she'd been on the wrong side of that expression before. Erroneously. And it sucked.

"I don't know. But two sets of hands have to be better than one. Even if one of the sets is compromised."

"David, sit down." She stood up. "I'll go get you a fresh set of scrubs and the first aid kit. We'll get you dry and properly bandaged."

"That's okay. You clearly have everything in hand. Since you don't need me, I'm just going to go home."

"I'd really like to take a look at your arm. Are you cut? Is your shoulder out of place?"

"Just a puncture wound. I impaled myself on a branch."

"You need to see someone."

"It didn't go deep. I'm fine. A hot shower, a little gauze, and I'll be good as new."

"I don't know what your fear is about doctors, but you need to see one."

"I don't have doctor-fear."

"You do. You definitely do. White coat syndrome."

"I do not."

"The night we met, you refused to go to the hospital. And now, here you are injured again, and you won't go to the trauma center."

"That's not fear of doctors. That's aversion to wasted time and money."

"Taking care of yourself isn't a waste of time or money."

Again the sound of tires on gravel sounded.

"That's probably the pizza," Faith said. "Join us?"

"No, thanks. I just want to go home."

"I'd love it if you'd stay," Carter said. "We don't really know each other very well. We could talk."

"Another time, maybe. Thanks." David made a hasty retreat down the hall.

Faith stood. "He's probably going to let the delivery guy in. I'll go pay."

"Sit," Carter said. "I got it."

"Here's some money." She reached into her pocket.

"Don't be ridiculous. You saved my dog. I can cover pizza."

"I'm still going to bill you."

"I wouldn't have it any other way, Doc." He walked down the hall, and she retrieved paper plates and napkins from the cabinet. Soon he returned with two boxes and put them on the table.

"Mmm." She opened the smaller box. "Smells divine."

"I think that's the sausage you smell."

Faith shook her head and put a slice on her plate.

Carter put two slices on his plate and sprinkled red pepper flakes on them from a little portable packet Scuderi's had sent. "So, you met David when he had another injury? Is he accident-prone, or something?"

"No." She took a bite of pizza. It burned the roof of her mouth, and she threw it back to her plate and guzzled some water. "I was working triage the night of the terrorist attack. He came to my station with a gunshot wound."

"And he didn't go to the hospital?"

"Calling it a flesh wound would be generous. It was more like a surface scratch. He didn't want to wait for the emergencies to be over before he was seen at a hospital, so he begged me to stitch him up. After arguing over it for a while, I finally agreed. We got to talking, and the rest is history."

"What a coincidence, him getting an injury that you could treat, and getting you rather than a different emergency worker."

She took another bite of pizza, sucked in air to cool it off even as she chewed it. "It was a coincidence. One that worked out for me."

Carter ate the two pieces on his plate and took a third out of the box. He didn't say anything, just stared at the floor and ate in silence.

And she was glad. David was an excellent employee, and she didn't appreciate Carter starting another witch hunt. Especially when it pertained to someone else in her circle of friends and family.

When she was finished, she rose. "I'm going to go check on Max."

"Okay. I'll refrigerate the leftovers."

She walked past the table and glanced down at the spot that Carter seemed focused on. There were tiny droplets of blood on the floor. When she walked into the hallway, she saw they led toward reception.

Had to be from David.

Should she call him and insist he go get his arm looked at? He had to know how badly he was injured if he was bleeding that long after falling.

Maybe she should just go check on him herself. But she didn't want to leave Max.

A quick peek at the dog, and she saw he was resting comfortably. She grabbed a spray mop out of the utility closet and scrubbed the hallway, intending to go all the way to the door. When got to the lounge, she found Carter crouched on the floor, examining the droplets. He stood and stuffed something in his pocket. Ruby padded over and sniffed at it.

"Ruby, heel." The dog walked over to her and sat by her feet. "Carter, what are you doing?"

"I'm a cop. I was checking out the stain on the floor. It's blood. Fresh. I think David's hurt worse than he's letting on."

"Me, too." She sighed. "But I don't want to leave Max."

"I'll go check on him."

"You don't have medical training. And you get sick at the sight of blood."

"I did fine today."

She bit her lip and studied him. "Yes, you did. And I never thanked you for helping me."

"Technically, you still haven't. But don't worry about it. You saved Max, so thank you."

She smiled and leaned on her mop. "I'll call Jensen, see if he can go check on David."

"Tell him I'll meet him there. What's the address?"

"Let me pull his personnel file." She bent down and quickly mopped up the stain on the floor.

"I'll finish that." He took the mop and headed to the hallway. "You go get the address."

She left the room and went to the filing cabinet behind the reception desk. She looked under every heading she could think of, but she couldn't find his paperwork. And she knew she'd asked him to file it there.

She checked her office. Still nothing. Did a web search for the address, but didn't find him listed.

Finally, she called him, but he didn't answer.

Faith gave up and returned to the lounge. "I can't find his file. And he's not answering his phone. Can you track him down through some cop database, or something?"

Carter sighed. "No. Let's just hope he's okay."

But something about the tone of his voice made Faith question whether he really meant it.

CHAPTER 20

CARTER BLINKED AND SAT UP, trying to figure out where he was. Then realization dawned on him.

He'd spent the night at the clinic, in part for Max, in part to protect Faith. Every fiber of his being told him the perp he'd shot at would be back, and he wanted to be there when it happened.

But the night passed uneventfully.

He and Faith had taken turns checking on Max, even though her phone would indicate any change in his condition. They brought Ruby to see him once, but both dogs got too excited, and they had to take her out of the room. Faith needed Max to stay still and rest, but Ruby had the opposite effect on him.

They chowed on leftover pizza around nine, and he'd passed out before eleven. But it was a comfortable evening, spent with easy conversation and easier silence.

At least, it was comfortable after they got over the awkward mood following David's departure.

Carter didn't believe for a second that David had been hiking. He suspected David was the perp who had shot at him and Max, and when Carter returned fire, he'd hit him.

But he couldn't share his suspicions with Faith. Even in the face of the missing personnel file, she was David's staunchest supporter. She'd be angry with him, and he'd be unable to stay with her, to protect her.

He stayed the night for not only his dog, but for Faith, too.

David didn't show, though. No one did.

And Carter had to believe it was because David was holed up somewhere with a gunshot wound in his arm.

If only he could figure out why. The motive was all that was missing.

David had access to the clinic. He didn't need to break in. So what was he up to?

Carter stretched and looked around in the early morning light. He had a crick in his neck from how he'd been sprawled in the chair. Faith, however, seemed quite comfortable on the couch.

She looked like an angel. Ethereal. Her light hair spilled over her shoulders, and the sun reflected off the tresses and made them glow. Her face had a peaceful expression, one he hadn't really seen since he'd met her. So often she was angry or scared, suspicious or worried.

And he had to admit, he was usually the cause.

But lying there, her features were soft with a relaxation only deep sleep could induce.

And she was beautiful. Breathtakingly so.

His blood chilled thinking about what David's motives were, about him hurting her.

The evidence was mounting, and Carter gathered every minuscule bit, analyzed each one by one as he would pieces of a puzzle. They were starting to fit together, and a picture was forming.

He just needed to keep Faith safe until he had the whole thing figured out.

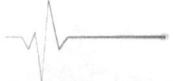

SHORTLY BEFORE LUNCH, FAITH DECIDED she wanted another observation day with Max. She just wasn't ready to release him yet, although she insisted he was doing fine. Better than expected, actually.

Hopefully it was just her being overly cautious, and she wasn't lying to spare Carter's feelings.

He would have spent the day with her and Max again, but Tony had called him in to help with something. After Faith assured him it was okay for him to leave, he called Manny.

"You busy today?"

"It's Sunday, man. I just got back from church, and we're going to have carnitas."

"I'll call Moto, then."

"What do you need?"

Carter brought him up to speed on the events from the day before. "I'm worried about Faith out there all alone. The department isn't going to approve surveillance, but I want someone to keep an eye on her."

"Then why are you leaving?"

"Cooper called me in."

"I'll call Moto, and we'll go out there."

"You're doing me a solid, man. Thanks. I owe you. Moto, too."

"We won't forget."

"Carnitas keep, right?"

"They'd reheat okay, but there won't be any left. The family's all coming over, and those will be the first to go. As well as the tamales *and the* taquitos. *I'll make a plate to go."*

Guilt washed over him. He'd love to be home, sharing a meal with his extended family. With any family at all. But they hadn't really done anything like that since his brother had died. He knew how special that time was, and he didn't want Manny to miss it.

"Don't worry about it, Manny. Stay with your family."

"It's no problem."

"Actually, it is. Faith will see you, and she won't appreciate me sending someone to spy on her."

"I won't be spying. I'll be doing my job."

"But that's not how she'll see it. I'll call her family. One of them will do it, and they'll be far less suspicious."

"You sure?"

"Yeah. Enjoy the day."

They hung up, and Carter called Royce. Voicemail. Tried Jensen, too, but he got the same result. He didn't want to leave a message, so he planned on calling back regularly until he reached one of them. In the meantime, he drove to the station.

Tony wasn't at his desk, so Carter looked around for him. Found him in the conference room.

"Hey, man. What's so important you're working on a weekend?"

"Something weird popped up with the Yavin case. Seems to relate to yours."

"What?"

"Pull up a chair."

Carter sat and looked at the papers and evidence spread over the table. He didn't see anything that related to the drug operation he was looking into. He looked up at Tony.

"Remember that disease the doctors said Yavin had?"

"Crusty-brain something-or-other."

Tony shook his head. "Close enough. It got me thinking, though. If his dexterity was that compromised, he'd never be able to build a bomb."

"But it didn't go off. Probably because he didn't assemble it right."

"I talked to Royce and Stanford. They both agree that a man in Yavin's condition couldn't have made anything even remotely resembling a bomb."

"How's this relate to my case?"

"He had help."

"Yeah, I get that. But what's that have to do with pushing drugs?"

Tony handed him a sheaf of paper. "Here are all his calls. Incoming and outgoing. See that highlighted number? Over the course of the last eight months, they went from communicating once every two weeks to several times a day."

"Whose number is it?"

"Burner."

"I still don't see what this has to do with my case."

"We've recovered some of the texts."

"Okay."

"No names, but look at these." He handed Carter another sheaf, this one with printed text messages. "Check out the phrases highlighted in pink."

Carter jumped around, skimming certain passages, looking for a connection between the two cases.

July 12

Unsub: We have common interests. I'll help u achieve your goal, and u can help me with mine.

Yavin: I don't no what I can do to help you.

Unsub: Motives r mine. Don't worry. Let's meet.

Yavin: When and whre?

Unsub: I'll call u with deets tomorrow.

August 27

Unsub: Studying online. Think I no how 2 do what u need. Will practice on smaller scale.

Yavin: Anf what do u wnt me 2 do?

Unsub: Keep up protest. School needs 2 pay 4 discrimination. We'll shine a spotlight so bright on your cause, no one will ignore it.

Carter looked at Tony. "This is all well and good, but it still doesn't tell me why our cases are related. We can't even swear it's Yavin. Could be his caregiver using his phone to cover his or her tracks? You check on that?"

"It's not a caregiver. Look at the texts. He's already displaying dexterity issues. Some of the words are spelled wrong. It just gets worse as time progresses."

"But what's that have to do with—"

"If you don't want to read all the messages, skip ahead." Tony grabbed the sheaf, flipped forward several pages, and handed it back.

January 17
Yavin: Uo rn't aswerin my calls.
Unsub: Had phone off.
Yavin: Need 2 talk.
Unsub: Busy. Almost got caught 2nite.
Yavin: Doin wht>
Unsub: Procuring product. Will call tomorrow.
Yavin: What prduvt?

January 19
Yavin: How des K hep us?
Unsub: My business. And never mention in writing. Will call u.

February 7
Yavin: Meed tp meet.
Unsub: Why? Dangerous.
Yavin: Scnd thoghts.
Unsub: Fuck that. 2 much at stake 2 back out.
Yavin: Wha ypu gomna do bout it? Kill me?
Unsub: Tomorrow. Midnight. The patch.
Yavin: Too dsrk and sxary. Hw bout diner?
Unsub: Can't be seen in public together. And I have 2 harvest some product.
Yavin: Majuna grows in winter?
Unsub: NOT IN WRITING!
Yavin: Byt cold nd dark ovt thre at nite.
Unsub: Greenhouse.
Yavin: Tredpasng.

Unsub: Trespassing? Fuck that. u want me, that's where I'll be.

February18
Yavin: Wrk out hw 2 bld th bomv yet? Tim shrt.

March 9
Unsub: Stop calling all the damn time. I got this.
Yavin: 2 hrd 3 hld gun. Cnt go
Unsub: STOP WRITING THAT SHIT!
Yavin: Al th pwopl.
Unsub: All the bigoted people. We're going to make 1 hell of a statement.
Yavin: Leas I wpnt liv tp see afttrmqth.
Unsub: NOT IN WRITING!

March 10
Yavin: Rolld ankl at pot frm lst nite. Dpnt think I cn evn walkl into gym for gme
Unsub: Stop fucking texting this shit. You want to leave a trail?
Yavin: dsnt mttr. Nwithr of us wlkn out offff thr

March 10
Yavin: Pkn me upp>
Unsub: An hour before tip off.
Yavin: Yu ger th gun smugld in

March 10
Yavin: Drpd drgs to soon. Lpst them.
Unsub: It's fine. Someone will find the vials. Be brave, E. Tonight, u make your stand and we'll see each other in paradise. Throwing away phone now. Good luck.

Carter tossed the pages on the table. "What the fuck was that all about?"

"The attack wasn't Yavin's idea. He was manipulated into doing it. Someone played on his fears, his deteriorating thoughts. It was like programming a robot."

"No. I get that. But why? I mean, why plant drugs at a terrorist attack? To what end?"

"Misdirection? Garnering awareness? The press has talked about nothing but this attack since it happened. Everyone knows drugs were found at the scene. Could be it was all a red herring, just to get free press about a burgeoning business."

"Awfully risky. He had no guarantee the press would even find out."

"I think he did."

Carter raised an eyebrow.

"We didn't release the discovery of drugs to the public. Someone called in a tip to the media. Who would do that? And why, unless to get the info out there that the drug business is back in Cathedral Lake."

"The damn business never left." Carter stood and looked over the stuff on the table again. "What's this?"

Tony took it. "DNA report. We were so lucky the bomb didn't go off. Or maybe we weren't. Maybe it was intentional. Either way, the unsub must have cut himself when he put the thing together. Found a trace amount of blood inside the casing."

"Run it against arrest records here? ViCAP and CODIS?"

"Ran it through every database we could get our hands on. No matches in any system."

Carter pulled a napkin out of his pocket. "Try comparing it to this."

Tony took the napkin and raised his eyebrows.

"I'm pretty damn sure I know who the unsub is. And that means Faith is in danger."

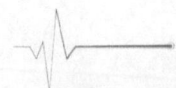

CARTER NO LONGER HAD THE luxury of waiting for one of the Kellers to answer their phones. It wasn't safe to send them to her, anyway. Instead, he had Tony send units out there while he tried calling her.

No answer.

A trickle of sweat ran down his temple, and he swiped it away. His gut was in knots—he knew something was wrong. Desperate to get to her, he fished in his pocket for keys and headed for the door.

"Carter. Where you going?"

"The clinic. I need to make sure Faith is safe."

"We need to brief the Chief."

"You do it. Max is out there recovering from surgery. If the Chief doesn't want me rushing out there, explain I'm just checking on my partner."

"Max had surgery?"

"He got shot."

Carter made to brush past him, but Tony grabbed his arm and spun him around. "I can't read the Chief in, because apparently I don't know the whole story."

"I'll call you from the car."

"You'll wait right here until he arrives, and then we'll brief him together. Units are on the way out to Faith's clinic as we speak. She'll be fine."

"Tony, please. I need to do this myself."

Tony's phone rang, and he grabbed it. "Cooper." He listened for a moment, then he looked up at Carter. "We've got a problem."

CHAPTER 21

FAITH SHUT RUBY IN HER office, then she checked on Max again. His energy was returning. She redressed his incision, looked for signs of infection, but found none. Barring some unforeseen circumstance, he not only was going to live, he was going to make a complete recovery. Would probably even return to duty.

Max was overdue for a potty break, so she took him out the back door and into the open field between her office and the barn. Salem had been on the prowl out there, and he hissed when they strolled past. "It's my property, dummy. I'm allowed to be here."

He darted toward the office, and Max turned to follow.

"No, boy. You need to take care of business first. And you aren't ready to play tag, anyway."

She stayed outside with Max for about ten minutes. Ruby's barks carried all the way out to where they were, and the disruption seemed to be distracting him from the purpose of their walk. He snuffled and sniffed, walked in circles and explored the field, kept trying to go back to the office. God, she wished Ruby would shut up. They'd never be done if Max stayed focused on her dog. At the rate things were going, they'd be out there all day.

God, she hoped this wasn't a complication from the surgery. She didn't want to have to open him up again.

Faith had no desire to stay out there any longer. The day was chilly and the grass was wet from all the rain. Soggy, too. A few times she sunk or slipped in a mud patch.

"Come on, Ma—" Her foot hit a mud slick and slipped out from under her. Next thing she knew, she lay on her back in the field, the wind knocked out of her. She struggled to breathe. Tears stung her eyes, and panic welled and crescendoed, a maelstrom of frantic gasps and frenetic tremors. When she at last managed a deep, satisfying inhale, Max barked and licked her face. She lay on the cold earth, suffering both bruised tailbone and pride. Tailbone injuries were the worst—they hurt like hell and took forever to heal. While she waited for her breathing to stabilize, she tested her range of movement. Everything hurt. She didn't know how she was even going to climb to her feet. And because she wasn't miserable enough, the cold muck she lay in saturated her clothes and chilled her to the bone.

Wonder if Tide was strong enough to get those stains out.

She scrambled to roll over, managing only to get dirtier. Then finally she found purchase in the sloppy mud and the strength to clamber to her feet. Standing, she surveyed the damage. Filthy and sore, but no real injuries to speak of.

"Come on, Max. I need to go inside." Finally, he squatted and took care of his business.

God, she hoped it was only mud she fell in. This was where she told all her clients to take their animals when they needed to go out while waiting to be seen.

It was also Salem's litter box.

No point in dwelling on those unpleasant details. She'd change when she got inside. Probably just toss her clothes.

Faith took Max back to the office and led him back to his kennel. She had to coax him inside, as he kept trying to get to her still-barking dog.

He was probably well enough to stay with her rather than being caged, but he wouldn't keep still around Ruby. If she let Max stay out, the two of them would frolic, and he wasn't well enough to socialize yet.

"Sorry, big guy." She rubbed behind his ear and closed him back in the kennel. "I know she's your girlfriend, but you aren't up to the task of culminating a date." When he wagged his tail, she laughed. "Feisty. That's a good sign. But even if you could, you shouldn't. Carter wasn't thrilled the last time you and Ruby… spent time together."

What the hell was wrong with her? She was talking about sex to a dog. And not even about her sex life, but about his. What a sad commentary.

Not that a clumsy, nervous, filthy woman even deserved a sex life.

"I don't know, Max. Do you think Carter and I are going to figure this out? And if we do, what about my family? You've met them. They aren't his biggest fans."

His ears perked, and he sat up.

"What is it?"

Right, like he could answer.

Faith patted the cage in lieu of petting the dog, and she headed toward the hallway. She badly needed a hot shower and fresh clothes. She'd settle for a sponge bath and a clean set of scrubs.

Max let out a few loud barks and scratched at the floor of his cage. Ruby's barking joined the melee. "What's wrong with you two?"

She toed off one of her muddy shoes while she checked on Max again.

A sharp pain radiated through her skull, and all went black.

HER HEAD THROBBED. THE SCENT of stale earth and moldering decay tickled her nose. She sneezed, then her eyes snapped open.

Icy panic caromed through her. For a moment, she thought she'd been rendered blind, but soon her eyes adjusted to the darkness.

A tidal wave of hysteria crashed over her.

The ruins. She was in the cathedral ruins, in the same spot she'd been held before.

And damned if she wasn't bound to the wall again, too.

Her lungs refused to cooperate. Chest threatened to burst from lack of oxygen. She gasped. Tears stung her eyes.

What the hell had Tod told her to do? Thoughts reeled, yet her mind was blank.

Panting for air, praying for release. Time spiraled. Or stopped.

Unbearable agony.

Find a cadence. Hum a melody. Center. Breathe. Calm.

She didn't know where those commands came from, but she grasped at them like the mental lifelines they were.

Despite the restraints binding her hands, she managed to tap out a measured beat with a few of her fingers. The rough wall scraped against her knuckles, the coarse rope abraded her wrists. But still she drummed a rhythm that matched a wordless mantra she moaned to herself.

Soon her pulse slowed, regulated. She managed to calm her breathing and released a long, slow sigh. Her right foot was freezing. Right. She'd been about to change out of her muddy clothes when someone cracked her in the head.

Finally she looked around the room.

Someone stood in the doorway. He clapped—a slow, sarcastic slapping of palm against palm that echoed in the dark chamber. "Fought off another panic attack, did we? How many more times do you think you can manage that?"

Sour swirls of dread and despair whirled in her stomach, and she thrashed against her restraints.

He stepped into the room and sauntered over to her. In the dim lighting, and she barely made out the sneer on his face.

"David?" The blood rushed from her face and settled like a coagulated ball in her already-queasy gut. "Why?"

"Name's not David. And when I tell you who I really am, you'll know why."

"**WHAT DO YOU MEAN YOUR** name's not David?" Faith couldn't process what was happening, what he meant.

"I've been planning this for almost a decade." He linked his fingers behind his back and paced back and forth in front of her. "I've studied your whole family, and after careful consideration, I knew you were the way in. You were my ticket to revenge."

"A decade? Revenge? Why? For what?"

He ignored her questions. "You want to know the best part? I didn't even bother establishing a fake identity, because I knew you were too trusting to even run a background check. But man—" He turned, faced her, and scoffed, little flecks of spittle spraying her face. "Even I didn't expect you to offer me a job on our first meet."

"Who are you?" She had a handle on the panic, but not the rage. It roiled inside her, threatened to burst out in a torrent of hostility. But nasty retorts wouldn't get her answers. Nor would they get her free. She tamped down her anger and tried to keep him talking while she intuited a way out.

"Davis Henry Anderson." He leaned in, his nose almost touching hers. "Make sense now?"

"No. Should it?"

"The name 'Anderson' should be familiar to you. To your whole family. You ruined us!" He spun around and stormed around the room. "Davis Anderson. *Anderson*. It doesn't mean a thing to you, does it?"

Her right binding was slightly looser than the left one. If she wriggled against it, she could possibly slip her hand free. Had to keep him talking so he didn't notice what she was doing.

Or worse, decide he'd done enough talking and put an end to it all.

"I'm sorry. No."

He screamed and punched the wall. Then he rounded on her. "All right. If that doesn't ring a bell, maybe you know my parents. Frank and Sally Anderson."

Shit. She *knew* that name. They were Jimmy Salvo's guardians. The same Jimmy that got Hope killed. And that made David—Davis—Jimmy's stepbrother.

David James. Davis *Anderson.*

How could she not have realized?

The Andersons were a nice couple. She'd never met their son, though. And he clearly wasn't as kind and easy going as his parents.

Maybe she should lie? A surreptitious glance at Davis, and she knew that would be the wrong course of action.

"I know Frank and Sally. They're really sweet. My parents get a Christmas card from them every year."

"Funny. My folks are dirt poor, but they still manage to shell out money on a card for your family. What have the Kellers done for them, though?"

God. He was demented. What were they have supposed to have done for the Andersons? Jimmy Salvo was the reason Hope was dead. His parents did what little they could to make up for a wrong that wasn't theirs to right—a wrong that couldn't be righted—although they tried.

He jabbed his finger into her sternum. Pretty sure that was going to bruise. Poked her repeatedly to accent his words.

"Well? What. Have. They. Done?"

"I—I don't know."

Davis spun away and paced again. He ran his hand over his face, the raspy sound of five o'clock shadow sounded eerie as it echoed off the walls.

Her wrist felt like it was on fire. Something wet trickled down her arm. She'd managed to rub her skin bloody in her quest for freedom.

If she used the blood as a lubricant, she just might get free.

"Do you have any idea what it's like to be the town pariah? To have everyone stare at you, whisper behind your back?"

She remembered how they'd been ostracized for a while when Hope had first died. She knew first-hand how difficult it was. "Actually, yes, I do."

He scoffed. "Pretty little rich girl? I don't think so."

No point in arguing. He wouldn't believe her anyway.

"Because of *your* sister, our name was dragged through the mud. She destroyed us!"

It wasn't Hope's fault. Salvo had threatened her. She'd been trying to do the right thing, was even working with the police to put a stop to it.

But Davis wouldn't see things her way. So she stayed silent.

"Did you know that Haggerty bastard sued us for killing his wife?"

Of course she knew. Her parents had initially been named in the suit, too, but their lawyer had gotten them out of it. Hope was as much a victim as Paula Haggerty had been.

"Did you?" he yelled.

His voice echoed around her, like it came to her from all directions.

"Yes!" Her tone asserted her frustration, her defiance, and he slapped her across the face. The sting stole her breath, and she blinked back tears.

"Did you know your parents were initially named, too?"

"Yes." This time her voice was soft, nearly unintelligible.

"But only my parents went to trial. Why do you think that is?"

She lifted her chin. "Because Hope was an innocent victim, but your stepbrother was guilty of corrupting her."

He backhanded her across the same cheek. Her vision blurred. Felt like her eye swelled.

"Innocent? She was a *whore*. A dirty slut who got my stepbrother killed!" He punched her, once, again, all with the same hand. His arm. She'd forgotten. Maybe she could exploit that weakness. If only she could get free.

She spat at him.

"Bitch!" He pummeled her in the head, in the gut. Knocked her around so hard that she jerked violently in her restraints.

And jostled her hand free.

The pain was nearly unbearable, but she couldn't let him know what he'd done. She held onto the bloody rope so it appeared she was still suspended, arms extended, against the wall.

Out of breath, he spun away from her. Walked in circles until he'd calmed.

"Your dirty lawyer kept your family from paying for Jimmy's death. Meanwhile my parents lost everything trying to set things right. Things that weren't even their fault!"

He was right about that. None of it was Frank and Sally's fault. But they'd been responsible for Jimmy, and Jimmy's estate—not that he had one—had been ordered to make restitution.

"You're right. It wasn't their fault. I'm sorry."

"You're sorry? Sorry doesn't bring Jimbo back. Or our money."

"But this is all in the past. Why now? Why us? We didn't sue you. Mister Haggerty did."

"You might not have taken our fortune, but you took my stepbrother."

"I didn't take anybody!"

"Your family did!" He struck her again.

She listed to the side and clutched the rope to keep him from seeing she'd freed one hand.

"Your slut sister got Jimmy killed. That Haggerty dick stole our money. So I plotted revenge."

"And you decided I was the easiest target to punish." Lucky her.

"Second easiest. I already killed Daniel Haggerty. He went down easy."

The blood drained from her face, ran cold through her veins. "And now you're going to kill me?"

"Eventually. But first, I'm going to destroy the Keller name."

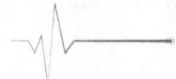

DAVIS HAD BEEN GONE FOR what felt like an hour. In reality, it could have been minutes, it could have been days. Faith had no concept of the passage of time in the dark chamber.

That she was equally panicked and enraged didn't help matters, either.

She had no idea what he would do, where he had gone, but he had spoken with maniacal glee before leaving.

And since he'd walked out, she'd picked at rope that still bound her. It was knotted so tight, she'd begun to lose circulation in her fingers. They were cold, and they tingled.

Her free hand, sticky with blood, hadn't been able to even loosen the binding. She'd hoped to be free before Davis returned, but she was stuck there.

She checked her pockets, but either he'd taken her phone or she never had it. Hell, she might have lost it when she fell in the mud.

Seemed like a lifetime ago. Seemed like a different life altogether.

Tears streamed silently down her cheeks. She was stuck there. Nothing she could do but wait for Davis to return with news of how he ruined her family… and then kill her.

At least she'd get to see Hope again.

The sound of shifting earth and sliding gravel intruded on her thoughts. He was back.

"Did you miss me?"

He sounded far too pleasant.

"What did you do?"

He laughed. Cackled, more like it. Sounded like he'd completely gone off the rails. "Oh, Faith. What indeed."

Davis continued laughing to himself. The sound set her teeth on edge.

"Let me tell you how my plans all came to fruition. It started with me leaving home and joining the Aryan Nation."

A freaking skinhead? He wasn't only certifiable, he was indoctrinated into a cult?

She didn't like where this story was headed.

CHAPTER 22

THE CHIEF HAD COME IN while Carter and Tony bickered about whether he had to wait. Answer made for him at that point—and not the one he wanted. Chief called half the force into his office to discuss the evidence. He lost valuable time bringing everyone up to speed.

Finally he was released, and he sped out to the clinic. Tony and several other cops followed.

A parking lot full of cars greeted him when he got there. Most were official units, a few he recognized as belonging to Faith's family.

And he hadn't wanted to involve them until he knew more.

No crime scene tape was up. No perimeter had been established. Any and every clue to Faith's whereabouts was probably contaminated and useless.

He headed to the officer at the door. "What the hell is going on here? Why isn't the tape up?"

"I talked to the sergeant when I arrived and saw she wasn't here. He said not to do anything until her family and friends were contacted and we could establish she was actually missing."

Damn it. That explained why the Kellers were there and the tape wasn't. Didn't mean it was the right call, though.

"I'm the one who requested protective detail for Faith Keller. Why the hell wouldn't you check with me, instead?"

"Sorry, Emerson."

Carter shook his head and walked inside. The Kellers were all in the reception area, talking to a detective. Faith's friend—Kacee something?—was with them. Vonni Smith was also there, but she sat away from their group. She had Max on one side of her, and Ruby on the other. Both wagged their tails when he stepped into the room. He went immediately to them, stooped down, and rubbed behind their ears.

"Hope you don't mind me being here. The Kellers called when they found Ruby locked in Faith's office and Max in a kennel."

"No. It's fine. Are they okay?"

"The dogs or the Kellers?"

He tilted his head.

"The dogs are fine. Can't say as much for the family."

"Mind keeping an eye on them for a while longer?"

"Take all the time you need."

Carter petted them again, stood, and hurried to the Kellers. Tony was already with them.

"I just got them up to speed on what we know," Tony told him.

"Okay. What about any evidence here?"

Detective Franklin flipped through a notepad. "Not much to go on. Found a muddy area out back where it looks like there might have been a struggle. Seems to have upset a cat."

"That's Salem. He's always ornery."

Franklin shrugged. "Okay. No signs of struggle in here. We did find one muddy shoe."

"Is it Faith's?"

"Parents seem to think so."

"Yes, it's Faith's," Vanessa snapped.

"Anyone check her car?"

"It's not here," Franklin said. "But GPS is disabled. Can't track it."

"Anything else?"

Franklin shook his head. "We have enough to consider her officially missing now. I'm going out front, have them establish the perimeter."

He walked off, and the Kellers all turned to Carter. "Now what?"

Wasn't Tony, as a detective, supposed to take charge? Carter didn't know what the hell to do. Where was she? What was happening to her? If James so much as hurt one hair on her head…

He took a deep breath. Was glad Tony didn't step up. He needed to see this through to the end.

He needed to bring her home, safe and sound.

"All right. We need to figure out where she is."

"Her car's gone," Jensen said. "She could be anywhere by now."

"True. But she's not anywhere. She's somewhere. Somewhere specific." Carter sighed. "If we only knew who David James really was, we might have an idea of where he'd taken her."

"I never trusted him," Vanessa said. "I told Faith he looked familiar to me. We know him from somewhere. I know it."

"Okay. Let's work with that." Carter didn't have any idea how to jog her memory, but he had to try something. "Was he a regular at the nursery?"

She shook her head. "I don't think so. But I could give you access to the security footage. Maybe he'd been in there and bought something with a credit card. Or had something delivered somewhere."

"That's a start." Carter beckoned an officer. "Can you work with Missus Keller on getting the security video from her store?"

"You got it." He led Vanessa out of the room.

"What about you guys?" Carter looked at Royce and Jensen.

"I never met him," Jensen said. "I don't even know what he looks like."

"Vanessa's right. There *is* something familiar about him. Something shady, too."

"Shady *how?* What bothered you about him?" Tony asked.

"When he met me… He was weird. It was like he was trying to hide his face from me. He didn't want to look at me directly."

"So you probably do know him," Carter said. "But not well. Not if there isn't instant recognition."

"Some kind of acquaintance," Tony said.

"Shit, he could have been a one-time patient on a really busy day. He could be anybody."

"No," Carter said. "Not anybody. He didn't expect his face to blend into a bunch of others. He feared you'd recognize him. That you'd know and remember him from somewhere. Your meeting might have been a one-off in your past, but it was a memorable one. He wasn't lost in a sea of other patients."

"All right. So a one-time meeting. Probably not a recent one." Royce thought for a moment. "How am I supposed to remember what I don't remember? It could be anything!"

Tony clasped his shoulder. "I know you're scared, Royce. But you can do this."

He had to remember something—He was the only lead they had.

"I don't know." Royce looked at Jensen. "You sure you never met him? If we could bounce ideas off each other…"

But Jensen shook his head.

Carter's phone rang. "Emerson."

He listened for a moment, felt a glimmer of hope. "We'll be right there."

"What?" Royce asked.

"Missus Keller found footage of him at the nursery. Buying fertilizer."

"Let's go check it out," Tony said.

They headed back to Faith's office and found Vanessa behind the desk, staring at the computer screen. When they entered the room, she turned the laptop to face them. "It's only a little better than a profile of his face, but that's definitely him."

"Did you call the—"

"Yes, Royce. I'm not stupid. Kaitlyn is going through the records now and looking for the delivery address."

"It's probably going to lead back to the plot of land by the nursery," Jensen said. "The pot farm."

She shook her head. "No. I'd remember if we had a delivery right there."

Royce peered at the screen. "He does look familiar. Maybe if he had hair. Or a beard. Something."

Vanessa's phone rang, and she jumped. Almost dropped it before managing to answer it on the fourth ring. "Hello? Kaitlyn?" She listened for a moment, then grabbed a pen and a piece of paper. "Thanks." She disconnected the call and handed the paper to Tony. "Can you find out whose address that is?"

Closed his eyes and exhaled slowly. "Don't have to. I just saw that address today when I was reviewing old case files. I know whose it is."

"Who?" Royce asked.

Tony hesitated, and Carter understood why. The information might be useful to help jog the Kellers' memories, but it was also an ongoing investigation into the disappearance of their daughter.

"If you don't tell us," Royce said, "I'll just drive there myself."

"Frank and Sally Anderson."

"What?" Jensen said. "The Andersons? Wait a minute." He glared at Carter. "Why were you looking at that old case? Do I need to call Bella?"

"Settle down, Jensen," Tony said. "It's not what you think. The two cases are connected."

"How?"

"Oh, my God!" Vanessa jumped out of her seat.

"What?" Royce asked.

"I know who that is. That's the Andersons' son!"

And the puzzle pieces all fell into place. Carter tuned out the cacophony of voices as he thought through the evidence. David James, or whatever his real name was, had been targeting Faith and her family on behalf of his dead stepbrother. It was all about vengeance. Frame her family for illegal drug distribution, terrorize her. Eventually abduct her—the twin of the girl he probably blamed for his stepbrother's death.

And make her pay.

"All right, all right. Quiet down." When they'd all settled, Carter said, "We know the who and the why. Now we need the where. Ideas?"

"Site of the accident?" Vanessa said.

Tony shook his head. "That's one of the main streets into town. A busy intersection. Way too public."

"The Anderson's house?" Jensen asked.

"Doubtful," Royce said. "They're just too nice to go along with a scheme like this."

It was about revenge. About terrorizing Faith. About making them suffer. Where would Anderson take her to torment her? Carter snapped his head up and looked at Tony. "The ruins."

"What? Why?"

"That's where that dirtbag Sturgis held her before, so it's a trigger site for her PTSD. And I already caught him scaring her there. Maybe it was a dry run for him. Maybe it was just luck that he stumbled on her there. Maybe he saw and opportunity and followed her. I don't know. But I bet that's where he has her."

"Can't hurt to check. Let's go," Tony said. They all headed for the door, but Tony stopped and turned around. "Where do you all think you're going?"

"To the cathedral," Vanessa said.

Carter shook his head.

"No way," Tony said. "This is police business."

"That's my daughter!" Royce said.

Carter wasn't going to wait to hash that one out. He slipped from the room and hurried to the front of the clinic while Tony argued with them. He was about to run to his car when Max barked.

The poor guy had undergone two surgeries in the last week—the most recent for being shot. He should be home resting. But he looked in Max's eyes and saw the heart and soul of a cop.

He deserved his shot at bringing this guy down.

Carter whistled to him, and Max bounded over. He had to be in pain, but he didn't show it.

"Thanks, Vonni."

She waved, and Carter headed to the parking lot, Max at his heels.

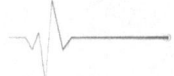

CARTER LOST CONFIDENCE IN HIS plan when he got to the beach and the lot was deserted. He thought for sure Faith's car would be there.

It wasn't designed for off-roading, so he knew Anderson hadn't driven up to the ruins.

He was just about to give up and leave when he saw disturbed brush at the far end of the parking lot. A quick examination of the foliage showed a large gap where branches had been broken and crushed. He walked into the opening, looked over the hill, and found Faith's car. Anderson must have rolled it down the hill to hide it from view.

Hadn't hidden it well enough, though.

"This is it," he said to Max.

They started up the hill, and Carter worried about his partner. Having Max there for the arrest was one thing, but making him hike that steep, rough terrain was another. What if his stitches didn't hold? Guilt washed over him, but he didn't have time to take Max back to the car. Every second Faith was with that maniac brought her closer to—

No. He wouldn't think of it.

They crested the hill, and Carter paused to let Max catch his breath. He petted him, and the dog's tongue lolled. Poor guy probably needed a drink, too. Soon. Soon he'd have Faith safe and Max resting comfortably at home.

A primal scream echoed out of the basement of the ruins.

Time was up. He gestured to Max, and they breached the perimeter.

CHAPTER 23

FAITH SIMPLY STARED AT DAVIS in disbelief. Never in a million years did she expect this.

"We didn't have the money for me to go to college before the lawsuit. I was going to work for a few years to earn some dough, then go. But all that went out the window when my folks lost everything. So after we buried Jimmy, I ran.

"I didn't know where I was going, but I ran into a group of people who understood persecution."

"You think you were persecuted because you couldn't afford college?"

He backhanded her. "Shut up, bitch. This is *my* story."

She saw stars, and she refrained from replying. Instead, she continued to try to work her hand loose and listened to his warped version of reality.

"My brothers put me on the path. They showed me that my family was persecuted, punished by the cabal of rich Jews like you who take advantage of government loopholes—"

"We aren't Jewish."

"What?"

She decided to try to build a rapport with him while she tried to get free. "We aren't Jewish."

"You're not?"

"No, we're not. We certainly aren't members of a cabal. And I assure you, the government has harassed us a lot more than they've helped us since Hope died. We're in the same boat, you and I."

"Really? You had to go into debt to pay for something you didn't do. All the while mourning your stepbrother's loss?"

"I was a minor when Hope died, so I can't speak about my parents' financial obligations for anything that happened. But I did have to mourn my sister."

Davis paced for a moment, then he turned to her. "So what are you?"

"What do you mean?"

"What are you? What religion?"

"Christian." Skinheads were Christian, right? She was safe saying that.

"What sect?"

Sect? She sighed. She might not practice, but she'd never deny her faith. Even knowing he wasn't going to like the answer. "Catholic."

He strode over to her and shoved his face in hers. "That's just as bad, rosary rattler! You aren't going to trick me into thinking we're similar. We're nothing alike! You understand?"

She nodded, afraid he'd beat her again. But instead, he walked away again. Sounded like he paced.

It took him a while to calm down. When he did, he continued. "I was almost happy living with my Aryan brothers. I'd found a calling."

He'd found a cult, the crazy bastard. And by the sounds of it, they corrupted his anger for their own purposes.

"About a year ago, my high school basketball coach reached out to me, wanted to tell me goodbye."

"I thought you said you didn't play sports in school."

"You are such a stupid cunt. I lied to you. And you had no idea. My brothers told me you were the weak link. And boy, were they right."

Her whole body ached. Her energy flagged.

She feared when Davis stopped talking, she'd stop living. But she didn't know how much more she could take. Every time she tried to extend the time he talked, he abused her. Faith already feared he'd broken her ribs. It grew increasingly difficult to breathe, and the pain in her side was excruciating. She couldn't bear another assault.

"My old coach had gone and contracted a Jew disease." He spat the word like it tasted bad on his tongue. "He was dying. It was perfect. After that, it all came together."

"I don't follow."

"Of course you don't, you dumb bitch." He sighed. "I befriended my old coach. He was so sick, so gullible, so easy to manipulate. It didn't take much to convince him he'd been discriminated against because he was a Jew. Ha! Nothing could have been further from the truth. He'd been given special treatment because of it, but he was so fucking stupid, he didn't even realize it. I was the one who convinced him he'd been taken advantage of. And I got him to retaliate."

"But... why? How did that impact my family?"

"Are you stupid because you're a girl or a Catholic?"

Faith didn't answer. She kept working to free her bound hand and struggling not to pass out from the pain.

"Probably both. Anyway, I'd been stealing your drugs for weeks leading up to the basketball game. And, predictably stupid, you never reported it. Worried it would bring up questions about your dad and your family again, weren't you?"

She nodded. Maybe she was stupid, because hearing him voice her deepest concerns showed her just how foolish she'd been.

"The night of the shooting, I made sure your drugs were planted at the gym. I knew the pigs would find them and trace them to you. But you hiring me that night? That was the icing on my cake."

She thought back to how they'd met, the things he'd said. He had played her. And she fell for it. A simple check of his references, and all this could have been avoided.

"I was the best of all of us! I got my evil Jew coach killed, and managed to tarnish his reputation in the process. Let folks see him and his race for what they really are. Invited my brothers to that ridiculous vigil, gave them a platform in the press. And then I managed to frame you for the increased drug distribution in town. It was perfect!"

His story was over, and she still wasn't free. She was out of time.

"You're ruined, Faith. Your business is toast, your family reputation is gone. And now, to avenge my stepbrother, I'm going to kill you. I'm going to beat you to within an inch of your life, long and slow. It's the least you deserve. And when your body is bruised and broken, I'm going to leave you here to suffer. Then there's going to be an explosion while you're cooking meth, and I don't think you're going to survive it."

Tears fell down her cheeks. All the panic attacks she'd had fearing this very thing, and now that it was happening, she was totally self-aware. Calm. Well, exhausted, anyway. She prayed she'd hyperventilate and faint, taking her away from the horror and the torture and the pain.

No such luck. She'd be lucid for the whole agonizing thing.

Until she died. And felt nothing at all.

"Goodbye and good riddance, bitch." He hit her so hard, her teeth rattled and her arm jerked. Her wrist slid in the restraint.

He hit her again. Her vision hazed, but her hand slipped a little more.

"Cry for me!" He kicked her in her injured ribs. It stole her breath, but the haze vanished. Adrenaline kicked in, and she yanked at the rope.

Free!

He came at her again, and she raked her nails down his face.

"Bitch!"

She lunged for his injured arm, squeezed with all her remaining strength.

Davis howled, the sound echoing off the walls.

Faith covered her ears and dropped to the ground. Without the ropes holding her up, she lacked the strength to stand. She curled into a fetal position and tried to protect her ribs.

Davis fell on top of her.

Then pandemonium broke out in the chamber.

CHAPTER 24

CARTER BREACHED THE BASEMENT OF the ruins in time to see Faith crumple underneath Anderson. Both of them seemed injured. She was in a ball on the floor, and he lay on top of her, injured arm out to the side, other hand clutching his face. He couldn't tell more than that in the dim light.

Anderson sputtered various obscenities. He clearly didn't know Carter had arrived. When he rolled off Faith, his face looked black. He kicked at her head, but missed.

"*Freeze!*" Carter yelled.

Faith didn't move, but Anderson skittered back into a corner. Carter couldn't see where he'd gone. He heard the click of a safety and dropped to the ground.

Max growled.

A gunshot rang out, the flash momentarily blinding him. The explosion reverberated off the walls, didn't seem to dissipate but instead echoed in Carter's head. He covered his ears. Squinted into the corner where Anderson had gone.

Something brushed his arm, something warm and strong. He heard growling and yelling. Groping in his pocket, he pulled out his phone and flipped on the flashlight.

Max had lunged at Anderson and had him pinned. He stood on his chest and snapped at his face and neck.

Carter knew he wouldn't actually bite unless Anderson tried to get up. He didn't reveal that knowledge to the perp, though.

Anderson cried and thrashed under his snarling dog. Relief washed over Carter. It was over.

Tony burst in, his own flashlight adding to the wash of light brightening the room. He bounced the beam back and forth between Anderson and Faith.

"Cuff him, Tony. I'll see to her."

He heard the bustle of activity behind him, but his attention was only on Faith. He knelt beside her and gently stroked her hair away from her face.

Good Lord.

He barely recognized her. Her face was swollen and bloody. She wheezed with even the shallow breaths she managed.

He wasn't even sure she was conscious.

"Faith?" He whispered, trying not to frighten her. "Faith? Can you hear me? It's me, Carter."

Nothing.

"Faith?" He spoke a little louder, hoping to rouse her.

Still nothing. Not even the wheezing.

"Faith!"

Her family burst into the room. Flashlight beams bounced around the chamber, then settled on Faith.

"She's not breathing," Carter said.

"Not again," Royce said.

Jensen dropped to one knee next to Carter and checked for a pulse. "Dad!"

"Out of the way, Jensen," Tony said.

"But she's—"

"EMTs are here. Move!"

Jensen scrambled back, but Carter couldn't seem to budge. Tony grabbed his arm and pulled him out of the way.

EMTs wasted no time getting Faith out of the chamber, onto a stretcher, down the hill into an ambulance, and on the road. Her family piled into cars to follow. Carter could do nothing but stand there and pray they saved her.

"Carter? Carter!" Tony snapped, breaking into his thoughts.

"I have to go to her."

"You have to deal with Max."

Carter whipped his head around. Max lay on the cold ground, panting, eyes half closed. "Max!" He ran over to him, dropped to one knee, and petted him. His hand came away warm and sticky.

"Were you shot, boy? Or is this your old injury?"

Max whimpered.

Carter leapt to his feet and charged at Anderson. "My dog!"

Tony shoved Anderson into the custody of two officers and struggled to hold Carter back. "Cool it, Carter."

"But Max…"

"Let's get him to the vet. Come on. I'll help you get him into the car."

He didn't want to take Max to his old vet. He wanted to take him to Faith. But Faith fought for her life even as Max might be losing his.

Carter thought about his brother, prayed softly to him. "Help us out, Mark. Put in a good word for us. Get both Faith and Max through this."

He kept imploring his brother silently as he and Tony struggled under Max's weight, slipping and stumbling down the hill to his vehicle.

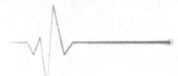

CARTER SAT IN THE WAITING room at the vet's clinic and bounced his leg. He couldn't stay still, but Tony had made him sit. Said the pacing distracted him.

"How long has it been? It's been too long, hasn't it?"

Tony sighed. "It's been about two minutes since you asked me the last time. And no, I don't think it's been too long."

"You didn't even bother to look at your watch."

"Don't have to. There's a clock right there." He pointed to a clock mounted on the wall across from them.

Carter hadn't noticed it. Hadn't noticed anything since the ruins. Didn't even remember driving there. Had he driven? Had Tony?

He had no idea.

"Have you heard from Royce?"

"And I'll tell you what I told you the last time you asked that two minutes ago. No."

"You've been typing shit into your phone since we got here. You telling me not one of those texts is from the Kellers?"

"That's what I'm telling you."

Carter growled and popped to his feet. He started pacing again.

"Carter. Sit down."

He sighed, but he took a seat. And started bouncing his leg again.

Tony shifted his weight so he could look at him. "You know, you aren't alone in this."

"You mean because you care for the Kellers, too? I know." He did know. Didn't think it was quite the same thing, though.

"No, that's not what I meant. I mean, yeah, I do care for the Kellers, but I was talking about something else."

Carter stopped bouncing his leg and turned to face him.

He sighed. "I know I'm tough on you. Maybe too tough. And maybe you hate me a little for it."

"I don't hate you, Tony." Couldn't be farther from the truth. He idolized the guy. Felt miserable when he let him down.

"Carter, I know I don't often say it. Hell, I don't think I ever said it."

"Said what?"

Tony cleared his throat, looked down. Looked up and met Carter's gaze. "You're family to me. Always was, since we were kids."

"Tony, I—"

"Let me finish." He inhaled, let the air out slowly. "I always thought of you as the kid brother I never had. But when Mark…" Tony looked down, took a few more deep breaths. "Before Mark and I deployed, we promised each other if anything happened, we'd look out for the other's family. You get that? I promised Mark I'd look after you. And I've kept that promise."

"I know."

"But I didn't do it for Mark. Not entirely. I would have done it, promise or not."

Carter stared at him. This was the closest they'd ever come to an emotional conversation, and he wasn't sure where Tony was going with it.

"I feel like you feel isolated here. Alone. But you're not. I'm glad you moved here, because I'm glad to work with you. But mostly, I'm glad you're here because you're my brother. Okay? You get that? You are family to me. So stop with the macho shit right now, and stop thinking you need to hold yourself apart from me. I might outrank you, but I still love you. I'm here for you."

Invisible bands constricted around Carter's throat and lungs. Tony called him his brother. He had a brother.

Tony wasn't Mark, but he was the next best thing.

Carter threw his arms around Tony and swallowed the lump in his throat. He spoke the words into Tony's shoulder because he couldn't say them while looking him in the eye. "I'm scared, Tony." He took a trembling breath, and Tony patted his back. "I can't be in two places at once. I need to be here, I want to be there. And I'm terrified I'm going to lose one of them. Or both of them. And not get to say goodbye. If I had only been better, been faster—"

Tony pushed him to arms' length and forced him to meet his gaze. "You listen to me, Carter Emerson. We aren't going to lose them. Either of them. You did a damn good bunch of police work. Even when we all told you to back off, you stuck with it. Without you, we might be having a very different conversation right now. Understand?"

Carter nodded, and Tony let him go.

"Now, positive thoughts, right?"

"Right. Positive thoughts."

Carter resumed bouncing his leg, and Tony resumed doing whatever it was he was doing on his phone. A few minutes later, the vet came out.

"He's resting comfortably."

"Is he going to be okay? What happened?"

"He's going to be fine. There was no fresh gunshot wound. He lost some staples and pulled some of the internal stitches. I had to open him up to stop the bleeding. Doctor Keller did his surgery, right? Did a damn fine job. He won't even have much scar tissue. But he's going to need to take some time off. Maybe even retire, I don't know. We'll have to reassess him once he's healed. You shouldn't have had him in the field with you today."

"I know. There were extenuating circumstances." He wasn't going to tell the doctor he wanted Max to have the satisfaction of being involved in Anderson's arrest.

"Well, no more extenuating circumstances, okay?"

"You got it. Can I see him?"

"He's still pretty out of it. It'll be a couple of hours before the anesthesia is fully out of his system. But I guess you can say hello."

"So, you aren't releasing him tonight?"

"Absolutely not. Go see him, then get out of here."

"Thanks, Doc." Carter shook his hand. "You coming, Tony?"

"You go. I'll see him when he's ready for visitors."

Carter followed the vet back to a recovery kennel. Max lay on his side, his tongue out, his eyes half closed. When he saw Carter, he tried to roll over and whimpered.

"Ssh. Stay, boy. Stay right there."

Max seemed to relax, but he kept his eye trained on Carter.

"I just wanted to see you. Tell you I—" Tell him he loved him. Carter took a deep breath. He opened the kennel door and petted Max's flank. "You're a good boy. You're a hero. You probably saved my life. And you got the bad guy. Good boy." He paused a second, then added, "Daddy's proud of you."

Max seemed to smile, then he drifted off to sleep.

Carter closed the door and walked back to the waiting room.

Tony was already on his feet. "They want us at the hospital. Let's go."

"THEY DIDN'T TELL YOU ANYTHING?" Carter asked. "Is it bad news? Good?"

Tony used his lights and siren to speed through town. They were almost at Oakland Regional Hospital.

Carter hadn't stopped peppering him with questions since they left. Hadn't gotten any satisfying answers, though.

Tony raced through the parking lot and whipped his vehicle into the fire lane. He left his lights on but turned off the siren. Then they both piled out of the car and rushed inside.

Carter reached the desk first. "Faith Keller? Emergency room? Regular room? Come on!"

"Tony. Carter."

Carter didn't wait for the receptionist to answer. He headed down the hall toward the doctor who'd called them. Tony was on his heels.

"Doctor Hammond. Hi. Have you spoken to Royce? Is Faith—"

"She's fine. Just fine. They're moving her up to the third floor now. Her parents are with her, but she's allowed non-familial visitors. Why don't you go on up?"

"Thanks." Carter pumped his hand up and down.

Tony did the same, then he led them to the stairs. Carter took them two at a time and flung open the door. He ran down the hall to the nurses' station. "Faith Keller, please."

The nurse looked up at him and smiled. "She's a popular woman. Room three-twelve. Right down this hall and around the corner."

"Thanks."

He and Tony hurried down the hall. When they turned down the aisle, they saw a large group of people clustered outside a door. They made their way to them, and Bella noticed them first.

"Carter! Tony!" She wrapped Carter in a hug and whispered in his ear. "Thank you."

The rest of the group took turns embracing him and Tony.

Looked like things were going to be okay.

CHAPTER 25

FAITH HAD INSISTED TO TOD that she didn't want to take any drugs for her PTSD. And even though she was now brave enough to admit her fears and face them, she still wouldn't want to try any medicine to help push past the anxiety. It was imperative to her that she remained lucid so she could properly assess her situations.

But for the abuse she'd suffered at the cathedral? Hell, yes, she wanted drugs. God bless morphine. Knock her out, let her drift on a cloud of purple sheep... she didn't care. Suck it, clarity. She wanted big pharma.

She'd blacked out at the ruins and woken up in the hospital who-knows-how-long later. Groggy and pretty much out of it, her initial memories were hazy fog and blurry forms talking in crazy, garbled voices. And a lot of blackness. She'd drifted in and out of consciousness a lot.

At the moment, niggling discomfort in her chest and head demanded attention. Her eyelids fluttered open—didn't expect that to hurt, but it did—and she managed to make out her parents, Jensen, and Bella sprawled on random chairs throughout the room. She tried to sit up and groaned as a pain shot past her rib.

"Faith? Faith! You're awake!" Mom burst to her feet and rushed to the bedside. "Oh, thank God."

She tried to swallow, but her mouth was dry. Tried to talk, but her tongue felt thick and glued to the roof of her mouth. Would have sighed if deep breaths didn't hurt. She reached for the bedside table, but IV tubes tangled in her sheets and the needle tugged on her hand.

How was it possible that even her hands hurt?

Right. The bindings.

She turned her head and, despite the throbbing, nodded at the water pitcher, which looked blurry. Everything and everybody looked blurry.

"You thirsty?" Jensen asked. "Here, let me." He held a glass near her ear and tipped a straw into her mouth.

Sucking through the straw hurt her face, but she was so thirsty, she suffered through it.

Jensen took the glass away before she'd had her fill. "Not too much at first."

"Why don't we sit you up?" Dad grabbed the controller and pushed the button that elevated her head. Rising hurt, but not as much as doing it on her own. "Better?"

"I hurt. Everywhere." Her voice was hoarse, her throat scratchy.

"You're on a PCA and probably due for another dose."

Patient-Controlled Analgesia pump. Nurses, doctors, and patients all rejoiced when those happy machines hit the market.

"Can you do it," he asked, "or do you want me to?"

Faith tried to reach the button to activate the administration of the drug, but the motion caused too much pain.

"I got it." Her dad pushed the button for her.

Just that little bit of movement tired her, and she rested against her pillows.

"Do you want us to let you rest?" Bella asked.

"She's been sleeping," Mom said.

"She needs rest to recover, Ness. Sleep's good for her." Dad stood. "We can come back later, when you're feeling better."

"Please, don't go." Faith felt like crying, but just thinking about it made her face hurt. "Can you tell me what happened?"

"Don't—don't you remember?" Jensen looked from her to their father. "Amnesia?"

"I'll page the nurse, get a doctor in here."

"No." Faith shook her head and regretted it. "I don't have amnesia. I remember everything Davis said, everything he did. Up to when I blacked out. What happened then?"

Dad pulled his chair closer to her bed, sat, and took her hand. "Are you sure you want to go through this now."

"Yes." She coughed, and searing pain ripped through her chest. Tears sprung to her eyes, and she sucked shallow gasps of air to avoid further aggravating her lungs. "Water."

Jensen started to lift the straw to her mouth again, but she snatched the cup from him and sipped with greed. Didn't stop until the straw sputtered, signaling she'd drained the glass.

"More, please?"

"No." Jensen took the cup and put it on the table. "We should have started you with ice chips. You're going too fast."

"My mouth is so dry."

"Will it be worth it when you throw it all up? Great for your lungs."

"You're so bossy."

He stared at her, eyebrows raised. "Guess you're feeling better."

She leaned back on the pillows, again, and ignored the barb. "So, what happened? Fill in the blanks."

"You'd managed to get your hands free from your restraints." Dad hadn't looked so grave since Hope died. "They had to use an abrasive to get all the dirt and rope fibers out of the flesh. You're going to hurt for a while."

She looked down at her hands. Both wrists had bandages around them, one of them dotted with blood. But she didn't even register any pain from them. Morphine must be kicking in. "My chest?"

"Carter got to you first. You were already free of the restraints by then, and you and Anderson were fighting. You took some nasty shots. Two broken ribs."

"By the time Tony and the other cops got there, Max had pinned Anderson down." Jensen clenched his fists and took a deep breath. "You were fading. Fast."

"Your father feared he'd have to do some kind of field operation to save you." Tears fell down Mom's cheeks.

Faith looked at her father. "Like with Hope? I'm so sorry."

"Before Jensen and I had to make that decision, the EMTs got you on a stretcher and rushed you down the hill to the ambulance. They had you stable before you got to the ER."

"You've got three broken ribs, a concussion, several contusions on your face." Jensen looked away. "And you know about your wrists."

She raised her fingers to her face and explored with her fingers. Didn't even recognize what she felt. Even the softest touch seemed to hurt.

"I want a mirror."

"No." Mom took her fingers and squeezed gently. "It doesn't matter how you look. What matters is that you're going to be fine."

Her stomach lurched. "It must be bad then. Really bad. I want to see. I need to see."

"Faith," Dad said. "It's going to heal. All of it. We were so relieved to hear he hadn't shattered your cheekbone or jaw. You took quite a beating."

Her fingers explored her face again. "My nose?"

"Broken. But set." Mom squeeze her fingers again. "You're going to be fine."

Faith sighed and wondered how bad it really looked. The way they all stared at her, she figured she must look like a carnival sideshow. But they wouldn't let her look and she couldn't do anything about it, anyway.

Something picked at her brain. A memory, or a fragment of one. She tried to latch onto it. Click. Bang. A gun. "Wait! No gunshot wound?"

"What?" Bella sat at the foot of her bed and grabbed her foot. "Gunshot wound? No. No. You're fine."

She heard the terror in her voice, knew how hard it had to be for her to relive it all again. "Was anyone else shot?"

"No one else is even injured," Mom said. "Except that no good, lousy—"

"Okay. Got it. Good, then."

"Why'd you ask?" Dad asked.

"Must have been delirious or something. But I thought I heard a gunshot before I passed out."

"No one was shot. It's all over, honey. And it's all going to be okay."

"I can't believe this has been hanging over our heads for almost a decade. How could none of us have known about Davis Anderson?"

"Why would we? We never even met him. Your father and I only saw him once, at the cemetery. And we weren't introduced. I never gave him a second thought."

"It's not right, though. What happened to his family. We didn't have to pay the Haggertys after the civil suit, but they did. And it was really all Wade's fault."

"Their attorney didn't do them any favors," Jensen said.

"Not their fault they couldn't afford good representation. Or that we could."

"Faith," Dad said, "you shouldn't be getting worked up. You need to rest. We're going to step out and let you sleep."

He always did know how to shut down a conversation.

Dad patted her arm, Mom squeezed her fingers, and Jensen smiled at her. No one kissed her, so her face had to be a disaster.

They headed for the door. Bella blew her a kiss and followed them.

"Bel? Hang back for a sec? And close the door."

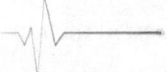

FAITH TOOK A DEEP BREATH—as much as she could with her lungs on fire—and waited for Bella, who closed the door and then took the seat her mom had vacated.

"I know you have a compact in your purse. Give it to me."

Bella stood. "If that's why you asked me to—"

"That's not the reason. Not the only reason. But before we talk, I want to see the damage."

"Oh, Faith. No. It doesn't matter. It's bumps and bruises."

"Feels like a lot more. And given everyone's looking at me like I'm a freak, I need to see."

Bella bit her lip.

"Give me the mirror, or I'm getting out of this damn bed and walking into the bathroom."

It was an empty threat—there was no way she was moving anywhere for any reason—but it worked. Bella plopped down in her seat, fished in her purse, and pulled out a compact.

"I want it on the record that I'm doing this under protest."

"So stipulated, counsellor."

Bella handed her the mirror. She braced herself for the worst, then she looked at her reflection.

Blood drained from her face. She knew that by feeling, not by sight. Her face was every color imaginable but white.

Okay, so she hadn't really been prepared for the worst.

Both eyes had deep purple bruises under them and were puffy, but the right one was swollen half closed. Her lower lip sported a wide gash—that explained why her mouth hurt when she used the straw. Her cheeks looked like she puffed them out while holding a mouthful of air, every expanded inch of it some shade of bruise. Her nose was full of packing and had a splint taped over it.

Miss America, move over. Here comes Faith Keller.

She's seen enough, and she passed the mirror back to Bella.

"You okay?"

"Now I know why no one kissed me. There's no safe space to land even the smallest of smooches."

"It's going to heal, Faith. And you'll be fine."

The morphine made deep breaths bearable, and Faith took one before continuing. "About that."

"What?"

"Being fine. I owe you an apology. And a thank you."

"What for?"

"The apology is for when we went to the cathedral and I totally flaked on you."

Bella shook her head. "Don't be ridiculous. We were both terrified. It's understandable why you reacted the way you did."

"But we were supposed to be supporting each other. And I wasn't there for you."

"It was a big day, Faith. I'm just happy to have gone there. And to have gone there with you."

"Which brings me to my thank you. I— I'm grateful you took me there."

Bella sat back, her expression turned stony. "Yeah, clearly you're going to have nothing but happy memories of that place."

"That's the thing. I'm okay. It's all okay."

"What do you mean?"

"If I hadn't gone to the cathedral with you that day, I think I would have been a basketcase when Davis held me there. But I'd already faced that place with you. And it didn't hold anymore terror for me."

"You weren't afraid?"

"Oh, no. I was scared shitless."

The corner of Bella's lip quirked up.

Faith was glad she saw even a little humor in the situation. "But I would have been catatonic if I hadn't been there first with you. Us going there gave me the strength to face my fear of that place, to manage it. And to face Davis. To fight him, long enough to survive it. At least, as long as I could."

She gave Faith's fingers a squeeze. "I'm just glad it all worked out and you're safe and this whole thing is finally over."

"It is over. Time for us to move on."

Bella smiled.

"So, are you ready to set a date and get married at the lake?"

Her smile faltered. "Uh…"

"When I get out of here, I'm going to go to the lake. And the cathedral.

I'm going to go everyday if I have to until I've mastered control over my fears. The lake is too beautiful to miss out on. The ruins are just a place. I may have a lot of work ahead of me with respect to trusting strangers, but I'll be damned if I'm going to fear my hometown anymore."

"Good for you."

"Want to come with me?"

A huge grin broke out over Bella's face, and she giggled. "Yeah. Yeah, I think I do."

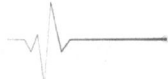

AFTER BELLA LEFT, FAITH TOOK a nap. It was the most restful sleep she'd had in years.

When she woke, her room was dark and she had trouble seeing. She made out a figure in the corner, cloaked in shadow.

Terror burbled up in her throat. She opened her mouth to scream, but snapped it shut again.

She was in a hospital. Secure in a bed, hooked up to IVs that were helping her get well. Anderson was in jail, and she was safe. Pursing her lips, she breathed out slowly.

The figure stepped into the light. Carter. She smiled.

"I hope I didn't startle you."

"What are you doing in the corner?"

"I didn't want to disturb you."

"You could have had a seat."

"I sat enough today. The waiting room at the vet, the waiting room here. Out in the hall. I just wanted to stretch my legs a bit."

"The vet? Is Max okay?"

"He's fine. He ripped some stitches and pulled a staple or two. The vet sewed him back up. Said he'll make a full recovery."

"I'm so glad to hear that. Ruby will be thrilled, too."

"Those two have grown quite fond of each other, haven't they?"

Faith bit her lip, hissed when it hurt.

"What is it? Do you need a doctor? I can get the nurse."

"No, it's not that. I have something to tell you, though."

"Go ahead."

She fidgeted with the nubby blanket that she'd pulled up to her chest. Couldn't meet his gaze. "About Ruby and Max."

"You mean what happened at your house? I'm sure they won't always do that. They'll become the best of friends, and we'll never have to think about it again."

"See, that's the thing. I think we'll have to think about it again."

"Why?" He sat and stared into her eyes.

"When they—well, you know." She sighed. "Ruby was in heat."

He blinked. And again. Didn't speak, though.

"I mean, I don't know for sure yet, but there's a good chance she's…" He could finish the sentence himself.

"You mean we're going to be grandparents together?"

She chuckled. "I thought you didn't call yourself 'Dad' with respect to Max."

"He's family. No two ways about it." He stood, walked in a circle, and sat back down. "Puppies, huh? Wow. What do you even call that breed? German Retriever?"

"If she's pregnant, her puppies will be Golden Shepherds. I don't know if you've ever seen that mix, but they're adorable."

He took her hand. "Grandparents, huh? Would have thought I'd have had kids first."

She tried to swallow, but ended up coughing. He reached over her for her glass and held the straw to her lips.

"Sorry," she said. He was almost on top of her. So close, she could see the dark indigo ring around the frosty blue flecked iris. His eyes were gorgeous.

He was gorgeous.

Carter put the cup down, but he didn't sit up. She felt his body heat through the scratchy covers, wondered what it would be like if they were in bed together without injuries and tubes and unsightly hospital gowns.

She groaned, and he sat up. "Did I hurt you?"

"No. I was just thinking about something."

"Couldn't have been anything too good if that was your reaction."

Her cheeks flamed, but he wouldn't be able to tell through all the bruises. "Just now realizing I'm in a hospital gown, with messy hair and an unrecognizable face."

Carter leaned in again, his face so close to hers she felt the heat of his breath. Coffee and mint. Two of her favorite things.

He studied her for a moment, then leaned over and kissed her cheek, the brush of his lips across her skin so soft, she wasn't sure she felt it at all. He must have found the one square inch of her face that didn't hurt.

Or he was a magical medical breakthrough in pain management.

"You're beautiful, Faith."

She smoothed her hair and pulled up her blankets.

He sat back, took her hand. "Don't. Don't worry about how you look. I'll take you any way I can get you. I'd rather you felt better, but I'm just so damn glad you're alive."

Tears stung her eyes. "My family says you saved me."

"I think Max did more of the saving than I did."

"Thank you, Carter." She squeezed his fingers. His hand felt warm, solid. *Safe.*

"You know, even when you were determined to arrest me, something about you interested me."

"Even when I was determined to arrest you, I wondered if I'd be able to do it. You were under my skin even then."

She smiled. Her gaze traveled over him—wavy hair, brilliant eyes, soft lips, muscular body. Something on his jacket caught her attention. "Lean over a little."

His brows furrowed, but he complied. His jacket gaped open, and she grabbed the edge of it, examined it closely. She poked her finger through a hole and wiggled it. "Carter, what's this from?"

He sat back, the jacket slipping from her fingers.

"Carter?"

After he cleared his throat, he mumbled something, but she couldn't make it out.

"What?"

"It's a bullet hole."

"A bullet—Davis. I knew I heard a gunshot. Are you all right?"

"I'm fine. He didn't get me." He grabbed her hand again.

"That was an awfully close call. Too close." She didn't even have him yet, and she almost lost him.

"I've been shot before. This is nothing."

"You've been shot!"

"I'll tell you about it sometime."

"To think I almost lost you before I even had you." She couldn't believe she'd said those words aloud. Was it the drugs? No way he couldn't see her face color after that blunder.

"Well, now you know how I feel about you. So we're even."

She smiled. "Hardly."

"Let's make a pact to never get hurt again."

"I don't know if I can keep that promise, but I like the sentiment."

They sat together for a while in companionable silence. Soon a nurse poked her head in. "Visiting hours are ending. You need to say goodbye."

Carter looked at Faith. "I have to go, but I'm not saying goodbye."

"Goodnight, then?"

"Better than nothing, I guess." He kissed the top of her head. "I wish I didn't have to go."

"Pull rank. Say you're a cop and you're watching over me."

"I am a cop. And I am watching over you. But you need your rest."

She didn't argue. She was tired.

"Can I come back tomorrow?"

"Come as often as you'd like."

"I was thinking, when you get out of here, maybe we could try dinner again."

"Dinner?"

"Well, yeah. Don't you think it's a good idea for us to get to know each other better? You know, for the sake of the dogs."

"When you put it that way…"

"I want to get to know you, Faith. I want to take you out and spend time with you. I think we might really have something here. If we can just put the past behind us."

The nurse came in again. "Sir, you have to go now."

"He's a cop," Faith said. "He's here on official business."

"I'm sorry. I didn't know. Try not to keep her up too late. She needs her rest." And she walked away.

"Stay as long as you like, Carter. The past is in the past… and I'm not going anywhere."

He smiled and settled back down in the chair.

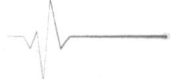

THE WIND BLEW FAITH'S HAIR in her face, tickling her cheeks. She loved the feeling. Her face no longer hurt, even her nose was merely a little tender. The simple things, like swiping at stray tendrils blowing in her face, brought her joy.

Because she was pain free.

And because she was alive to feel anything at all.

She pulled the wilting bouquet out of the vase and replaced it with a fresh bunch of multi-colored tulips. "Thought you might want something more vibrant than the muted, monochromatic displays Mom's been leaving."

The colors popped against the warm granite stone. If it wasn't a cemetery, it would be cheerful.

The wind picked up, and Faith knew her sister appreciated the gesture.

"It's finally over, Hope. We can all finally move on." She kissed her fingers and touched the tombstone, then tugged on Ruby's leash and headed for the car.

She and Bella were going shopping for bridesmaid dresses appropriate for a lakeside wedding. Then they were meeting Carter and Jensen for dinner and followed by a bonfire at the Square. There would be huge crowds, but she could handle it. The town was celebrating the high school basketball team's championship victory.

And she was celebrating a victory of her own.

A NOTE FROM STACI

HI! THANKS FOR READING *Pride and Fall.* I loved writing it and bringing these characters to life. I hope you enjoyed it as well. If you wouldn't mind investing a few more minutes in this work, I'd really appreciate it. Please let me know what you thought of this story by leaving a review online (Amazon, Barnes & Noble, Goodreads—wherever you share your opinions with other readers). It doesn't take long, but it really helps me craft stories you enjoy, as well as reach other readers. I value your comments and am grateful for whatever your share.

The other way we can connect is through social media. Stay up to date with both my Cathedral Lake and Medici Protectorate series by visiting these links:

Facebook: Author Staci Troilo • Twitter: @stacitroilo
www/stacitroilo.com

I'm really looking forward to hearing from you. Until next time....

STACI TROILO GREW UP KNOWING family is paramount. She spent time with extended family daily, not just on holidays or weekends. Because of those close knit familial bonds, every day was full of love and laughter, food and fun. Life has taken her a thousand miles away from that extended family, but those ties remain. And so do the traditions, which she now shares with her husband, son, and daughter... even her dogs. And through her fiction, she shares the importance of relationships with you. Mystery or suspense, romance or mainstream—in her stories, family is paramount.

Facebook: Author Staci Troilo
Twitter: @stacitroilo
Amazon: http://amazon.com/author/stacitroilo

WWW.STACITROILO.COM

* 9 7 8 1 6 3 3 7 3 6 1 7 7 *